Michael Wilson was born into a government family outside of the nation's capital. On scholarship he attended Carnegie Mellon University with a painting major and literature minor. After university he was a bartender, received two literary grants, wrote and produced a television show for deaf/hearing children, owned an eclectic store, and was lead teaching artist at a program for children at risk. His paintings have been displayed in gallery shows and can be seen at artbymichael.net.

For all the women who fought for their country on the home front.

Michael Wilson

GOVERNMENT GIRLS

A Novel of Hope During WWII

AUSTIN MACAULEY PUBLISHERS®

LONDON * CAMBRIDGE * NEW YORK * SHARJAH

Ordering Information
Quantity sales: Special discounts are available on quantity purchases by corporations, associations, and others. For details, contact the publisher at the address below.

Publisher's Cataloging-in-Publication data
Wilson, Michael
Government Girls

ISBN 9798889108023 (Paperback)
ISBN 9798889108030 (Hardback)
ISBN 9798889108054 (ePub e-book)
ISBN 9798889108047 (Audiobook)

Library of Congress Control Number: 2023922865

www.austinmacauley.com/us

First Published 2024
Austin Macauley Publishers LLC
40 Wall Street, 33rd Floor, Suite 3302
New York, NY 10005
USA

mail-usa@austinmacauley.com
+1 (646) 5125767

My mother and her stories about the War years.

Chapter 1

Mornings is when I miss you the most, Ma. I know I squawked when you came in and shook my toe saying 'Morning Merry Sunshine' to wake me, but I miss that now. I miss Pa chewing his tobacco and spitting it in that can he kept hidden under his chair thinking you don't know about it. I miss the kids all fighting as we cooked breakfast. I miss getting my feet muddy and wet in the Mississippi.

Most of all, I miss feeling safe there at home. Sometimes, maybe too much of the time now, I want to be someone who isn't afraid all the time, someone who is brave like you.

I have enclosed a little money to help out.

Love you so much
Mary

Mary picked up the letter and looked at the stationery. Her mother had given it to her when she first left for college to make sure she would write home (like there was a chance she wouldn't). The paper was a creamy white that reminded her of the froth when she milked the cows back on her Uncle Bud's farm. Across the top and down the sides were delicate purple violets on green twirling vines.

It must have cost Ma a fortune! But I was the first to leave home, and I guess that was hard for her. And now she has to get my older sister Priscilla to help out taking care of all the kids! That will never happen.

Folding the letter, she let out a long sigh as the room filled with the dusty blue of early morning. She turned off the man in the moon lamp that had been Muriel's son's before he left for one of those big cities Mary dreamed about, sometimes a good dream, sometimes a nightmare. She should have been thrilled here with her own bed, her own room but she actually missed being crowded in with her three sisters. Their room had smelled of washed hair and the vanilla they used for perfume. This room smelled of dusty furniture, no matter how many times she dusted.

This wallpaper of cowboys bucking on horses was faded and peeling along the seams.

But it was what she could afford on her salary and she was grateful to have a place to live and a job where she could send some money home. Stuffing the letter in the matching envelope, she heard the long squeak of the screen door then the sudden slam. Sunlight began to poor into the room and she knew she better hurry or she was going to be late.

The blood red of the morning sun oozed across the horizon and splattered gold on the silk of the corn. The blue and purple shadows of night fled, the shadows of day leaped up. The light reached her feet as Muriel stepped onto the lawn, letting go of the door with the screen that her lazy husband never seemed to get around to repairing. It was another day in Spring Grove, Wisconsin, another day she expected to be like all the others of her seventy-seven years had been. She had grown up on this farm as had her grandparents since they came over from Denmark. They all had been buried in the small graveyard on the property and she expected she would lie in this rich soil too.

"Morning, Ma and Pa," she said tilting her head over to the gravestones as she passed them on her way to the chicken coop.

She lay her raggedy basket down on the ground and laughed to herself. Her body was just getting old and it was harder and harder to get her arthritic body loosened up and ready for another day on the farm.

The screen door screeched and slammed again as Bart, their farmhand who slept up in the attic ran from the house to the outhouse. His thin frame disappeared inside the structure and Muriel laughed again. She hoped he made it in time. Better get a new pot of coffee going before he came out.

Picking up the basket again after she had stretched her back, she opened the door to the coop.

"What's all the noise about, ladies? You act like I wasn't here first thing in the morning, every morning, come rain or shine!" The cacophony of noise from the chickens grew softer as though they were actually comforted by her words as she lay down her basket.

Bending over the bucket of feed, she dipped her left hand; the one not gnarled by arthritis, and pulled out a handful. She tossed it on the floor of the coop as the chickens swarmed around. Then she picked up her basket and began to collect the eggs. She always loved the way eggs felt warm in her hand. Silence and the smell of the coop surrounded her. One hen came up to her and clucked as if to protest.

"What would you do with these eggs anyway? You ought to be glad you don't have kids. I'm just saving you the trouble of waiting for him to call."

The chicken clucked back and though she knew they were only dumb animals, she still suspected they could understand her. She was sure the cows did when she talked to them.

"Where's that big cock anyway? Almost an hour late with his cock-a-doodle-doing."

Opening the door to the henhouse, the smell of fresh grass and manure arrived on a cool breeze from the west.

"Men."

Best hurry up and not dawdle. She needed to get some of these eggs fixed for breakfast. Bart always spent quite some time in the outhouse but when he came out he was starving and ready to go milk the cows.

The house had been there for three generations and she had grown up and expected to die there. It was still standing but that was about the only thing that was special about it. It was just a box with white peeling clapboard and green peeling window frames. The rooms were laid out like most homes in the area, the largest being the kitchen. It was a room filled with years of good smells of great hearty meals and fresh baked breads and cakes. In the center of the kitchen was an old table that they had found by the side of the road, better than the one they already had, which they burned up in the front room fireplace. The five chairs were mismatched and most needed gluing. In the chair near the old black stove sat Gunther, thin but with a gut, and still good looking in a rugged way despite his eighty some years. His face was hidden behind the Dubuque Herald News. A snake of gray smoke rose above the paper.

As she put down the basket of eggs a bit too hard to get his attention, Muriel read the headline MORE AMERICANS DEAD. Gunther folded down a corner of the paper, a cigarette with a long ash dangling from his mouth, and said, "Yesterday. President Roosevelt announced…"

"I swear," she said loudly, and then began to mutter, "I swear up and down this farm that you never get nothing done no more 'cause you're always reading about that war. Our son is safe working in a recruiting office and so this war doesn't mean diddly squat to us."

After years of living with this woman, and even though his hearing was not as good as it used to be, he could hear her. He tried to fold the paper up neatly but gave up and laid it on the table next to his empty coffee cup.

"War changes everything, everywhere," he said emphatically.

"Horse plop, why…"

This was about to become one of their frequent arguments on the subject, but they stopped abruptly when they saw Mary standing in the doorway. With her pale yellow cotton dress pressed and ready for work, she looked lovely he thought. That was the word, not beautiful or cute, but lovely. And she had that smile that only a young woman can have, not from innocence but from hope in the future. But right now she had a toothbrush in her mouth.

"Morning, Miss Frank," Gunther said and winked. Muriel saw the way he looked at her and felt sad. *He'll never look at me like that again,* she thought.

"Morning," muttered Muriel.

"Good morning," Mary said walking over to the sink. She pulled down hard on the pump as a stream of water came out. She wet the toothbrush and gave her teeth a quick scrubbing. She was late again.

"We should never have gotten in that war. Last one caused that depression and you know that…"

Before Muriel could continue, Mary spat in the sink and spun around.

"But we are in it and my brother is over there."

With a 'humfff', Muriel walked over to the stove. As her back was to the table Mary went over and took an egg from the basket and nodding to Gunther, put the egg on Muriel's chair.

Chapter 2

The morning held her in rapture. Mary's auburn hair shone with reds and browns glazed with a shimmering gold as she briskly walked up the dirt and dust road. The freshness of the air after the night's thunderstorm astounded her and she said a prayer of thanks to God. Ma always said that if you only say one prayer let it be thanks. And she was so thankful, for the green fields that stretched out lazily to either side of her in rising and falling undulation. Thankful for thoughts and memories of her family, thankful for her friend, and thankful for a job where she could make some extra money to help out now that she wasn't at home to help Ma with things there.

As for so many families, times had been hard for her family, four boys and five girls. Pa limped with a slide of his left leg and a limp right arm that hung useless from his shoulder down. He had been a victim of polio as a child. It had left him crippled but at least he had survived. Polio was the dreaded disease that stalked healthy men, women and children. When he was six, his sister, five years his senior, had complained of a headache one night at dinner. Not like her she pushed her chair out from the table and leaving a full plate of food, left to lay down upstairs. Not like her at all. By morning, the disease had found her and she was dead.

Movie theaters had closed, church service was suspended. Schools were almost vacant. Everyone in Dubuque, Iowa was afraid of contracting the disease. In spite of his mother's efforts to avoid it, a year later he too had contracted polio. But despite how high his fever he had survived, but left crippled.

It was then that his father set up a trust fund for him. He was a successful cabinet maker with a shop downtown. He realized his son would not be able to take over the family business one day because of his disability.

Pa may have lost all of his trust fund with the arrival of the Great Depression but not his spirit. He had lost everything but knew that the land and the good Lord would not let them starve. So, he moved his new family to Harper's Ferry, Iowa, a small farming town beneath the bluffs and on the banks of the Mississippi River. There he knew they could fish, plant a garden and take on odd jobs from the farmers around the county. And anything else they could think of.

Mary had found a job as a teacher. Pa had gotten the idea of having his boys and some of the locals dive for clam shells. They cleaned them out and piled them up behind the house. Once every couple of months, the kids saw the arrival of a mysterious Asian man who bought the shells, had them carted off, and made them into pearl buttons and buckles. Somehow they had managed to put away enough money for Mary to go to Iowa State Teacher's College.

It had been her first time away from home and it frightened her to the bone. There was so much to learn yet so little of it was common sense. She had learned more about children helping to raise her brothers and sisters and cousins. But she was determined. She needed to help her family, so she worked hard. Everyone seemed so naturally smart and dressed so smart. She wore the simple dresses that Ma had made for her, nothing store bought. The problem was that her mother didn't sew that well. After a series of badly cut patterns and being poked time after time with a needle, Mary would receive a box with a new dress in it. Sometimes there was even a spot of blood on it.

But she did turn heads on campus. Her hair was thick and she wore it in a wave that accentuated her round face. Her lips were full and she had a natural blush. Her breasts were ample and when the few boys that were on campus took a nice long look at them, she was embarrassed.

While in college, Mary found a job taking care of an older woman and her teenage son (who was always looking at her breasts). The woman had narcolepsy and needed someone around if she had one of her 'fainting episodes' as she called them. It was pretty much the three of them in the house because the husband was off selling Hoovers in three counties.

Gradually, she had learned to control her fear, curling a strand of hair between her fingers seemed to help, and finished college. Right away, she found a job in Polk County that no one else seemed to want: teaching all grades in a one room school house.

Her prayers to Saint Theresa had borne fruit.

She looked down at the watch that had been her grandmother's. It was much later than she had thought. *Too much time counting my blessings!* She had wanted to be at school early too; today was the performance that the students had been preparing for. They would be excited that the day had finally come. They were putting on a puppet show for the kids in the next town over. With fifteen kids of all grades crammed into one room, it seemed a good solution to tie all their lessons together.

And she was going to be late for it. Even picking up her pace wouldn't get her there in time. She was going to have to do something rash. She had no choice.

Mary stopped and looked to her left. On the other side of the old rail fence lay the pasture of Mr. Boyd's dairy farm. Through the songs of birds muffled by the leaves in the trees along the road, she could hear the buzz of flies as they circled around the fresh cow pies.

She had no choice. Making sure her papers were stuffed in her note book, she held it tight. She managed to climb over the rough fence without either getting a splinter or getting her dress caught. Jumping down, she saw that she had barely missed a large cow pie. It was going to be a challenge to run through this mine field. She took off.

Then she saw him; she had forgotten about him, Mr. Boyd's nasty old bull. She stopped when she realized that from where he stood, under a tree twenty feet away, he was looking right at her.

"Why aren't you snoozing?" she asked as the bull raised his large head and let out a snort.

"Nice Adolph," she said as though she was trying to soothe a frightened child. The bull only shook his head and snorted again. She wasn't sure what that meant in bull language but she was pretty darn sure it wasn't good.

She gingerly took a step forward. Adolph took two.

"Look over there!" she yelled as loud as she could and pointed back the way she had come from. To her surprise, he turned his head.

Curse the cow pies; this was her chance to make a run for it! Mary took off running. She waited for the earth to rumble with the bull close behind her. She stepped right in a large wet cow pie and began to slip. She lost her balance but then regained it in time. Reaching the other side of the field she made it over the fence. She leaned over panting then stood up and took a chance to look back at Adolph, who stood under the tree still looking off in the other direction.

Chapter 3

The sun left a pale smear of yellow as it slides up the side of the sky. Birds sounded restless in the trees and the leaves tremble in a quick puff of wind. Sweat ran down Billy's freckled face and soaked the fabric of his blue and yellow striped cotton shirt. He was not late for school. He had always loved the tumble of words and numbers, the rumble of kid's feet against the wooden plank floor as they ran outside for recess. He loved his friends, even a few of the bigger kids, some of whom were older than his eight years, some of whom were his age but just bigger. He was a small boy. He especially loved Miss Frank, her wide and frequent smile, her patience with him when he reversed his letters in words or his numbers. He even loved how stern she could be at times. He loved school but he had not run to get there faster but to get away from the small lake that ran beside the road on his way.

Four walls: one with a chalk board filled with old ghosts that could not be erased; two with cork boards which held samples of lettering, pictures of barns, families, and a tank; and one with a door by which hung pegs that Mary had hammered in the walls. In the walls there were four windows, not just along the two side walls, but scattered haphazardly. Outside, the school house had been freshly painted red at a picnic last fall. It was a project for the students and their families, and the paint looked as fresh then as it did now, eight months later.

Mary had not pulled the rope on the large iron bell that hung on the post beside the door yet. She was still trying to clean the cow manure from her shoes as her students began to arrive.

"Can I ring the bell?" a small girl named Alice asked as she walked up holding the hand of her teenage brother.

Mary smiled and before she could say anything, Alice let go of Ben's hand and reached for the rope. She pulled and pulled again. The bell moved but did not swing far enough for the clapper to ring. Her eyes welled with tears but before she could let loose a sob, Mary reached over and pulled the bell so it began to ring. Satisfied, Alice ran up the stairs into the classroom.

"Will you be with us today?" Mary asked turning to Ben who had stood waiting for the question.

"No, I gotta help Pa on the farm today. But you can send any homework for me when I come to pick up Alice." Mary liked this kid. He was tall for his age 15, just like one of her brothers. His brown hair was always disheveled and his crooked smile gave him a goofy look. She knew he was anything but. He didn't want to get behind. He had ambitions; he didn't know what they were, but he knew they didn't involve farming.

"How about if I drop it off myself, and then if you need any help, I'll be right there?"

Ben smiled that crooked smile. He already knew she would be glad to help him. She had before.

Mary reached over and rang the bell again.

A dozen kids filled the room and a dozen individual whirlwinds around her. Papers on the bulletin board flew up as one of the kids ran by. But Mary managed to remain calm. It's not that she was some saint of patience but she had learned with all younger brothers and sisters to focus on one thing at a time. And that one thing right now was getting the puppet show together. It was a lesson on colonial life, of tobacco and plantations, of shipping and tea. And about the founding of the country, the Revolutionary War. She wanted them to try to understand war. They were hearing parents and older kids talking about it every day that it was horrible. But it could be for a cause, an important cause, freedom, and that someday, she prayed soon, would be over.

John, Grace, and Steven were in one corner practicing the script they had put together from essays they had written. "And then Paul Revere rode across the landing yelling, 'The British are coming, the British are coming'!" Mary stopped for a minute worried that the other class was coming in the door. The younger students were practicing operating the puppets, soldiers and civilians made from stuffed socks and strings they all had helped put together. The youngest kids were looking for props while making the sound effects they had practiced. Clack, clack with their tongues for the horse's hooves; bangs for the guns.

Mary looked up from where she was setting up the stage of old boards painted red and yellow when she heard, "Oh no!" Going over to Davey and

Becky, she saw that they had gotten the two lead puppets, one British and one patriot hopelessly tangled. They had started to try to tug them apart.

"Whoa there, not time to fight the big battle scene now!"

Davey, the toe haired boy with the perpetual cowlick even spit could not hold down, said, "Miss Frank, she got me tangled again on purpose because she wanted the British to win!"

Becky's rosy checks turned even redder as one of her hands grabbed tight to her pink dress.

"Well, I think there is only one solution. Suzy!" Mary cried out to the other side of the room. A ten-year-old with her blonde hair streaming out behind her came running over with a giant pair of scissors. Without a word, she cut the strings letting the puppets fall to the floor. Both Davey and Becky looked at each other.

"Could you get them the ball of string?" Mary said as she felt a tug on her dress. Looking down was crazy Tina, as she actually liked to be called, one of the smallest but not the youngest girls in the class. She loved acting crazy and getting laughs and attention but Mary could see a serious look on her face.

"What's wrong, dear?" Mary stroked the young girl's soft brown hair.

"Billy is in the corner, and I don't think he wants to read."

In the corner of the room Mary found Billy curled in a ball, his script in a crumple beside him. His jeans were clean and pressed, ready for his part in the show, to read the introduction he had written. In his hand he held some of the pencils and was breaking them in half, concentrating on them. His deep brown eyes were almost closed, and there was darkness around him that she couldn't understand. She knelt down beside him and whispered in his ear.

"Good idea, Billy, we're always short of pencils. Maybe you can sharpen both ends for me."

He looked up and his brow furrowed and he gave her a strange look.

"They are hereeeeee!" shouted the children in unison except one by the door who said in a voice loud enough for everyone to hear, "They smell like poop!"

Marge, Mary's best friend who taught in the next town, also in a one room school house, stepped into the room after her dozen students. She was tall and slim, with a sway to her step that swung her long brown hair that ran down from a wave across her fore head. Her eyes were dark and her skin had the slight tan from her Ojibwa heritage. With full lips, shinning with a bright red lipstick, she displayed a wide smile. As she smoothed down her dress flowered with roses, she said, "We're here for the show. So, take the empty seats, except the one of you that needs to use the outhouse. Out back now."

Mary came running up to Marge, who reached in her pocket and handed Mary a torn piece of newspaper. "Look at this later." Mary stuffed it in her pocket. "Now what are you so riled up about?"

"Dissention among the troops. Our star has stage fright. Can you try and talk to him? He's over in that corner." She pointed to where Billy was still huddled with a few of Mary's students staring anxiously at him.

"Do you think he will appreciate the way I bat my eyelashes?"

Marge and Mary walked over to Billy as the kids rustled in their seats.

Leaning over and whispering in her ear, Marge whispered to Mary, "I know the family, the Bartletts. They got news yesterday that Billy's brother died in the war."

Mary knelt down and took Billy's hand. "How about I take and read your script? Then at lunch time, Miss Colbert can watch the class and you and I can go down by the lake and eat lunch together."

"I can't go by the lake."

"Why?"

"Because I can't skim rocks on the lake with Danny any more. How am I going to learn to skim rocks without him?"

"I'll help you learn, I'm real good at it." She didn't say it was because one of her brothers had taught her how.

"I hate Mr. Roosevelt."

"I wish…" and she did.

"Things will never be the same."

Out of the corner of her eye, Mary looked over to see if the puppets were getting tangled up again. Marge sat at the old oak upright piano in the corner playing 'The Battle Hymn of the Republic'. She ended with a crashing chord as Mary stood up from where she had pushed her desk under the window and walked to the front of the class.

"The colonists knew they would die to be free…"

Looking down beside her, she saw Billy with his hand out. She gave him the crumpled paper and he began reading.

"They were going to fight the British and kill them until they were dead," he adlibbed, "at the Battle of Bumper Hill."

Billy stood aside as Alice got down on her knees and pulled the old curtain made from one of Mary's old towels open. When she moved, two puppets entered from opposite sides of the stage. They both still had some loose strings dragging along behind them. The kids laughed then clapped.

Suddenly, the room became silent. Mary heard someone at the door clear his throat again. She saw Marge roll her eyes as she turned to the door. There in a rumpled brown suit with a wide green and brown striped tie stood a pudgy man of about fifty. With the light behind him, reflected off his bald head, they couldn't be sure what expression was on his face, but they were sure it was not pleasant.

"Children, get out your lessons now." His thin voice trembled with a suppressed anger. He motioned with his head for the ladies to join him outside.

Marge held onto one of the ropes on the swing that hung from the old maple tree and swung it back slowly back and forth. Mary gave her a look. It was only infuriating Mr. Warner, superintendent of schools for the two adjacent towns. But Marge, as was her stubborn character, refused to be intimidated.

"I really am sorry," Mary began.

"I'm sorry, but that won't work this time," he said.

"I really did forget to send you an invitation to our puppet show, it was…"

"I can't put up with straying so willfully from the curriculum. Last time I believe it was some silly play. And don't you say anything, Miss Colbert, because after that field trip you went on without permission…"

"It must have been 110 degrees in the classroom that day and we only went over to the police station." Marge swung the rope harder though she spoke in a soft even tone.

"And did you get permission to come over here? I think not. Reading, writing, and arithmetic, the three R's is all you are supposed…"

"That's an R, a W, and an A." Marge now had a slight smirk on her face.

"I'm taking over your classes for today and until I have decided what to do about this insubordination."

As Mr. Warner stormed up the stairs, Marge gave the swing a hard push.

"This is my first teaching job. How will I get another? And my family needs the money," Mary said as her eyes welled up with tears.

Marge reached in Mary's pocket, pulled out the newspaper clipping and handed it to her.

The Bureau of Investigation needs ladies to replace the men who are off fighting for our country. Apply to our Washington Representative in Des Moines, Iowa, April 17, 1942.

Chapter 4

At first, Freddy Bower thought this was the dream job. He was fairly tall, 5'7",
with what had been called by his last girlfriend, a killer-diller body. A little on
the heavy side, but she said that made him all the more huggable. At least until
she went off to hug that idiot, Steven Owens, but back to him.

I'm a nice looker even though I have a crooked nose, thought Freddy, but
*I still got all my sandy blonde hair even if it is thinning a bit. But I got one big
drawback, I'm a dead hoofer. Can't dance a step, can't keep a beat, the only
thing I can keep doing is stepping on some little missy's feet. These girlies
don't know that though. Or could they tell somehow even though I'm sitting
here at this desk in the police station all day. The FBI told me this was going
to be field work in the Midwest and I thought maybe gangsters in Chicago. I've
been trying to make the most of it with these little ladies, but too few of them
go for my line, I better get another one.*

"Would you be willing to go to Washington, DC, away from your family?"
It was the last question he had to ask.

"Yes, I've been living away from my family for some time now, trying to
earn some money. You know how times are," Mary said, across from Agent
Bower, leaning forward in her chair unaware how appealing it made her breasts
look. She was stacked.

"Do you live here in town?" Freddy was getting excited. This was his
second to last interview for the day and the innocence in her eyes made her an
easy target.

"No, over in Harper's Ferry. I'm staying overnight with a friend at a hotel
(that makes it actually sound nice) down the road."

"Maybe you and your friend would like to go out and get some dinner with
me after I finish interviews for the day, I've only got one left." He leaned

forward in his chair, getting a better look at her pale skin and the curves beneath the cream and dark blue dress. Two of them, now this could get interesting. "Why don't you ask your friend if she would…?"

"Oh, you can ask her, she's your next interview. Did I get the job?"

"I have to look over the application, but I'm sure everything here is in order and I can let you know by mail next week."

When Marge walked in the room, her heels clacking across the polished wood floor, he felt his groin responding to this looker. She wore a red dress, with a tight belt at the waist, and walked with a sway of her hips that didn't seem put on.

Now this is getting even better.

But the look in her eyes and the screech of the chair across the floor as she pulled it out told him that she was all business. She had done it, read his mind; that crazy thing women could do when they knew just what you wanted. And she would have none of it. Well, on with the interview, as she laid her completed application on the desk. He would ask her out to dinner too, but he could already tell by the way she sat back in her chair and crossed her legs, that he would be eating dinner alone again tonight.

I love coffee, I love tea, I love the java jive and it loves me
Coffee and tea and the jiving and me
Cup a, cup a, cup a, cup a, cup a…

Mary hadn't heard that song by her favorites the King Sisters in quite a while, and she began to sing along in her thin sweet voice. In the kitchen where the radio was, she could hear the rich voice of her mother singing along, and then to her surprise, Pa started singing in a low rumble. She laughed and began to hum so as not to be rude. Tessy, her rambunctious little sister with the big eyes and big heart kept talking and talking as she ran a comb through Mary's newly washed hair.

"And then he pushed me, so of course I pushed back and stepped on his toe as hard as I could so…"

"Tess! You're not supposed to beat up the boys. You could get hurt."

"But he's a bully to me and I just…"

"You should go to your teacher. Ow!" Mary said as Tess caught a tangle in the brush. She began working it out with her fingers.

"Sorry, but she never does anything but call his yucky mother and she does nothing."

Mary would have gone to talk to the teacher but she realized she wouldn't be here to do that. The month here at home with Ma, Pa, and the kids just made her heart ache that she was going away again, this time to a big city, Washington, DC.

"Honey, I have to finish packing. You can help me."

"I don't want you to pack, I don't want you to go. Who will brush your hair? You'll look like a mess and people with laugh at you. You need to take me along. I've never ridden on a train before. Does it go all the way there or will you have to get off and walk?"

Mary hugged Tess so tight she couldn't continue talking. Just then they heard the ca-lump, ca-lump, ca-lump, up the stairs, with other pairs of footsteps following behind. They sat on the edge of the bed in anticipation. Mary felt her nerves tingle and a lump in her stomach although she knew it was for no reason. When she was a little girl, she knew that sound meant Pa was coming up the stairs to talk to her about something; something she had done wrong. But she was older now and wasn't going down to the river when she wasn't supposed to or chasing after the boys when they went hunting for rattlers for the bounty.

The half open door slid all the way open and Kathy smiled big, missing one tooth, as Ma and Pa came in holding a package. Like a rushing stream, Po and Margaret Ann, her two other sisters, fifteen and seventeen, came in trying to suppress giggles like little girls. They pushed Pa forward.

As he held out a box wrapped with the funny papers and a red bow left over from Christmas, he said, "We got you something for your new life."

Tears came to Mary's eyes. This life of family here on this mighty river was about to be over, just a memory she would call up from its tender place in her heart when she looked at the few photos she was taking with her. It all made her heart ache. And the smiles in the room went bitter sweet.

She took the box and pulled off the bow putting it on the bed knowing they would use it again. Unwrapping it, she saw beautiful dusty rose material. As she pulled it out of the box, she realized it was a women's suit. She gasped.

Then everyone was talking at once.

"It's from a store over in Prairie du Chien."

"We all saved money for it."

"I did babysitting for the Falco kids."

"I helped bake cookies and went door to door and then…"

"I know I don't sew so well, so we figured…"

And all of a sudden everyone was silent. The music from the old radio in the kitchen had stopped.

And the news from the war front is…

I'm going down the road feelin' bad
I'm going down the road feelin' bad
I'm going down the road feelin' bad
I ain't gonna be treated this a way
I'm going where the water tastes like wine
I'm going where the water tastes like wine
I'm going…

Marge reached over from the back seat of the big old black Pontiac and turned off the radio. She was too excited to hear the exuberance of the music right now. She needed to breathe, calm down. Her mother held her rough hands tight together while her father's, stained with oil from the service station where he worked gripped the steering wheel tight. Something deep in her heart felt guilty about being excited to be leaving again. It wasn't that she hated her parents; it was just that they were always butting heads about the stupidest things. They were a stubborn lot. And it didn't help that her widowed grandmother had moved in with them a couple of years ago. Mom was stuck in the house all day with her, the two of them arguing, and when dad came home, she was ready to take it out on him. Nobody yelled at each other, they just bickered and bickered. But the silence was worse because that meant that they were really mad at each other.

And there was silence in the car right now. She couldn't figure this one out though. Were they mad that she was leaving and not trying to find a job closer to home, where she could help take care of her grandma, whose health wasn't so good lately? Was it that she had lost her job teaching and decided to go to the big 'evil' city? Or were they genuinely sad that she would be gone?

She pulled open the ashtray on the back seat, took out a Camel cigarette and lit it. She rolled down the window and saw they were now passing where the bluffs ran along the river and the sign up ahead read 'DANGER FALLING

ROCKS'. Not that she or anyone else had ever seen one. But she and her mother had always ducked down anyway. She felt like doing that now, just to be silly, so she did. Out of the corner of her eye, mom saw her and smiled. Then dad smiled too.

Marge saw tears in her mom's eyes, tears in her dad's. And there on the train platform in McGregor, she saw tears in the eyes of Mary and her family as they stood there waiting for her. There were no tears for Marge though. She was off on an adventure and the world seemed wide open in front of her.

Chapter 5

The future rumbled down the tracks, the smell of coal and soot came in the cracks around the window even though they had tried to close it tight. They had changed trains in Chicago and at least the cracked green leather seats on this one had thicker padding. The train hit a smooth patch and slipped along the rail. The swaying died down as did the rattle on the tracks.

Mary looked around at the people on the train: a mother with two young children, both asleep with their heads in her lap as she dozed off. A gentleman getting his suit coat wrinkled as he sat leaning into the corner between the seat and the window. He was snoring. Other people were snoring too, including a group of four soldiers in uniform. She had never actually seen a man in uniform before. Somehow their youth was smothered in the khaki cloth and they looked like the men in the newsreels, men who went to war, men who could die in battle.

She leaned over and put her arm through Marge's who was engrossed in watching the night and its lights go by. Neither of them could sleep. *Will I ever get a good sleep until this war is over?* She wondered as Marge turned to her.

"It shouldn't be long now. We should be there by morning."

What had passed them by in the night they could only guess. Large areas of darkness were punctuated by the white glow of lights. Sometimes in the distance, groups of lights seemed to warm and flicker like lightening bugs as they rushed by. The countryside heaved up and gave way to the late night city lights; lights of warehouses and factories where men and women worked in shifts all day and night for the war effort. And right along the tracks the sad apartment buildings, smeared with soot on the bricks and windows through which shone a pale light and the shadow of a person passing across it. The air had given up the fragrance of grasses and manure to give way to odors of exhaust and asphalt and the smell of coffee and hamburgers raced by. Mary was hungry but knew she was too nervous to eat, though she took an apple from her purse. It was from the front yard of her house back in Iowa—she cupped her hands around it holding on to the past.

Marge could not take her eyes away from the window, naming in her mind the towns and cities they must be passing through. She had sat down with a map the night before they left and tried to memorize each place. Changing in the hustle and bustle of Chicago, crossing two rivers, they went through the outskirts of Pittsburgh, and then Philadelphia which meant they could not be far away.

The blue of dawn rose like flooding waters around the train and Marge knew sunrise would not be far behind. In the seat in front of them a man with a puffy sun burned face, took out a cigar and slide down the window with a screech. The dull black wind blew in.

"Just love a shovel full of soot in my face," Marge said loud enough for the man to hear, though she could tell he couldn't care less. But she turned to Mary and with her infectious smile said, "Good for my complexion." Though she could be a bit crabby from time to time, especially after staying up all night (something she never had a reason to do), she was happy. Happy to be away from home, happy to be going someplace new and exciting, just plain happy.

The red sun sipped away at the night as the light now rose up around them. It was there in the distance, the shadows of buildings, of her new life. Marge pulled down the window and stuck her head out as the wind slapped her in the face.

"Look out big city, here come the government girls!"

Chapter 6

Lou Schweitz sat with his gut squeezed behind the steering wheel of the bus, took a puff off his cigar, and looked out the window to the river as it soaked up the dusk blue of evening and said goodbye and (Lou added) good riddance to the day. Still he had to laugh to himself. His pasty white skin turned a splotchy red as he broke out in a laugh. He knew why the band had hired him back in New York. They said they needed a white man to drive them down south, but he hadn't until today realized what they meant.

They had been driving along Route 1 in Georgia, a hot afternoon where every heat mirage splattered puddles over the asphalt. The widows were all open and most of his passengers were asleep. They had been performing late the night before. They worked hard. They weren't one of those soft and sweet swing bands that he used to be so fond of. That was, until he got this job and heard real swing for the first time. This band could jump and how he had come to love it. Even though he was fat, or rather heavy set as he preferred to say, he could get himself moving and jiving to the sounds. He slept in short shifts with their music always playing through his dreams.

Then he had heard the wail of the siren and in his rearview mirror saw that he was about to meet his first southern cop. He pulled over and pulled out a cigar which he didn't light. He liked the feet of it in his mouth, made him feel secure. He knew he hadn't been speeding nor doing anything else wrong, but he was still nervous and felt himself sweating even more.

"Afternoon, officer." He pulled the cigar from his mouth and rolled it in his fingers.

"Afternoon ya'll," the young fresh faced officer managed to drag out his words, for what seemed to Lou, like thirty minutes. "You from up north."

It wasn't a question. And Lou knew there were some blood feelings in the south for the north and began to get even more nervous.

"I saw the sign you got painted on the side of your bus." The cop leaned against the side of the bus as he spoke, smiling.

"Yes, did a nice job, didn't they?"

"It says 'Swing Sisters, swing like you never heard it before'. Sounds like one of those girl bands to me, mind if I take a look?"

The cop was already walking around to the other side of the bus.

"All the ladies are sleeping now," Lou said loud enough so the girls would hear him and lie low.

Lou opened the door and the cop climbed the stairs.

"Ladies?" he almost yelled. "These are just some bunch of niggers!" But he kept looking at the women.

Dotty, knowing she was one of the prettier of the girls and sleeping near the front of the bus was afraid her eyes would pop open involuntarily, and who knew what might happen then.

"These ain't ladies, mister, and don't you go calling them that and defiling our good women." The cop turned to Lou with a smirk on his face.

"I'm sorry, officer, I mean girls. It's only a New York slang we use. This is the first time I've taken my niggers here down south."

"So, these are your girls?"

"Yes, they're my girls."

As the smirk changed into a grin, the cop looked back at Dotty (she could feel him looking at her) and began to smile even more as he said, "Your girls, I guess I can understand that. Mom's got a couple works for her. And I guess I can excuse the language. You bein' a yank and all. Where you takin' 'em?"

"To the Stardust Ballroom over in Spottstown. Know the place?"

"Yeah, nigger dance hall. Some white guys go sometimes though; stand in the back where the stench isn't too bad. It's down Pickett Road, right on the water."

And that is where the bus sat with Lou in it waiting for the rest of 'his' girls to get off the bus so he could take a nap before he went in to hear their last set of three. God, girls could be noisy with all that chatting and giggling and laughing. 'His' girls, he kinda liked the way that sounded. Of course, he wouldn't say that to Rhea, the leader of the band, who was now acting as their agent too after she had dropped that louse from Indiana.

"It's all right down here, Mama, as alright as it can be with the police watching you all the time waiting for you to break their silly laws." The whole thing, having to step off the sidewalk when a white person walked by, using a crummy separate toilet with no toilet paper, it made her mad. But deep down it hurt, it really hurt. But she didn't want Mama to worry about her so far from home.

Lamar, a large guy whose white skin and bald head almost glowed in the dark, stood in the corner listening to Dotty but mostly looking. She was a tall light-skinned Negress with those nice full lips, moist as she talked into the phone in the hall. Backstage, around the corner, he could hear the girls laughing as they got dressed behind a sheet they held up for privacy. They didn't have dressing rooms. This wasn't that kind of establishment. And he loved booking these girl bands. If he wasn't in his sixties maybe he could have taken better advantage of the situation.

Twirling the phone cord around her finger, Dotty felt that homesickness beginning to churn her stomach and tighten around her heart. She only had one nickel left for the phone, but could have stayed on the call all night.

"No, Mama, I'm not afraid down here. We actually had a barbeque with a white man and his family the other night in Springfield. He had been a fan of our time on the radio at the ballroom in Indianapolis and loved to entertain us. He lived a ways out of town so he felt it was safe to have us over. It was nice to have a real meal after all these one night stands. It was four in the morning but we had all this great southern food, chicken, collard greens, corn on the cob and the best peach cobbler I've even had.

"Yeah, I miss home too. It's like a lazy dog down here. Don't feel like living down here. Everything is too slow, the way they move, and talk, and think."

"So, you think I'm slow, do you?" Lamar said stepping around the corner. Dotty was about to say something but Patsy came up out of nowhere and placed her hand on her shoulder. She knew Dotty had a quick tongue and if she wasn't careful, it would get her in trouble down here. She had been chatting with Barb who had toured the south before, with another band, and frankly, the stories she told scared her. If it wasn't that she needed the job so bad, she would have stayed back in New York and let the Swing Sisters go on tour without her.

"We were all talking the other night about how you southern men are such gents. You take your time to think what you are going to say, not like the men up north who can't even think and just blurt out whatever comes into their thick skulls," Patsy said realizing as she said this it sounded stupid but perhaps Lamar, who was about as smart as a manhole cover, didn't notice. But when she saw the look in his eyes she knew that what he noticed was her and her light skin for a Negro.

"Mama, I gotta go, the band is warming up, yes I know, but tell the neighbors and the kids that I love them, yes, gotta go." She put the phone back in the rack and heard her nickel click in the box. Sally was giving her that 'we gotta get out of here' look.

Patsy took Dotty by the arm and walked her toward the stage. "Nice chatting with you, sir, we have to get to practice or Rhea will have our behinds for being late."

Dotty looked back when she realized she had left the pile of nickels she had intended to pay for the call with back on the phone. Lamar looked right at her with a smarmy smile, then pulled a red hanky out of his back pocket, picked up the receiver and wiped it like she had left germs all over it. The heat of anger rose in Dotty's cheeks but she turned and looked ahead. What else could she do?

Thank Jesus she doesn't sunburn, Dotty thought as she pulled back the tattered blue velvet curtain and walked behind Patsy onto the stage. When they had arrived and the other girls still slept, as best they could in the wet heat, Patsy laid out in the bright sun to make sure her skin was dark enough to pass for a Negro. She had talked to other girls before they left and she knew the importance of keeping up the appearance of being colored.

As Dotty slipped the strap of her sax over her shoulder, Patsy sat down behind the drums. They both smiled at each other and slipped off their high heels before Rhea came out and saw them do it. She thought the taller the woman the more elegant she looked to the men who came, not only to dance with their girl but to ogle at the band. For Dotty, it was a matter of comfort. It could be hell standing through three, maybe four sets in heels. And she couldn't even imagine how Patsy could have used the pedal on the drums.

The shoulder strap hurt on her bare skin and callouses had finally started to form on her shoulder. The dresses the girls wore were ones that Rhea had picked out for them and then had copies made by a local seamstress back home. She thought they made them look elegant. The dresses were not as beautiful as the 'International Sweethearts of Rhythm' wore, but not like the suit jackets some of the other girl bands wore. They were long dresses of a blue shiny material, off the shoulder but not too low cut. "Just enough to get the boys hot," Rhea had said. But they were expensive. Dotty had done some freelance typing for different offices around town and had managed to save up the money.

The ceiling had turned dusk blue with the lights reflecting off the cigarette smoke that filled the room. The shining bodies of the boys and girls swirled and strutted as they jitterbugged to the music.

Dotty smiled. It was time for one of her favorites. Barb, their lead singer, chosen because she was a looker as much as for her voice, stepped back and turned to Tracy at the piano. She took a breath and leaned over the keys, her exposed back glistening with sweat. She began to play slow and romantic. Then Barb stepped forward as Dotty put her sax to her lips and made it wail. The rest of the band broke out into…

It don't mean a thing, if you ain't got that swing
Do-wah Do-wah Do-wah
It don't mean a thing, all you gotta do is swing
Do-wah Do-wah Do-wah
It makes no difference if it's sweet or it's hot
Just give that rhythm everything you got.

And Dotty loved the way the crowd cheered and set themselves in motion. She glanced to the back of the hall where the two white police officers, the 'security', stood and despite themselves they were smiling, one even mouthing some of the words. Then he winked at her and Dotty looked away.

Dotty held the newspaper and stared at the front page where the photos were out of focus and grainy, and the news of the war distressed her. Men were dying. That was the real news behind the headlines. And what was she doing? Playing with a band.

She folded the paper as best she could and looked down at her breakfast. She was famished. Dotty could eat a horse, but it being morning, she was having eggs over easy, grits with lots of butter, and biscuits and pan gravy.

The cafeteria, for her race only, was a large room with cinderblock walls freshly painted a pale green, about the only color it seemed you could get once the war had started. Long tables filled the room and the food was served family style with the plates heaping with food. The cook came out and smiled with his hands on his hips. Of course, the regulars were there, and some of the kids from the dance last night, but the real satisfaction came to him serving the band, his honored guests as he saw things.

"I'll eat so much, I'll pop the seams in my dress," Patsy said as she lifted up a piece of white toast with a lake of butter in the middle. She had to admit she liked this southern cooking but still missed a good meatball that Mama made.

There was a loud screech as the door to the cafeteria slid slowly open and the crowded place slid into silence, with only the clatter of forks being put down on plates. In the doorway, surrounded by hot yellow sunlight, stood the silhouettes of two men. Dotty looked away from the light and to the faces of the locals around them. A polite but nervous smile hid at the corners of their eyes. A look of panic skidded across the faces of a few of the girls in the band. Looking over at Patsy, she could tell that she also thought something she didn't understand was happening.

The two men stepped into the room, letting the door slam behind them, the curtain on the window of the door swaying like a ghost. One was larger than the other, large enough to intimidate anyone with the smirk that was wiped across his face. The other was a skinny guy also dressed in worn jeans and a stained white shirt. They wore their clothes like a uniform. They both had guns tucked into their belts. And both were white beneath a hot shimmering sunburn.

They looked around the room with their eyes resting on each member of the band. Suddenly, the room burst into talking but this time with a nervous edge to it that cut like a dull knife.

"We're just here to make sure no laws are being broken," the bigger man said in a slow, wet drawl. Dotty recognized the man. He had been standing at the back of the ballroom, with, but not really with the policemen from last night. The smell of bacon frying was overwhelmed by the smell of fear as the locals tried not to look at the men.

"Morning, gentlemen," said Pete, the owner and chef. "Can I offer you anything to eat?"

The skinny man ran his finger along the handle of his gun, an obvious gesture of intimidation.

"You know we wouldn't eat with niggers."

"I thought you might like a cup of coffee to take out."

The big man smiled as if to say, "Oh, trying to get rid of us?"

"We heard there was a new band in town and came to see for ourselves."

Dotty knew the man had already seen the band. She put her hand down beside her and grabbed the handle of her purse. She nodded to Patsy to do the same as the act subtly spread among the band members.

The two men walked through the tables as every customer averted their eyes and tried to act as if nothing was wrong. At the table next to Dotty and Sally sat an older couple, both with snowy white hair. In the middle of a sentence, Dotty heard the man say 'civilian patrol', and Dotty knew it was meant as a warning to her though she didn't really know why.

The two men came up to the table where Dotty sat and stood behind her chair. She could smell them, a mixture of tobacco and sweat. They were looking at Patsy. As casually as possible, she lifted her cigarette and took a drag then put it back in the ashtray. Smoke hovered in front of her face as though she was trying to hide behind it.

"You're awful light-skinned, girl," the skinny man said. There was a tone to his voice that was even more frightening than the bulk of the other man.

"Yes," said Patsy, "my daddy was a white factory owner."

"And where was that?"

"In Newark, New Jersey."

The other man stepped in front of his companion. Dotty could smell the sourness of his breath.

"I'm not so sure you are colored. I've been up north, and you sound like an Italian to me and that would mean your white and associating with colored. That's an insult to real ladies."

"And," the other man spoke up with a chuckle, "will send you to jail here."

Sally could guess what would happen to a white girl who tried to pass as colored when she was in jail. Her eyes darted around. She could feel herself beginning to panic. There must be a way out but she couldn't see one.

More light flooded the room as the door opened and two men stood in the doorway. They stepped into the room holding the door open in surprise at seeing the two white men there. The black skin of the two men shone in the light. They were both dressed in uniform.

The older man at the next table had been wringing his napkin in his hands as he watched what had been going on. He quickly stood and saluted the two soldiers. As the two white men turned around to see what was happening, the other customers stood. There was a moment of silence. Then the crowd began to clap. The big man turned to his skinny partner and they both looked around flustered.

Dotty, already standing and holding her purse glanced around at her fellow band members. They held their purses and Rhea was already moving toward the door. Like a flood of dark water, the women rushed out the door, all of them pushing Patsy to the front.

As they broke from the door, they began to yell, "North. North!" and ran down the road where Lou had parked the bus. Through the sound of chewing his sandwich, Lou heard the code word he had set with the ladies. 'North' meant get the bus started—we gotta get out of here fast!

Chapter 7

Like a great stream after a damn had broken, Marge and Mary were swept off the train and down the platform hanging onto their suitcases and each other. There were men and women and children, and many soldiers. Washington had been a sleepy southern town until the war, but now had been transformed in a flash and 200,000 thousand people passed through Union Station every day.

Union Station, Architect Daniel H Burnham, assisted by Pierce Anderson, was inspired by the Arch of Constantine for the impressive exterior and the Baths of Diocletian for the ninety-six foot tall vaulted ceiling, decorated with receding squares of gold leaf. The room shone like wet stone; marble and white granite. This was a palace in the grand European style yet uniquely American celebrated in six colossal statues designed by Louis St. Gaudens: Prometheus (Fire), Thales (Electricity), Themis (Freedom and Justice), Apollo (Imagination and Inspiration), Ceres (Agriculture) and Archimedes (Mechanics). They watched over the huge room, rumbling with the trains below and the crowds of soldiers and civilians hurrying across the marble floors from their trains to restaurants, shops, barber shops, ticket windows, or out the huge doors.

It was into this almost overwhelming room that two young women from farm country were swept. People jostled around them and the cigarette that Marge was trying to smoke was knocked from her hand by a soldier's elbow and landed on the floor, which she noticed was covered with other smashed butts.

Mary wanted to say something to Marge, something about the size of things, her fear all mixed up with excitement, anything to try to connect with her. She tried reaching for Marge's hand but they were being pulled apart. Finally, she stopped, having reached one of the long oak benches in the center of the room, and the crowd rushed by them. A group of GI's sat smoking and almost yelling at each other above the roar of the trains and the slam of a thousand feet on the hard surface of the floors beneath them.

On the bench with the men, one of the soldiers was slumped over asleep. Mary could tell by the way he was blowing through his mouth, he was snoring. She laughed to herself when she saw someone had stuck a tag into his hat that said, "Wake for the 2:00 train to Raleigh."

"What's buzzin', cousin? How's it going?" A thin but confident voice said behind them. They turned around to see a boy, almost a man, with a thin face and a thin body in a tight brown and white checkered suit.

Mary stood, confused. He wasn't her cousin so why…

"Byron Fillmore here at your service, a one man welcoming committee. Let me take those bags for you," he said reaching for their worn brown leather suitcases.

"Oh, is this that southern hospitality I've heard about?" Marge said with a big smile.

Byron smiled back as Mary asked, "Did Mr. Hoover send you?"

Before he could answer he had taken the bags and jumped into the stream of people. Marge was the first to realize what had happened.

"Somebody squash that bug, he's got our bags!" she tried to yell above the noise.

Just before he totally vanished, they saw a tall light-skinned colored woman swing her carpet bag around and threw it across the floor, landing right in the thief's path. He skidded to a halt as the bag traveled under his feet and knocked him to the floor. Mary ran over to where he lay with the wind knocked out of him.

"Are you hurt?" he asked kneeling beside him.

"He woulda had a better day if my bag hadn't run into him," the colored woman said picking up her bag. Marge arrived and grabbed their bags off the floor just as Byron jumped up and raced for one of the doors to the street.

"Thanks for saving our vast fortune," Marge said as the woman helped Mary up off the floor. "And Mary here who was ready to nurse that crook back to health."

"Dotty Mason," as Marge and Mary both extended their hands. They shook hands and look relieved. "You gotta be careful here. *Newsweek* called this city the murder capital of the United States." She saw the surprised look on the two women's faces start to change to fear, so she quickly added, "Here to find a government job?"

"Mr. Hoover already hired us," Mary said taking her bag. The three of them began to walk toward the door, jostled by the crowd. "How about you?"

"I'll be looking for a job, but I gotta find a place to hang my hat first."

"Any ideas?" Marge asked.

"Sister, I wish I did."

They had reached one of the huge doors. Mary was about to push it open when a soldier rushed forward and opened it for her.

"Thank you."

"Anything for you," he said with a silly grin on his boyish face. He tried to catch Mary's eye again as they all walked out of the building.

But across the park-like setting in front of the station, rose the gleaming white dome of the Capitol Building. Mary found she had tears in her eyes.

In Washington, hot days may come in the spring, but not the heat of day that the women were used to. This heat was not dry, nor damp, but with a humidity that verged on wet. The city shimmered: the white buildings of marble, the mirages in the street above the asphalt, the foreheads of the men, women, and children they passed by. The air shimmered with sound: laughter from a group of women standing on the sidewalk in front of a newsstand, army buddies punching each other as they laughed in a playful way, the hissing of the grass, the growl of a car, and the clang of the trolley bell. This was paradise for the GI's that were passing through town. So many men had gotten drafted that women stepped up to take their jobs and the new ones created by the war machine, which seemed to live off of paper. Two soldiers hung out of the trolley window whistling as it passed by Mary, Marge, and Dotty.

Smiling Mary said, "I heard cities weren't friendly, but I never have seen so many friendly young men."

As they crossed Connecticut Avenue in a hurry, all but Dotty astounded by the traffic, Marge said, "I think by their cat calls, they wanted to be more than just friends."

They had crossed over into the park in the middle of Dupont Circle. "Face it, Mary," Dotty said laughing, "you are stacked."

The fountain, round and ornate, was surrounded by women in summer cotton dresses and a fewer number of men in uniform, trying to strike up conversations with the women. Being outnumbered by the women, the men were puffing out their chests like roosters and trying to impress them.

Marge walked over to the fountain and sat down on the ledge, taking off her shoes.

"We walked all the way from the station, and my dogs are barking." She swung around and plopped her feet in the water. It felt so good she let out a long sigh.

Dotty and Mary sat down too, as Marge splashed her feet in the water.

"We've been walking and walking and stopping at every boarding house but everything seems to be full. We need a better strategy. I thought we would find something in the *Washington Post* but diddly squat."

Dotty lowered her head and was silent.

"We'll find something. I just know we will," Mary said putting down her suitcase and sitting on it. "I'd rather walk through cow pies than on these hard sidewalks."

Three GIs, buddies since they found out they were being shipped to Europe together, walked through the park trying to enjoy their last hours in the city. They were looking for an escape from the thoughts of what lay ahead. Although with their boasting and bravado, they acted to each other as if they were excited to go off on some great adventure. Their names were Bill, the tallest, John, the shortest, and Steven somewhere in the middle in both height and looks.

"We need some help with these bags," Marge said to Dotty, knowing Mary wouldn't get what she was thinking. Dotty smiled and nodded as Marge reached over and unbuttoned the top button on Mary's tan blouse.

"Just so you won't get so hot," Marge said. Dotty laughed under her breath as she saw three GIs looking their way, well not so much their way, Mary's way. From the way they looked at her, Dotty surmised they were from the Midwest and had probably never seen a colored person before.

John grabbed his buddy's arm, smiling at the three gals they had spotted at the fountain.

They smiled back.

"Do you think they want us to pay them for…" asked John whispering as he stared at the women. He had heard from his buddies back at the barracks about such women, but thought they only came out at night.

"Shut up and wave back," said Steven his smile growing wider as he whispered back out of the side of his mouth, "They're nice gals, can't you see, they got a maid."

Marge dried her feet on a hanky she pulled from her purse and slipped on her shoes as the soldiers came over. She stood up.

"Ladies, could we be of service to you?" John said bowing.

"Why is he talking like that?" Bill whispered to Steven.

"He's only from Missoula not some highfalutin Englishman," Steven muttered.

Marge stepped forward batting her long eyelashes which, with her hazel eyes, were her best feature.

"We've just been resting after carrying these bags around all day. And you gentlemen, definitely officer material, could you be so kind as to carry our bags?"

"We'd be delighted," Bill said.

John grabbed for Mary's bags, and Steven, always a bit late on the up take, grabbed Marge's. They each still had a free hand but only Bill made an effort to carry Dotty's bags. She insisted on carrying the small case but let Bill take her big carpet bag.

"Sorry about them. Let me take that too," Bill said reaching for the smaller metal case.

"I can carry this. But thank you so much for offering."

As they began to walk away, Dotty leaned over to Marge and nodded her head toward Bill, "Definitely officer material."

The Fraser Mansion, and it certainly was a mansion, on the corner of R Street and Connecticut Ave., was impressive not only for its size but for the early eclectic Beaux style designed by the firm of Hornblower and Marshall in 1890. The building was three stories high with attic windows that could be seen under a tiled hipped roof. So different than the many white marble and gray granite buildings of the city, or the brick townhouses they had been searching for a room, it was red brick wrapped in rough lines of pink granite. There was a colonnaded entrance porch with a balustraded deck.

And there stood the girls after the soldiers left them, hurrying to catch a trolley back to their barracks, which had been constructed on the Washington Mall near the Washington Monument.

"This must be it," said Marge holding up the housing section of the Washington Star.

"The sign says Golden Parrot Tea Room and Restaurant, but I guess the place is so big they must have rooms to rent." Mary reached up and buttoned the top button on her blouse again.

"Get out your rosary, Mary." Marge folded the paper and put it under her arm.

"The city looks full," Mary said with just a hint of disappointment in her voice.

Marge reached for the doorbell, afraid to just walk in. Dotty stopped her.

"The last place was full because I came to the door with you and you know it."

"And that's the way it is," said Mary reaching across Marge and pushing the doorbell. "You are here and so are we. Ever occur to you, we might not want to live in that place anyway?"

"You are white, in fact, some of the whitest people I've seen."

"Are you sure?"

"If we're gonna be friends, I gotta know why you don't put me aside."

Dotty could see Mary had a determined look on her face.

"My grandmother is a full-blooded Ojibway and she wouldn't put anyone aside."

"Don't try to vote in the state of Louisiana. Marge?"

"I know her grandmother and she has a mean temper I wouldn't want to cross"

As the heavy door swung open, they saw a woman like no other they had seen before. Her dark hair was wild yet styled. Her eyes were surrounded in dark make-up and she wore a long dress in black, not an evening dress, but something far more interesting, with lace tufts like they had never seen before. Although all this darkness could have been intimidating, the smile on her red lips was wide and welcoming. She swayed her body as she spoke, her hands spun happiness around her and the gold hoop earrings shone in the sun that spilled in the door way.

The women stood there not really sure what to say. This was the kind of person you were immediately attracted to because she must be so interesting, like an ornate box from some far away land than you couldn't wait to open.

"I've been waiting for you," she began then paused. They might get the wrong impression once they learned of her reputation. "I saw you out there on the porch for the longest time and figured you might be sizing up my establishment. It's a very decent boarding house on the upper floors and the main floor is a fine dining establishment."

"Oh, I am sure that it is, we were just wondering…" Mary began but then started to fumble her words. *Were all city women going to be like her? A bit crazy?*

"Actually," Marge said pulling the newspaper from under her arm, "we were admiring the place. It's like a big pink White House, maybe bigger. We tried to get a room there but they were full."

They all laughed, not a polite laugh, but a genuine one when they were infected by the woman's loud laugh.

"Like the government asked us when they came by last year, we've opened up the third floor; it was actually the servant's floor from back when this was a private residence. The rooms are a bit small, but very clean and away from the street noise on Connecticut. It's warmer in the winter, which is good what with the oil rationing, and with very nice people, except for that pesky ghost. Oh, maybe I shouldn't have mentioned that." The woman was very apologetic. She had a good feeling about these girls and would love to have them stay here.

"Do you have a boarder who sleeps in a coffin in the basement too?" Marge quipped.

Mary was afraid if Marge was going to start making some of her smart remarks they would never find a place to live, but the woman only chuckled and gave Marge a wink as if to say, I love your wit.

"It sounds marvelous Mrs.…"

"Goldman, but known to all my boarders as Elaine. Actually I only have one room in the house…"

Disappointment turning to anger, Dotty said, "War changes everything but not this. I'll be on my way." She picked up her bag and the metal case.

"Maybe, we better too," a sad look swept across her face. Sad they would still have to look for a place to stay and sad for the way Dotty got treated. Mary understood suddenly that Washington was a southern town after all.

"Oh, actually I have two rooms. One is upstairs, and the other is above the old carriage house. That one has its own bathroom. Two of you could share one of the rooms and one could take the other if that works just fine for you girls."

They stepped into the foyer, into shadows and stairways. One led down on each side of a wide staircase, covered with an oriental carpet held down by brass rails that were shined bright.

They followed Elaine up the staircase into a room that almost took their breath away. None of them had ever seen everything like it: paneled walls in mahogany three quarters of the way to the mahogany beamed ceiling. Above the panels carved in the walls were shields with lions and horns and falcons and more on them. One could imagine suits of armor standing below each one. In the corner, flanked by benches was a huge gray stone fireplace. It was the grandest room the women had ever seen and through the doors around them they could see even grander rooms: one with floor to ceiling stained glass doors that lead to a garden, dining rooms to their left and right with fireplaces with grand mantels and crystal chandeliers.

They were astounded, thrilled and frightened. It was all so unfamiliar they could not image themselves living here, but knew it was unlikely that they would find anywhere else. "Once you make it in the door of any of these boarding houses," said one young woman they had encountered on their travels, also looking for a room, "be ready to answer lots of questions. It's like an interrogation. They know that they can search for the perfect boarder with so many of us looking and so few of them with rooms available."

The women waited for the questions to begin. At least they had made it in the door and up the stairs. But there were no questions, only a request.

"Give me your hands," said Elaine. She took the left hand of the three women, then closed her eyes and was silent. The women waited for her to say something. Finally, she smiled and opened her eyes. "Yes, you are the ones I've been looking for to live here."

Confused, Mary was about to ask what Elaine meant when she heard a cough down the stairs. The glare of the bright yellow light streamed in the glass from the door where the silhouette of a figure stood.

"Oh," said Elaine following Mary's eyes, "I have an appointment now. Why don't you girls go in and have yourself a nice cup of tea and when I'm done, I'll show you the rooms? Harry, we've got some new boarders!"

Chapter 8

The staircase was wide until they got to the third floor where it narrowed. At the end of the hall was a smaller, uncarpeted staircase which the three of them ascended with their new landlady. The hall they entered was narrower with the ceiling high above them. There was a small window at each end of the hall.

One of the doors opened and a woman about twenty-seven stepped out. Apparently, she spent much of her time putting together her exotic wardrobe. Draped in exotic patterns, lace, and fringe, she had an atmosphere of chaos with her long dark hair that was constantly in motion as her hands wove her words together. Her lips were full and pursed as if she had just tasted something sour. The olive of her skin led Dotty to determine she was probably Italian. And she was in a hurry.

"Hello," she said with an affected accent that had a hint of New Jersey that Dotty recognized. "I'm Brigette. I'm inspired right now. Can't get chatty!" with a gesture she swept them aside and rushed to the room with the sign on it marked 'Bathroom'.

"She calls it inspired, I call it going to the bathroom," Marge said.

"She's an artist," said Elaine as though that explained everything about Brigette.

It was not a large room; it had only one bed with a flowered pattern veneer that had mostly peeled off. The wallpaper, also with flowers, yellow, was peeling at the seams. A musty smell, accumulated over the years, seemed to cover the few pieces of furniture: an ornate oak chair with a faded and worn red horse hair seat, left over from the days this mansion had been built, a dresser with a large round mirror whose silver was tarnished, and a chest of drawers that matched the bed in style and disrepair.

Dotty went to the window, grabbed the green velvet drapes which, before they became thread bare had probably hung downstairs. She pulled them open and looked out across the city, the white dome of the Capitol and the

Washington Monument rising in the distance. *Girl, what are you doing here?* She thought.

Marge plopped down on the bed with a creaking of the springs and immediately took her shoes off and rubbed her feet. Then she hauled her suitcase up on the bed. With a struggle, she untied the knot of the clothesline her mother had wrapped around it, to make sure it would stay closed and so no one could easily get into it. Opening the suitcase, she took out what lay on top, a blue painted picture frame with a faded picture of her whole family, dad, mom, Jimmy, and her. They were dressed in their Sunday best. Ben, the old man next door, had taken the picture before had left for the city. She placed it on the chest of drawers.

Mary opened the door and came in the room. She closed the door behind her as Dotty turned around lost in thought.

"One bathroom for the floor, but it's gotta be better than sharing the basin and the outhouse with everyone in my family." Mary felt the room sigh as though it was relieved to be lived in again.

"I guess, I'm the lucky one that gets the room out back with its own bathroom. Never had one to myself before," Dotty said with a smile as Marge pulled another photo from her suitcase and leaned it up against the framed photo. It was of a young man, handsome in a dark and troubled sort of way, in a navy uniform.

"Well, look here, you got yourself a beau overseas?"

"That's my big brother Davey. I pray for him every day. God must have ears as sore as my feet with all the praying goin' on with this war," answered Marge.

Sitting down in the chair, Dotty said more to herself than to the other two women, "How did we get ourselves into this crazy war? What is wrong with people?"

"Guilt and anger, the two great motivators," Marge said sadly.

Mary sat down on the bed beside Marge.

"Where is love in the equation?"

"That's what I'd like to know," Marge pleaded as she lay back on the bed.

"Back home in an apartment in Harlem, in that picture there, and anywhere we can find it in this city," said Dotty as she walked toward the door.

Mr. Goldman, or Harry as he requested to be called, walked with Dotty, Marge, and Mary through the vegetable garden or victory garden as they were known, to the carriage house at the back, by the iron gate in the brick wall.

"We took up the formal gardens that were back here and put in a victory vegetable garden for the restaurant. We did it for the war effort, all the produce now gets canned and sent directly to the troops. You're welcome to come out and pull weeds anytime you feel the desire to," he chuckled.

The carriage house, painted a dark green with white trim, looked unlike the house, a gingerbread style Victorian building. The double doors to the carriage house were open, and as the others began to climb the stairs to the room Dotty would occupy, Mary saw next to the Chevy a Jersey cow was tied up. Walking over to the cow she patted it on the head.

"I never was that fond of cows before but you sure remind me of home. I better get upstairs."

As she ran up the stairs, Harry was coming down and squeezed past her.

"I gotta get back to the kitchen and make sure there is some cooking going on, not just horsing around. See you at dinner, served at six in the basement if Elaine didn't tell you." Harry had the body frame of a thin man but a large stomach, and he barely squeezed by Mary.

Dotty was admiring her new digs.

"This place is killer-diller!"

It was very small with only a single bed, more of a cot, and a chair like the ones in the dining rooms but with a broken leg that had been repaired. Marge pulled back the curtain with roses on a gray background at the far end of the room, to reveal a toilet and the smallest sink she had ever seen.

Dotty pulled open the shutters on the window on the back wall. She was staring out the window when Marge said, "We can hold big parties here with lots of fat people."

Mary looked around the room.

"Oh it's small but it's yours alone. Marge and I have to share a bed, not that you smell or anything, Marge," Mary said joking. "You are lucky."

"Yes, I am lucky," Dotty said looking out the window into the alley below. There were huts built from scraps of tin roofing and any loose boards that could be found up against the garden walls of beautiful large houses. One shack had a shingle nailed up to the wall with 'Betty's House' scrawled across it, another with 'Vicky's House'. She was aghast. Children of all ages played in clothes that had been patched so many times the original material was unrecognizable. She could see colored women and men milling about the alley. The women going to the one pipe with water coming out of it and filling up buckets and hanging out laundry on lines strung between the shacks. While the few men she saw sat on old chairs barely able to hold a person chatting with each other, whittling little toys for the children to play with or simply smoking a pipe or cigarette looking off to into the distance. With few prospects for making a decent living and even less hope for their future. From further down the alley came the sound of a sad harmonica.

African American men and women had been traveling north since the civil war, looking for opportunities they couldn't find in the south. Many headed toward Washington. When they arrived, they found that jobs as bellhops, wash women, or laborers were scarce. But the housing situation was worse, so many had ended up in shacks in the alleys on Capitol Hill and behind great houses throughout town. A commission had been formed in 1939 to clean up the alleys and build public housing, but the war had brought even more blacks to the city and many lived in squalor out of sight. Washington's dirty little secret.

Chapter 9

"Hi-de-ho," a soldier and his buddies said as they passed by. One of them whistled. But the women took no notice. It had been going on all afternoon as they toured the city with their eyes wide open. Marge had even forgotten her feet were killing her. No longer concerned with where they would be living, they had sympathy for the groups of women they saw hauling their suitcases and a newspaper turned to the housing section.

They had decided to go sightseeing in the capital city. They stood in front of the Capitol Building and asked a man with a briefcase passing by if he would take a picture with the camera Marge had bought at a Kresgie's department store. But instead of getting the photo of the three women, soldiers kept jumping in the picture. They decided to treat them like her students, "Move along" and quickly shooed them away.

"Now get out of here and go about your business," she said with a voice of authority, and like her students, they went off with their heads hanging low.

The picture was finally taken and they thanked the man. He thanked them for coming to "this great city to serve their country in its time of need."

They strolled down the trampled green grass of the mall lined with temporary office buildings and barracks and the sound of hammers as more were being built.

Arriving in front of the White House, they saw it was surrounded by an iron fence, piles of sand bags, and soldiers standing guard. Two of the guards swung the creaking gates wide open and a large black car emerged with American flags flying on the front fenders.

Mary was so excited she thought she would pee in her panties.

"That must be him! President Roosevelt!"

The car rolled past them slowly and they tried to get a glimpse of the man inside but could not see through the thick glass.

"Must be," said Dotty, fanning herself with her hand against the heat. "I hear tell that is Al Capone's former car. It's got steel plates in it and bullet proof glass. The Secret Service uses it to protect the president."

"Oh," Mary said, suddenly concerned, "who would want to shoot such a great man?"

"One guy with a funny little mustache, and I don't mean Charlie Chaplin." Marge turned to Dotty who had now pulled out the low neckline of her dress and was blowing down between her breasts. "I want to find a man just like Roosevelt. Only three decades younger."

The cherry trees were in bloom and the pink petals drifted lazily by on unseen currents of air and landed on the ground at their feet. They had finally reached the Jefferson Memorial. Though the monument was not quite finished the workmen had left for the day and silence surrounded them. With its white dome, Greek columns and the Tidal Basin in front, it looked like a Greek temple alone against a painfully blue sky.

Mary grew quiet as she wished her mother were here to share this moment.

Walking over to a sign Dotty said to the women, "It says here this statue of Jefferson is plaster for now, until they can use real bronze after the war is over."

"Will it ever be over?" Mary said brushing away some dirt and sitting down on one of the steps.

"It's been hard times for so long it seems back in New York. No jobs for a man, fewer for women, and then if you are colored…"

"So, you came here just like us and the hoards in hairnets." Marge sat down beside Mary.

"I had to get away from what I was doing and come here. If anything is to happen for this Negro woman, or any woman for that matter, it's going to begin here." Dotty sat down beside the other two women.

"A couple of weeks ago," Mary said softly, "I was doing what I had been expected to do, be a teacher. Now, I'm in a big city and going to work for the FBI. It's all so fast and so scary."

Dotty nodded. "Everything happens so fast during a war; love, death, changes."

"Everything happens so fast in a war except victory." Marge got up and walked over to the statue of Jefferson. It was hard to imagine he had once been a real person. "He looks like a god. If the Germans invade, they will probably think we've been offering up bureaucrats."

"It may sound crazy for one of my people to say this but I love and believe in this country. I pray to Jesus we can keep it." Dotty threw down her cigarette and crushed the butt.

Mary got up brushing down her dress. "We can never fall before Germany. Even if they invade, our spirit can't be broken and we will rise again. Because we believe in what it stands for."

"And all this Negro here wants right now is to find her a job."

"Well look at ya'll, dressed up like a movie star," Pam said and her 'sisters' laughed long and hard, and took deep drags off their Camels.

Dotty looked over at the group of three black women, all darker skinned than she was, something she had encountered before. They would be jealous of her because she was lighter skinned.

She had been standing out front of the five and dime for the last twenty minutes, smoking cigarettes and watching the young women going in the side door with nervous looks, sometimes expressed in giggling, sometimes in silence. Many carried their suitcases made of boxes that a sewing machine or a hairdryer had come in, wrapped round with rope so they could carry it. They all looked around to see what the other women were wearing, what skirt, what color lipstick, what hair-do. Most were new to a big city, coming from small towns or farms across the country, and they wanted to fit in with the big city that would be their new home.

She could tell by the accents of the black women they were from the south and she immediately thought of her experiences down in Georgia where she felt like a fish out of water. The group looked at her haughtily as she walked over to them, though Dotty knew that they were just feeling insecure.

"Hello, I'm Dotty Mason and thanks for the compliment. You can't imagine how hard I worked to look like I belong here in Washington. I just hope it is good enough to get a job," Dotty said putting down her case and extending her hand.

After shaking hands and introducing themselves, Effie said, "Oh, you look spiffy. We have to do some shopping now that we have jobs at the Navy Yard, wherever that is, though I guess it has to be on the water." They all laughed. "But we won't have much time to shop because we start work tomorrow!"

Pam said, "Whew!" and they all knew she was expressing a bucket full of emotions that had been dumped on her: fear, excitement, confusion. "I can't keep my feet on the ground this is all happening so fast!"

"Amen!" they all said and laughed.

"I found a place to live now I have to get up there and find a job," Dotty said refusing a cigarette that Pam offered her.

"Oh, we asked where the colored women could stay and we're staying at Lucy Stowe Hall, near that college for the colored. Are you staying there?"

"No, but maybe I'll be seeing you around town. Good luck!"

Dotty found herself in a cavernous room above the store. The echo off the high ceiling jangled her nerves. There were hundreds of women coming and going, lined up at tables with signs above them with an alphabet soup of letters WPA, OPA, OEM, BEW, and more. One made Dotty laugh: PWPGSJSISACWPB. Who could remember what all those letters stood for? She decided to just pick a line with a friendly looking girl to talk to and hope she got that job.

"Oh, we'll get a job, even you," said the young woman with her freckles going across her nose and between her breasts. "They need so much of every kind of work done they can't afford to not hire anyone, you betcha!"

But Washington after all is said and done is in the south, Dotty thought.

At a large table sat a handsome middle-aged man who had been developing a paunch. His brown hair was slicked back. He wore a gray suit that matched his eyes, which looked tired. He had just finished filling out the employment form for the girl with the freckles.

"Next," he said clearing his throat.

Dotty stepped forward as the other girl gave her a thumbs up.

"So, ya'll want a job?" This was a deep southern accent. Dotty smiled at his sour stare.

"We're lookin' for typists not laborers. Sorry."

"Oh, I can type, learned back in New York during the depression."

The man was stunned, a colored girl who could type.

"What is your name, please?"

Dotty took the form and went around the other side of the table where there was a vacant chair. She sat down.

Then Dotty placed the metal case on the desk and opened it to reveal a typewriter.

The Department of War had run an intense campaign to collect typewriters to handle all the paperwork waging a war required. 'Send your typewriter to war', had been on posters all over New York. There had been a jingle on the radio.

"An idle typewriter is a help to Hitler."

But the campaign was a failure even though Maureen O'Sullivan had appeared in an ad with a pile of typewriters in front of her, with tags that said, 'For Uncle Sam'.

"Maybe I can help you fill out these forms?" Dotty asked still smiling.

"But these forms, those morons, excuse me, bureaucrats printed are 18 inches and most typewriters are 12 inches. Sorry." The man looked startled and stumbled over his words.

"This typewriter is 18 inches," Dotty said as she took an empty form from the pile and ran it into the typewriter. "Next. You ask the questions Mr…"

"Hobbs, Eugene Hobbs."

"Dorothy Mason. And you, Miss are…"

A long hall with tall ceilings filled with whispers. Photos of men in suits holding guns lined the walls as did glass cases of Tommy guns and handguns. Marge and Mary pushed their way along in the group of women on the tour of the FBI's history, meant to impress them. It did. Would they have to carry guns?

"And this is John Dillinger's gun, confiscated when Mr. Hoover took him into custody," the guide said as he attempted to be loud enough to be heard over the 'Oh my' that came from the crowd before him.

"My sakes," Marge whispered to Mary, "it's just his gun. You would think it was some body part I won't mention or Cary Grant holding…"

With a passionate interruption Mary said, "But it is very famous, why he probably used it in…"

"Been here for months and I've seen the thing over and over." The voice, a bit harsh in a Lauren Bacall sort of way, came from behind them and they turned around.

Marge quipped, "Are you here today because you think they are selling stockings?"

"This is just the teaser. I'm here for the big pay-off to all this hoop-la. Let's see, from your accents I would say you are from the Midwest."

It had never occurred to Mary that to other people they might have an accent. "Iowa."

"Pennsylvania, Philly. Did they send agents out to investigate you all the way to Iowa before they hired you?"

Marge wondered what she could be talking about. "A man in a suit, very conspicuous among all those farmers in overalls, came and stood in cow dung while asking some not so clever questions."

"We don't even know what a union or a communist is," said Mary.

"They came by and grilled my mother while she was hanging the wash. You keep anything back when they interviewed you?"

A heavy set woman nudged Mary. "Don't talk to her, she's probably an informant."

"Don't listen to her; my name is Roz by the way."

"I'm Marge and this is my friend Mary."

They all shook hands while Mary took a long look at Roz. She stood just over 5'5" she guessed. Her smile was wry and contagious. Her red hair ran in waves that framed a pleasant face. What was an informant supposed to look like anyway, and who was she supposed to inform to?

A dark paneled room thick with silence. There was a slight slit where the dark blue curtains were not closed tight and dust sparkled in the sunlight that slid in. The room was thick with silence. Two men were in the room, one wearing authority like an over coat over his gray suit and red patterned tie, the other, taller, waited for the order. The man nodded to the other and he opened the door.

Mary, Marge, Roz, and two other women stepped carefully into the dimly lit room. J Edgar Hoover extended his hand and a smile of sorts quickly crossed his thin lips.

"It's so nice to meet you sir, I think you did a great job with Mr. Capone and those others that…" Marge began but Roz pushed her aside.

"I'm honored to shake hands with a truly great American."

"I'm honored too," but Mary was too nervous to shake hands and let the other two women move forward. She had never met anyone famous before. As they left the room, she turned and politely waved goodbye.

Once back in the hallway, Roz got between the two women, "It's Dillinger Marge, the Treasury Department got Capone. Got to run back to my desk girls. Watch your foot!"

With roaring bangs that shook their teeth, they entered the shooting range where a man with a nice but goofy face was doing target practice. There were six holes near the head of the paper silhouette of a man. One woman began to cry as the group was ushered through.

They were lead, without explanation, through another room where men dressed in suits sat over paper work or answering what looked like important phone calls. A few of the women winked at the men, who seemed impervious to such flirtations. But one looked up from his desk and while talking into the phone, flicked his ash in the ashtray and winked at Mary. She blushed.

Finally, they reached their destination. It was a huge room with a high ceiling. Windows with blackout curtains lined one wall. On the other wall were wooden filing cabinets that went all the way up to the ceiling. Desks filled the room, with women hunched over papers holding magnifying glasses. Beside each desk was a stack of cardboard boxes.

Roz sat at one of the nearby desks and was noticed by Marge and Mary. They nodded, then drew their attention back to the guide.

"…And when you have completed identification of the fingerprints, and we expect many to be coming in from every man in the service, you will wait for that man there to come and take them up to the files."

Many of the file cabinets were high up and a sliding ladder on a rail was in front of one row. The man was dressed in a gray suit, though it was not impeccably pressed like the other men they had seen. His was rumpled and his face wrinkled.

"He was beyond draft age in the Great War," Marge whispered to Mary who spoke up.

"Oh, I wouldn't mind taking them up there myself…"

"Absolutely not," said the guide emphatically. "It is against the rules."

Under her breath but calculatedly loud enough for Marge and Mary to hear, Roz said, "They are afraid that that man will look up our skirts. I say women here should wear pants."

Suppressing a giggle, Mary turned back to their guide who seemed about to wrap things up.

"This is the end of the tour, now on to your training session."

Chapter 10

It had all begun for Mary and Marge: the classes. The squeaky clean man with the slight lateral lisp conducted the classes in how to classify fingerprints. It's not that it was all that difficult, it was the way he spoke down to them, that tone in his voice that said, "I've got to go slow with them because women are dumb," that drove them to study even harder than was necessary. They came to each class ready to answer any question that he could have. They could tell he was also trying to give them the toughest prints to classify as if he could break them to prove his point. It was men who were really qualified for the job and it was men who would be doing it, if not for the draft.

Mary sat on the one chair in the corner of their room in the boarding house. The chair was hard and the horse hair scratched her skin where it touched her, but she didn't notice. It was just a distraction she could ignore. But there was one she couldn't.

Marge lay on her stomach on the bed with papers from the class around her. She had already gotten into the bathroom to get ready for bed, and wore a pale pink cotton nightgown. She had used cold cream to remove all the make-up she wore during the day and looked almost like a child without it.

"So, the loop is identified by…" Marge began but Mary interrupted.

"Could you please study silently?" She had gotten used to the thick silence of the library at college to study, and Marge studying aloud was driving her crazy, little by little.

"No problem," Marge said, sorry she had been annoying. Then she began to mumble everything she was reading and doing.

Enough, thought Mary. "I'm going to take a little walk out in the garden. You go on and study the way you like." Mary had an idea where to go to study.

The light in the carriage house was a harsh yellow on her papers but Mary really didn't mind. She stuck the Waterman pen her folks had given her when she graduated from college between her lips and tried to remember what they had gone over in class that day. From above her, she could hear Dotty's radio:

When a fellow loves a maiden
And the maiden doesn't love him
It's the same as when a bald man
Finds a comb along the highway

But that didn't bother her because while sitting on the fender of the Goldman's black sedan, she was with the cow. It made her feel like she was back on her aunt Lelia and her husband Jake's small dairy farm where she had helped out during the summers. The cow's smell brought back memories of early morning milking and how warm and frothy the milk was. They were lucky to have a milk cow, everyone else had to use powdered milk.

"So, this is a double swirl here and this is one loop. These prints are so hard to recognize." She slid off the fender and went over and petted the cow. "I hope they don't fire me and I hope they don't eat you."

There was a test and to the surprise of their teacher, each woman had received a perfect score. So, in a huge room filled with women, the work began. It was back breaking work, bent over hour after hour looking at the smudged lines in the prints, the uncomfortable wooden chairs making Mary wish she had a bigger behind. The day was long and as the sun began to set the blackout curtains were drawn. In front of the open windows, the heat built up and twenty different perfumes filled the air, along with the odor of cigarette smoke that they carried back on their clothes after their five-minute breaks. Unlike the male agents in the offices a floor up, they were not allowed to smoke at their desks with stacks of cardboard boxes filled with papers beside them.

Marge, Mary and Roz tried to sneak in an extra cigarette in the restroom. It was a long time between lunch and dinner back at home and the nicotine help to squelch their hunger. The door slammed open and a man yelled in, "You better be doing what you're supposed to be doing in there and not dragging on a butt!"

Mary and Marge were up to the work. It could be boring as all get out but they knew that these fingerprints were of the soldiers who were or soon would be fighting for their country.

As always, there was a line at the phone in the second-floor hall in the evenings, everyone had someone someplace far away that they missed. They stood in line jangling coins in their hand anxiously but patiently waiting. They understood they were all in this together.

Mary was last in the line when Dotty came up behind her to stand in line too.

"So, how is your work going?" Mary asked, noticing that she was next in line as a woman she hadn't had time to meet yet picked up the receiver and began to dial.

"It's hard being the only colored girl in the room, but let them stare at me. It's a small room and there are a dozen of us packed in like sardines in a matchbox. Some of the girls are trying to pick at the half dozen typewriters with one finger. The others are stuck filling out forms by hand."

"You are lucky you know how to type. You've got a skill that is in demand in this town. Actually all of us are in demand. At first I thought they might fire me because I work kinda slowly, but then I realized they need as many girls as possible."

"I wondered if I was going to get fired the other day. This man came in with some papers for Mr. Hobson and saw me. He gave me a look that could have brought me to tears if I had been anyone else. But when he came over and saw that I was typing like a bat out of hell, he actually smiled."

"Oh, she seems to be wrapping up her conversation. The tears are what tell you she is gonna hang up soon. I'll be crying too in a couple of minutes. I shouldn't because then Pa will end up crying too, he's the softy in the family. Ma, well she'll think she has to be strong for me. The funny thing is that I feel I have to be strong for them."

"Are you strong?"

"I never thought I was until just lately. I have been away from home before, but never far enough I couldn't visit once a month…war, even at home hardens you though."

"I think it's given me a hard head. I'm at the point where I just can't put up with the way all these white people see me."

"It was better at home?"

"I guess it was. We lived in Harlem in New York City where there are mostly colored, and I guess I would sometimes forget how the world beyond was, until recently."

"Do you miss your family?"

"Yes, it's my little sister, Debbie, she's 16, and my mom. Dad passed away two years ago."

"Oh, I'm sorry."

"I am too. But I'm real close to Debbie and my mom and we got through it as a family."

"Looks like it's my turn. I better get my hanky out now because no matter how hard I try there will be tears after I hang up," Mary said pulling her hanky out of her sleeve.

Brigette's hands had been covered with midnight stars splattered in her hair, and the raw umber of the branch filled the creases in the old man's shirt she wore when she was painting. But now she transformed from the eccentric artist to sophistication. She wore a white blouse and a rose colored jacket, tight at the waist. Her skirt was just below the knee and was also rose colored. She wore a simple necklace of white gold and emeralds her grandmother had given her before she died. The piece of jewelry accentuated her long neck. Her hair was freshly waved. She looked spectacular and she knew it.

Brigette opened her door, stepped out of her studio, and quickly closed it so no one would see the painting she was working on, a simple branch stretched across the night sky. There would soon be pale green leaves that looked like they were made from moonlight and the last pale petals of cherry blossoms adrift. It was the style of painting, with its Asian brush strokes quickly flowing across the canvass that she was known for. She always sold well when her agent, Bob, hung her paintings at an embassy party. Was a painting ever done? Only when she told someone it was done then she had committed to devote herself to other paintings.

Looking around to see if anyone could see how great she looked, she sighed. The hallway was empty and the only sound was of the shower in the bathroom.

The night air was humid enough to make her gasp as she walked down the steps of the Golden Parrot. She took a gold cigarette case with her initials BD on it in small diamonds. Taking out a cigarette, she saw an older man with a walking stick pass in a hurry. He had the look of a diplomat, haughty and reserved, probably from the French embassy just up Wisconsin Avenue. He slowed his pace and looked at her with a lust that gave her a quick chill. Yes, he was French.

A long black Cadillac snaked from the night in front of her. It stopped and the back door opened. She got in with a wide smile accentuated by the bright red lipstick she wore. As they drove away she thought she saw a face watching her from one of the basement windows.

Dotty couldn't think of anything more different from playing music than working in an office. But there was music to the typing, a beat in the rhythm of the keys, the dance of the bell ringing on the return, the ripping of each form from the carriage when she was done. She missed the camaraderie of the girls in the band though, the chatter of voices on the bus, the discordant but joyful sound of them tuning up before a performance. And the way they all fit together in the tapestry of each song. No matter what rivalry or argument, or bad feelings they might have had for another of the girls, when they played together they were a band and they all loved the band.

Not like the women in the office, sure they chatted with each other on cigarette breaks, but they had developed the art of ignoring her when she asked for a light or reached for the awful chicory filled coffee.

It was the touring with the band that she didn't love. One day as they were traveling on the bus down some highway somewhere in Ohio, they passed that sleek bus with the greyhound on the side. And she thought, "I feel like the greyhound on the side of that bus, only not some sleek creature but a skinny dog running in circles. I thought I would find what I wanted in music, but what I really want is love, and that's why I chose the sax, the sound of love."

Now she was in a city crowded with women looking for all kinds of things: a good job, a good man, a good pair of stockings. And here she was crowded in an office listening to her thoughts which became the lyrics to the music of her typewriter.

The door with the frosted glass window squeaked open and Mr. Hobson stuck his head out.

"Get your pad, Miss Mason." He said sternly to impress the women with how authoritative he could be, "I need you now."

He had a curious look on his face that Dotty couldn't place, a look of confusion perhaps like he had just spoken and foreign words he didn't even understand had come out of his mouth. She knew he was a shy man; a reserved man who she knew worked late, sometimes through the night. In a city filled with women he seemed to have neither a wife or a girlfriend. Yet even this shy man seemed to have a strange effect on the women she worked with, something about the furtive looks they gave him and now, the look that she noticed one of the girls giving her as she got up from her desk. Was it a smile, or perhaps a grin?

Mr. Hobson hadn't waited politely holding the door open for her. By the time she got there it was closed and she opened it quickly. Dotty wanted to get this over with. He gave dictation with a stream of words all rushing out and mixing together and she had to somehow make sense of them.

"Sit down," he said from behind the desk. "I just have a short letter for you."

She sat in the chair next to the desk and opened her pad and pulled a pencil out of her hair.

Rising, he said, "You are a clever woman, Miss Mason. You type, take dictation…"

"I learned to type in a government program during the depression. I never got a chance to use it though." She didn't tell him it was because she had decided to devote herself full time to her sax. "It wasn't until the war that I knew I had a skill that my country could use."

Coming around and sitting close to her on the corner of the desk he said as though they were talking about another subject, "There are a lot of girls in the city."

Dotty looked up and saw that even though he had a fan humming away on the table in the corner, he was sweating on his forehead. And his hands were tightly gripped together.

"You have something the other girls in the office don't have…"

"A typewriter?" Dotty was enjoying watching him squirm.

"No, a certain independence about you and you are a very pretty girl with that…"

"Steno book?"

"No, I was talking about…Is it true what they say about colored women?"

"Is it true what they say about you men from Vermont?"

"What is that?" He answered tentatively. The wind from the fan blew a strand of his carefully waxed down hair over his forehead.

"They have to keep their zipper up so their brains don't fall out."

He looked down to see if his fly was open.

Dotty couldn't believe she had said that, it came out with the speed of a hic-up. What did it matter anyway? Secretaries and typist were in demand all over the city no matter how many women showed up. She could always find another job.

A loud nervous laugh erupted from Hobson and he quickly went to his chair and sat down. He swung his chair toward the window and looked out across the mall as he began to dictate a letter.

Her boss had sent her all the way across town to the War College with a letter of what she thought was of little importance. But then it seemed to Dotty that most of what they did in the office was just generating more and more paper.

Walking up the steps of the large brick building, a few soldiers going down the stairs nodded at her. Surprised, she smiled back. There were gentlemen in the world. She found her way to the third floor and the office she was looking for after a half hour of asking directions. When she entered, there were two men standing there, both in uniform. One was tall and thin and rather handsome in a Frank Sinatra sort of way. He looked familiar, but then there were so many men in uniform in the city. The other man, black as a night without neither stars nor moon, was laughing with the other man. When he smiled she thought he looked real attractive.

The black man had his back to her and turned around when he saw his friend looking behind him.

"Yes, may I help you, ma'am?" He said in a deep voice with a thick southern accent.

"I have some papers from Mr. Hobson to deliver to Mr. Beam, from over at the Allotment office."

There was a moment when a hot breeze blew in the large open widow in the small room. Dotty felt a rivulet of sweat running down between her bosoms. The man's eyes followed it. A shiver went up her spine.

"I'll tell him that Mr. Hobson's maid dropped off…"

"His secretary, this woman don't clean floors for no one," she said with conviction in her voice.

"I'll bet you don't," said the tall thin man.

Chapter 11

The city was in constant motion, men, women, soldiers, trolleys and cars. So, Washington sweats on hot days. You can almost see it trickling down the sides of the buildings. Men carry handkerchiefs with their initials on them in their back pockets and pull them out to mop up the sweat from their faces. The women open their purses that hang over their arms and pull out a handkerchief with lace or crocheted trim, and pat their foreheads, trying not to take off too much of their powder.

Marge had just powdered her nose and put her compact away when Dotty came up, her skirt all but stuck to her legs she was so damp.

"Sorry, I'm late. I had to go all the way over to the War College," and saw the cutest guy she thought. "Thanks for waiting."

"No problem," Marge said not the least bit irritated. She had been having fun watching all the attractive men going by. "We're waiting for our friend Roz anyway." She was irritated with Roz, who had the same lunch hour as her and Mary, but never seemed to meet them on time.

"Oh, my back is tired," said Mary leaning back. "I worked a double shift yesterday. Between the shifts, I went downstairs to the file room with one of the other girls. We pulled out two of those big file drawers and took a nap."

"You never look the worse for the wear," Dotty said getting out her handkerchief. Maybe things can change she thought suddenly to herself. Here we are, three professional women, and one of us is colored. War changes everything, that's for sure.

Roz, however, did look the worse for wear. Her curly red hair had gone from style to frizz, her beige blouse was rumpled and he skirt looked like a dish rag it was so wrinkled. Still she didn't seem as exhausted from the heat as the others on the street, energy bouncing around her.

"Sorry, sorry, had to see someone about something."

Roz, you are always so cryptic, Mary thought. *But one day I'll figure you out.*

Scholl's Cafeteria was crowded with government workers. Roz had first taken Mary and Marge there, although it was not a well-kept secret. Everyone came for the fried chicken, meatloaf and more, but especially for the pies. They made a blueberry peach that Mary would die for. It was not one of her mother's pies, but was almost as good. Almost.

Marge grabbed the last piece of cornbread on the line and put it on her tray. The man beside her, some bureaucrat with a rumpled suit and a large nose, gave her a dirty look as he waited for one of the cafeteria girls to put out some more.

"I can't believe there are so many attractive men in this town. The town where men are boys and meat is well, who knows what. Pass me the meatloaf."

Mary picked up a small salad for herself then gave Marge some meatloaf. "All we see all day is boxes of fingerprints. The closest we get to men is their fingerprints."

"Swear off them!" Roz said.

"Meat?" Marge asked.

"Men are overrated here in town. They only want one thing and I'm not talking about love," said Roz. "Too many of these boys come from small towns and have never seen so many girls."

"And they are taking the opportunity to stare. Let them look, it won't be long before all they see is other boys and war." Dotty was thinking about her brother who had gone over to Europe, to where she didn't know. The city was exciting filled with hope and dreams of a war to be won, but also a certain stain of apprehension and fear. It was seeing all the GIs in the room, laughing and joking that turned her thoughts dark. How many would soon be crying?

"Don't let your face hang down to your knees," Roz said with as much scolding as enthusiasm, to change the tone. "Hell, we're about to eat the best pudding I've ever had."

An arm reached between Marge and Roz to grab some of the pudding. First a vanilla then a chocolate, topped with a swirl of whipped cream.

"Sorry, ladies, but I forgot my dessert and that's the real reason that I come here," said a man of about twenty-five. He wore a gray suit that somehow had maintained a perfect crease on his pants, though he had a casual tone of voice, something the women who worked in the bureau were not used to. And he was handsome, more in a Cary Grant way than a Clark Gable. He had said, 'ladies' and he seemed a real gentleman.

Marge took a good look at him. "I know you from the bureau. They taught you to say 'ladies', didn't they?"

"Yes," he smiled, "you know I recognize you too."

Marge could see it was a compliment, the first gentlemanly one she had gotten in the city. She was tired of all the cat calls and whistles.

"You know," she said, "they don't let us girls talk to the guys at work. You're breaking the rules."

"Oh," he winked, "you are worth breaking the rules for. Besides we're here now and where is Mr. Hoover to say we are breaking the rules?"

Marge wasn't sure whether to wink back or not.

"Since I can't say anything when I see you at work, I'll give you a nod." She let a quick smile run across her lips and she hoped her lipstick wasn't smudged.

"Well I got to get back to my buddies, eat this…"

"Both?" piped in Roz who was somehow feeling neglected.

"You betcha, nice to chat with you, ladies."

With that, he was lost in the room full of men and women.

As you came through the doors of the Golden Parrot, there was a stairway leading into the grand entry, and on each side of that another set of stairs, barely noticeable. One led to a room that had been a changing room for the ladies, where they could take off their coat and hat and shake of the dust from the dirt roads in Washington, at the time the house was built, and the other led to a room for the men. It was one of these rooms that Elaine had taken over as her private space, even her husband had not been in this room.

The curtains of red damask covered the two small windows of the room like eyelids closed to what went on in the room. The walls were hung with exotic tapestries that they had gotten on a trip long ago to Siam. And the floor was covered by a threadbare red oriental carpet. In the middle of the room stood two red velvet chairs that seemed to be waiting for an occupant to wrap its arms around. In the corner hung an ornate brass lamp where a candle burned. There was a hush to this room, not invaded by the street noise outside or the customers upstairs in the restaurant. It was a place thick with silence, though seemingly ready to speak.

What has lead me to do what I am about to do? Elaine thought, as she leaned back in her chair. The past had slid quickly into the present and seemed to have landed in her hands, which lay in the lap of her simple green day dress.

I was this way as a child, she remembered. Her family, father, mother, and two sisters, one two years older and one two years younger, had arrived twelve years ago from Prague, leaving behind what she had told her parents was about to happen to the Jews. They believed her, they always believed her for though she had the same gift as her mother, hers reached farther into the future. A future that she saw filled with horrors that still disturbed her even in the deepest of sleep.

Papa had worked in cheap theaters as a stage magician. His act was not much different from any other magician in the city, but his presentation was different. Mama was his beautiful assistant and while performing, they often bantered back and forth; she playing the surrogate for the audience, a doubtful wife, and he, the husband that was about to prove her wrong. Sometimes he pulled the trick off just as he said he would, and other times, he would produce a rabbit from a hat when he swore he was about to produce a dove. They were a great success. The girls, watching from backstage, always laughed at their father, the bumbling magician even though they had seen the act a thousand times. They were young, ten, twelve, and fourteen, but they waited anxiously for the dancers and practiced imitating their steps when not at their studies. Their parents looked on smiling knowing that someday they would be performing too.

But it was only a year later that they had left Prague, as their relatives said, or fled the city, as the predictions knew they must. Somehow, Elaine had never been sure why, they ended up in a small but decent apartment in Atlantic City, New Jersey. Papa went around town and took the train up to New York City, but found little work. The country was in the grips of the Great Depression and few people had money for such frivolous things as Vaudeville. Perhaps a movie, to watch Astaire and Rodgers lift their hearts and spirits, but that was all.

He did find some gigs though, performing in the Yiddish theater. But mostly, he was out of work. There was at least some solution to the problem though, Atlantic City was a beach town and tourists were attracted to strolling on the boardwalk. There he performed magic, and magically tips started appearing in his hat. Mama did something she had only done for friends and relatives back in Poland, she read palms. In the evenings when they were not at school, the three girls tap danced on the boardwalk and were quite successful drawing a crowd who always spared a few coins.

The most successful however was Mama. Scanning the lines on the palms of the passersby, she discovered she had a talent that was very popular. One day a man stopped by and had his palm read. He was impressed with the accuracy of her reading and decided to invite her to a party he was having at his apartment in the city, to read palms for his guests. He was a Broadway producer whose friends began to use her services. Papa suddenly started getting more gigs around the city.

The family moved to New York, and there began a life that Elaine could not have predicted for herself. She met a young man who was a composer and she fell in love. She must have had more talent than she knew and was cast as the ingénue in one of his musicals, along with her sister. Her career had begun in the theater, but was soon cut short, by her own choice. It seemed the composer was more interested in men than in her. But she moved on quickly after meeting another man she came to love, Harry. He was not as tall and not as handsome as the composer, but he had a good heart and that she had learned was what really mattered to her.

Harry had opened a restaurant in Washington, DC which he saw as an up and coming city, but his family lived in New York City. His father was also involved in the Yiddish theater, which is where she met him, through her father.

They fell in love and decided to marry. She still had her stage career, as did her sister; the oldest sister worked for a lawyer, but she would decide to end her career shortly. She became pregnant. Even though her career had taken off, she decided to move away with Harry, to what was then a sleepy town on the edge of the south.

It was there, after the birth of her son, she found that her gift of prediction had become stronger, the visions she received more intense. Elaine began to see that what she was able to tell people about their lives and their future could help them. Following in her mother's footsteps, she began taking on clients by word of mouth.

And that was how this client had come to her. The door opened as quiet as dust settling on the carpet and a figure all in black, with a black veil came in, walked silently across the carpet and sat down in the chair directly opposite her. Once the black lace gloves were off, she took the hands of the mysterious figure. They were immaculate and soft with perfectly manicured nails. There was a pause, and then the lace veil that hung from a modest black hat was lifted. There was a middle-aged man.

He put the veil up over his hat so she could see his cloudy eyes. Elaine knew this was the only way he could come to her, in disguise, for what would be said if the world knew that Mr. Hoover, director of the F.B.I. was going to a psychic. But there was so much he needed to know for his job.

Taking his hands again, she said in a quiet, almost motherly voice, "Yes, an opponent of yours is aware of your weakness."

"Then I must protect myself."

"But he had a weakness too."

"I know who you are talking about. I'll have to make him aware that I know of his weakness. He has too much information on me. And you have too much information on me," Mr. Hoover said, at first easily, then uneasily.

Elaine squeezed his hands to let him know that it was all right, we all have secrets that must never be told.

The air was thick in the fingerprint room, it was another hot day and the air smelled like the perfume counter at Woodword and Lothrop. Though a hush had fallen over the room, there was the continual rush of papers, occasionally a sigh as one of the women rose to stretch her aching back. The old man who helped with filing the fingerprints mumbled constantly to himself, no one was ever sure what he was saying. Sometimes he could be heard saying, "Mr. Hoover…" and it seemed he was carrying on a conversation with the director himself.

The women recognized the sound of a man's shoes echoing in the room. Many of the women looked down; others snuck a look to see who it was. Mary whose desk was near the isle, glanced up just as the man passed by her. It was the man from the cafeteria they had met last week. He winked but Mary was too embarrassed to wink back.

She saw him again, this time in a brown suit with a white shirt and brown tie, the next day when she went with the Marge and Roz to Scholl's for lunch.

Had he followed them there, or was it a coincidence that he was eating at the same time as they were? She got the feeling he had coordinated his lunch time with theirs when he nodded and smiled. When he was not smiling, he had a serious look on his face, his five o'clock shadow showing up at noon. When he smiled though, she noticed how wide his smile was and how his gums were pink.

"Okay, girls, where do you want to sit?" Marge asked as she took her tray off the line and looked around. "We could sit beside those soldier boys over there."

"They could probably use some company," said Mary. "They must have just gotten to town. They kinda have that lost look that I remember us having."

Roz only nodded. She was tired of all the GIs. They seemed to only want to flirt. She wouldn't have minded having a real conversation with them. But that only seemed to happen with her girlfriends.

As they headed between the filled chairs, two smartly dressed women sat down with the men.

"Change of plans," said Mary.

Roz pointed to a table in the back, "How about over there, you guys?"

They went over to the table way by the restrooms and took their food off the trays. It seemed more home-like to be eating off a table than a tray.

"Hello," said a voice behind Mary and she turned to see the man from the bureau. "May I sit down with you ladies?"

There were plenty of other seats in the cafeteria, with men in suits who might also be from the bureau he could sit with.

"Of course, you can sit with us," Marge said quickly.

Something is amiss here, thought Mary. *He is only speaking to me, but Marge seems intent on getting his attention.*

"As long as there is a chair you can always sit with us," Marge said.

"Where we come from, it's just being neighborly," said Mary as she began to sit, but he quickly pulled out her chair, then Marge's and was about to pull out Roz's, but she had already sat down.

"Where are you from?" He said as he sat down.

"How about we all introduce ourselves before we start answering questions." She didn't trust any man from the bureau. Why did they always want to know your business? She would have gotten up to leave, but there really wasn't a way to.

"I'm Rosalind, Roz, from Philly, this here is Mary…"

"And I'm Marge." She extended her hand and suddenly they were all a confusion of hands and arms, each trying to shake his hand. Then Roz seemed to leave the conversation and began eating her fried chicken as if she was in a hurry.

"Oh, and I'm Mary, we're from Iowa."

"Nice to meet all of you, I'm Agent Schaffly from California." He laughed at how the women stared at him as though Hoover had just walked in the room. "But of course, you can call me Greg. Small town girls, I like that," he said.

"What about me?" Roz said. "I'm from a big city."

"Oh sorry, but to me being from Los Angeles, which is one big sprawling mess, everything else seems small. I'm getting off on the wrong foot. Except Chicago and New York, now we are talking big."

"You've been from coast to coast," Marge said. She was sitting next to Greg and could smell his after shave, something that reminded her of Christmas cookie spices.

"Yes, well, there are criminals everywhere. Mostly it's either sitting in a car waiting for something to happen or back at the bureau doing paper work and waiting for something to happen."

"Is much happening with mobsters?" Mary asked.

Greg laughed to himself; next she was going to ask if he carried a Tommy gun. She had probably seen too many government 'G-Men' in the movies. At least they didn't expect him to sound like Jimmy Cagney. But wasn't it because of those movies he had joined the bureau?

"Mostly what we are tracking now is espionage. Some spies came into the country recently and we are tracking them now."

"How exciting and dangerous," Mary said.

"It's mostly boring if you want to know. Have you ladies been enjoying the city?"

They began to tell him how the city was almost overwhelming and sometimes lonely, even with so many people around.

"It's not like Harper's Ferry where I'm from. Everyone knows everyone else. And half of us are related to each other. I thought I didn't like that when I was there. Now I feel like life there, my folks and the kids, it's all going on without me." Mary put her finger in her butterscotch pudding and pulled it out and put it in her mouth. Greg watched her every move.

"All we know is the Mississippi River. Maybe someday we will get the chance to see the Atlantic Ocean. There must be a train that goes there."

"I have to go, sorry," said Roz. "There is someone I have to see before I go back and dive into an ocean of fingerprints."

Gray granite loomed over the street—the Federal Bureau of Investigation building. The doors were large and heavy for a small woman like Roz, but there was always someone going in or out of the place who was kind enough to hold the door open. Somehow it always made her feel guilty to have someone else hold the door for her, hell, to have anyone do anything for her, she thought as she entered into the cool of the building. Late at night, when she was working a night shift, (there were shifts twenty-four hours to try to do all the filing that needed to be done) the place was like a crypt. During the day, when it was busy it was still like a crypt, only a busy one. When she got back to her desk, Roz saw the pile of prints had gotten even higher. She quietly cursed the man who had dropped them off. Then again, he reminded her of her grandfather, though she could barely remember him, a bald head, crabby, a look to his skin like a wet dish rag. But she loved him because she knew he was keeping her and her mom safe and secure in their fifth floor walk-up. He would disappear for days at a time with no word where he was or what he was doing. Her mother fretted terribly, knitting a mile an hour until everyone in their building had a new winter scarf.

Then he would return and suddenly her mother was smiling again. They bought a radio, some new furniture and had money to go to the movies and eat ice-cream afterwards. Then he would take his crabby self out into the streets again and be gone for another couple of nights, returning with a wad of money. One day however, he never came back. Her mother cried of course, but mostly she sighed, as if she knew it was inevitable that the two of them would be alone one day.

Her mother had been wise; when she looked into the crystal ball of her fears, she knew she had to save and plan for the future. They continued to live well during the depression with the money her grandfather had somehow managed to give them. Secretly, she imagined him living in a foreign land having great adventures with the father she had never known. He had passed on before she was born, something her mother said her grandfather would always blame himself for, whatever had occurred. There were many things no one ever spoke of, and this was one of them.

Life was mysterious, she knew, that and being Roman Catholic now, a religion filled with mysteries, always kept her off balance, her sense of life slightly askew.

As she grew older, Roz had begun to feel a vague anxiety, like a swarm that might settle on some aspect of her life at any time. She felt she was walking on tissue paper just when she had gotten her feet wet. She managed, through the sheer force of her will to swat the anxiety away. But now she was sure it wasn't anxiety, that tragic form of formless fear, but it was the fear of that fear returning that was the problem.

Her shift would be over soon and soon she would be able to wrap the security of her little apartment around her and rest.

What was she doing with her life anyway? She knew she had to do something for the war effort. But women couldn't go and fight. She wished that she had taken her aunt's suggestion and studied to be a nurse. To be on the battlefield could be no more stressful than what she had been through in her life, at times death had seemed to be a good companion she knew she could rely on, if she needed to.

With the flip of a sheet of prints, she wiped away her thoughts, and went to work.

Chapter 12

Washington was a city in motion at all hours, a great engine churning people in buildings and out on the streets again as shifts began and ended. Dinner for the residents of the Golden Parrot was served at all hours and you never knew for sure who might show up.

Mr. Barille, an older man who was perpetually nervous and kept rubbing his bald head, sat beside Elaine. She had just sat down after putting a bowl of mashed potatoes on the table in the room off the kitchen where dinner was served. Bogey, a sleek black cat, jumped up in her lap and curled up for a nap. Next to her, Harry was tucking his napkin into the neck of his white shirt. After dinner he would go upstairs and welcome the dinner guests.

Ben and Bella, an older couple who never seemed to look at each other when they spoke to each other, sat in silence watching Mary with her hands folded and head bowed as she prayed silently.

When she was done and looked up smiling, Brigette said, "I think their skin is just beautiful." Everyone knew what she was talking about. When she sat down she had overheard Dotty's name in the conversation Ben and Bella were carrying on in Yiddish.

Picking up a bowl of peas and putting some on her plate, Bella said, "You'd think a dog urinating is beautiful." She let out a little laugh, pleased with her statement. She passed the peas to Mary who said thank you.

"Bella, my little buballa, would you pass the mashed potatoes and please put some of them in your mouth." Ben turned to her and gave her a look that surprised Bella.

"Well, I just never heard of such a thing as people of color eating with…"

With a restrained anger in her voice, Elaine tapped her fork on her plate. "Some people never heard of such a thing as Jewish people eating at the same table with them." She cleared her throat. "Dotty should be here soon for dinner, so you can ask her how her people came to America. Share stories. Now why was it you left Austria?"

"Because the Nazis…" Ben began, then let his voice trail off and looked embarrassed as though he had said some offensive word.

"We came because we had no choice…" Bella began.

"Please," Brigette interrupted before a fight broke out, "Please, I am an artist. The Nazis upset me."

"They should be upsetting everyone but they're not," said Harry as a silence fell over the table.

Elaine let out a huge sigh trying to dissipate her anger and frustration. "I'm Polish and I'm tired and at my wits end about the Germans. The Nazis are what happens when people are patriotic to their leaders instead of the ideals that the country once stood for, once a war is declared it is a giant monster that seems will only end when one side destroys the other."

"And war punishes the innocent," Mary said so sadly, everyone turned toward her. Sadness filled the hearts of all at the table.

Standing in the doorway, Marge suddenly appeared and with a loud ahhh took off her new brown and tight shoes. Everyone stopped and looked her way and a smile slowly drew across their face drawn by the hand of humor.

Mr. Barille rubbed the top of his head, took the napkin from the neckline of his shirt and stood up. "I can't take all this talk during my meal. War is horrible and so is my digestion." He picked up his plate that only had some potatoes and peas on it so far. "I'll bring this down later when…"

He quickly skidded out of the room passing Marge as she chuckled.

"He didn't have much on his plate, maybe I should take him…" Mary began but Marge put a hand on her shoulder.

"Sit, Mary. My barking dogs must have chased him away. Anyone mind if I put my feet in the soup tureen?"

Harry rose and pulled out a chair for her. "Welcome to the Saturday Evening Complaint Club."

Michael, his green eyes smiling as he came in the doorway and sat down, said, "What he means is, he threatens to feed us from the cans he hoarded in the basement that got the labels washed off; true mystery meals, unless we clean our plates."

"Now, there is a story for your column on the way things work behind the scenes in Washington. What is really in those cans of mystery contents?"

Michael could see by the way she was looking she was flirting with him and took it as a compliment, but wouldn't let on that he wasn't interested.

Mary began to serve herself. "After going through the depression without enough food…"

"I lived on the Mississippi," Marge said, "And it was catfish or walleye every meal."

But Bella had been stewing like a pot slowly boiling away what water was left. "That is why people of color flooded into Washington, isn't it? I mean because they heard the depression was over when you let the government give you a free ride, so…"

"Bubby," Ben said pointing to her mouth, "you have a piece of spinach dangling from between your teeth and the look of the slimy thing is making me a bit nauseous."

Grabbing her napkin, Bella covered her mouth.

"I hope you choke on the thing," Marge almost said but thought better of it and kept quiet.

Bella saw everyone was staring at her and she blushed. Mumbling something through the napkin, Bella got up and hurried out of the room.

"My humblest apologies for the conduct of my wife, however, her mouth is beyond my control."

"And hers," said Harry. "You are most welcome to stay here until you get yourself settled, however my cousin makes me want to check my family tree in the old country."

"And which branch she has been swinging on?" Marge startled herself that she had actually said that.

"Marge," exclaimed Mary. Marge was becoming much bolder since they had moved to Washington.

"Oops. Sorry, but apparently, my mouth is also beyond my control."

When Dotty walked in the room, she saw everyone looking at her in a well, peculiar way. Elaine immediately patted the empty seat beside her.

"Come sit here, dear. I want you to be sitting right across from my husband's cousin when she returns."

Dotty sat down.

"Dotty, you look as tired as my feet feel," Marge said.

"Well, hello to you too." Dotty laughed. "I was just looking for you and Mary upstairs." She turned to Elaine, "Who is that pale looking woman in the room next to Bab's room?"

Everyone was silent.

Brigette was the first to speak up.

"They say your people have a greater affinity for seeing beyond the veil."

"That room is only used for storage now," Elaine said.

"The ghost," said Brigette, "it was just the ghost."

It was late at night, a night filled with fears and hopes and dreams behind the hallway doors. Though she had to work an early shift, Marge stood in her bathrobe in front of the storage room door, waiting and wondering, hoping to catch a glimpse of something that might exist.

Mary hadn't realized yet that Brigette only ate at night when no one was in the kitchen. She would attend dinner but only push her food around on her plate to make it look like she had eaten.

She knocked on the door holding a piece of chocolate pie on a cracked piece of blue Delft China. After a few quick knocks, Brigette opened the door. She was dressed in a pair of men's pants and an old men's shirt, both spattered with yellows, reds, blues, brown, and greens. Her long hair was tied up. The room smelled of linseed oil, turpentine, and a musky rose perfume.

"Mary, how nice of you to come by," Brigette said opening the door wide to reveal her studio, double the size of the other rooms. Paintings with bold colors and strong strokes hung on the walls, leaned against the walls, and were stacked on the floor. They were of ordinary people doing ordinary things: a woman asleep holding a baby, a man sitting on a bench with vibrant mountains and clouds behind him, flowers that radiated life. But there were also landscapes, done in an almost photographically realistic style. There were many scenes she knew, of monuments and gardens around Washington, DC and places she didn't know but that looked like they were from all across the country. Then there were others from foreign lands, windmills, temples, churches, a seaside village, and many more. She could not take it all in; there was so much to see. But she found herself drawn to the ones that were not all that realistic and done in bold colors. It was almost as if they were alive and had greeted her when she came into Brigette's studio.

There was paint splattered and dripped everywhere. The studio itself was a work of art, thought Mary.

Brigette watched in silence as Mary looked around and was pleased. Not with herself, talent was something that seemed almost external and beyond claiming as hers. She was pleased with the paintings, whether realistic or not. She loved living with them.

"Your paintings, some are so colorful and some are so dark," Mary said standing in front of two canvases. One was of a woman standing with mountains behind her, large colorful strokes of bold pinks and greens. The skin tone was a bright yellow with a hint of aqua for the shadows.

"This is you, isn't it?" Mary said.

Brigette went to the painting and ran her finger along the cheek of the woman in the painting. "It's the woman that I was, abandoning the city and going out into the woods of Vermont. It felt so alive that day, so away, so gone from it all. It was done from a photograph."

"Who took it?"

Brigette ran her fingers through her hair and then shook it back.

"It was a young man I knew, he worked for my father. We met one day when I went to his office to talk with him. Actually, to tell him I was moving into the city, New York, the village of course."

"Of course," Mary said although she had no idea what she was talking about. But she liked the idea that she had moved to a village.

"And this painting," Mary said pointing to a small watercolor of girl with dark hair holding a cocker spaniel puppy. She looked so in love with the dog.

"I did that when I was twelve," Brigette said.

Mary was impressed for the watercolor was so real, so alive.

"But shortly after that, we had to get rid of my dog. We never got another one."

"Why did you have to get rid of him? You look like you don't want to let him go."

"Oh, he bit father, no wonder, the way he used to treat him. I would too!" Brigette laughed a sour sound that upset Mary. There was more to that story, but Mary was afraid to ask.

"But the boy who took the picture?"

"Yes, father owns an oil company and he was one of the delivery boys. He broke my heart you know, father that is. When he found out that we were dating, he forbid the boy to see me. Tommy didn't care, didn't care if he lost his job. But this was the depression and a job was a precious thing to lose. So,

I broke it off, I told him his hands were always stained with oil and would never come clean and that it repulsed me. And that he smelled of oil, he could never get the smell out of his pores."

"Was that true?"

"No, but I didn't want him to lose that job, the one that was supporting his whole family. Not for me. I wasn't worth it. So, I drove him away."

"Did you love him?" Mary asked turning and facing Brigette. Brigette averted her eyes and threw her gaze across the room.

"Yes, I loved him, but what has that got to do with it?" She sounded defensive.

Mary walked over to a painting of the Capitol Building at sunset. The building took on the light of sunset, the yellow and pink, but like a tarnished brass. The clouds were ominously strange. As if she could see images moving through them, images of war, not the war that raged over seas but one that was like the kind you participated in during foul dreams.

"This is yours too? It is so different. And so is this one of the ocean at sunset, where the waves seem a bit too high, the water a bit too dark, and the spray too frantic. But then what do I know, I've never seen the ocean."

"Oh, you should! The ocean is the heartbeat of the earth. We artists move in that heartbeat." An arrogant tone had come to Brigette's voice.

"Are you going to sell these paintings?" Mary asked stepping back to get a better look. And she felt they needed to be viewed from a distance.

"They are already sold. I have a friend who seems to know every diplomat in the city. When an ambassador has a party, he asks that my paintings be hung in place of some on the walls. I sell quite well. And these two were commissions by the French attaché."

"I can see why you left your village to come here to sell your paintings."

"Oh yes, but actually it was that the village was not far enough away from the town we lived in across the river in New Jersey. My father likes to control his world and I am part of that world," Brigette's words had become a dark umber. She was talking too much about her father and her hands began to tremble with a quiet rage and a subtle fear.

"But let's talk about you, Mary. You've never told me where you are from."

"Oh, a small town, a pittance of a town my mother calls it. Beneath the bluffs along the Mississippi River in Iowa. Harper's Ferry although there is no ferry there anymore. No reason to cross the river really. Most everyone in town is related to each other in some way and those that aren't feel like part of the family too. It was settled by the French although the Chippewa already lived there."

"It sounds very charming," Brigette said rummaging through her paintings to find another one to show Mary.

"It's my home and I miss it but I'm trying to feel at home here. What was it like where you came from?"

"That's what I'm looking for, yes here it is." She pulled out a twenty-four by thirty-six canvas with a house on it. It was a large looming Victorian structure against a sky that was a bit too blue. The house was a dark green with white trim. It looked more like the shadow of a house to Mary than the house itself. Brigette held it in silence as though she wanted Mary to understand the painting.

"It's quite large," Mary said.

"Yes, in a very small town that thought very highly of my father."

There was something disturbing about it that made Mary want to change the subject. "I love these colorful ones, with all the people you see here on the streets, this woman selling flowers, the man digging a hole on the mall, this one with the crazy little girl spinning around in the rain. It's almost like there are two of you."

"Two of me? Darling, there are so many of me I don't know what to do sometimes," Brigette laughed.

One floor lamp with the shade removed sat by an old and dusty overstuffed chair with a faded pattern of some undetermined flower. Another floor lamp, also with its shade removed, stood beside a small table where tubes of paint lay, and brushes stuck up from an old mason jar. To the right of the table stood an easel with a painting on it that was facing away from Mary.

Brigette was walking there with a smile and Mary followed.

The painting on the easel was done in the bright colors. It was of a nude man sitting on a chair.

"Oh my," said Mary under her breath.

"Does that shock you?" Brigette asked, strolling over to the painting.

"No, I have brothers. But I do love the painting."

Brigette was a bit disappointed.

"I almost forgot the cake. It's some of the best chocolate I've had."

"How nice of you, but I have my figure to look after all darling; a woman's greatest asset in a city like this!" Brigette had one of those figures most men would call voluptuous.

"Like this?"

"You did get off that train not long ago but surely you see that this city has so many men. And a good figure gives you such power over them!"

Brigette laughed and put her hands on her hips. She felt a kinship with Mary who had a figure like hers.

"More than the painting, I'm shocked by what you think of men. They just want to fall in love, like us."

Mary put the cake down next to the palette.

"Darling, if you believe that, then you have my piece of cake. You're going to do some growing up here. And have some ideas shattered."

"I don't put much stock in ideas made of glass. Mine are hard like diamonds."

"I thought that way too until I discovered real diamonds. And who would give them to me?"

"Anyway, I have to go visit the cow," Mary said turning.

Brigette laughed out loud as Mary walked to the door. "Thanks so much, Mary!"

Brigette found herself alone in her studio and it quickly had the life sucked out of it, and she felt lonely. But at least she had her art. She walked over to the front window of her studio which ran along the side of the building. Looking out the window, she once again saw that black car sitting across the street with two men in it.

Chapter 13

The day had sunshine skidding over a city that was just warming up. The humidity slowly descended from the sky like an invisible rain. A black Oldsmobile convertible with the top down drove up in front of the Golden Parrot with Greg at the wheel, dressed in a casual brown and tan shirt. He honked twice.

Out the door ran Marge, her yellow cotton dress already beginning to stick to her. Next came Brigette, in a loose red and green print dress with a bright orange silk scarf around her long neck.

"This is some car. I feel like I'm Rita Haworth going on an adventure." Marge said putting her bag in the trunk of the car.

"Yes, isn't it?" Greg said with the biggest smile on his face Marge had ever seen. She was used to seeing him in the context of other federal agents. "I checked it out of the motor pool. It's an undercover car."

Brigette had dumped her umbrella in the trunk and came around to the driver's side.

"I don't think we've met," Greg said extending his hand.

"This is Brigette. Mary invited her," Marge said with a hint of bitterness in her voice. "She's one of those artists."

"I'm intrigued, nice to meet you."

Brigette walked around to the passenger's side of the car as Greg swung the door open. Marge quickly ran up in front of Brigette. Brigette moved to the right. Marge moved to the right. Brigette moved to the left. Marge moved to the left.

"Going somewhere?" Marge asked as they continued the dance.

"I just thought you'd want to ride with Mary, your best friend, in the back."

"I just thought you'd want to ride in the trunk and blow up the spare tire."

"You have no sense of courtesy do you? Get your behind out of…"

"Your behind is big enough to rent billboard space…"

As they argued, Mary came running out of the house with a picnic basket. She put it in the trunk then got in the car and pulled the seat up for the other two women to get in.

"Get in, girls! I've never seen the ocean before!"

They reluctantly climbed in and sat beside each other in the backseat.

"We've got a three-hour drive ahead of us," Greg said as he put his arm around Mary.

She took it off her shoulder and smiled.

Marge had a terrible singing voice, it sounded like a flushing toilet. Mary had a sweet thin voice, Brigette a full and not so shy one. Greg chose to do an impression of Jimmy Cagney as they sang a tune from a movie they had all just seen:

I'm a Yankee Doodle Dandy
A Yankee Doodle, do or die
A real live nephew of my uncle Sam
Born on the Fourth of July
I've got a Yankee Doodle sweetheart
She's my Yankee…

But the sounds of their singing were drowned out as a convoy of army trucks rumbled by in the opposite direction.

Within the hour, they had reached a section of the beach just above Rehoboth, Delaware. The sand had flies swarming around some sea weed until they moved down the beach to a place where they could lie without the damn things. A large green blanket with satin trim lay on the sand with Greg, his eyes closed, laying between Marge and Brigette. Mary sat tying her hair back. She looked out at the water, blue/gray and churning up glistening foam. The Atlantic Ocean, how it moved, swayed, ran in and out, all so unlike the river at home, the mighty, but muddy Mississippi.

Greg turned over onto his back, sand, which had somehow snuck onto the blanket, now clotted in his chest hair.

"Marge, before you go in the water, would you pour some of that oil on my back?"

Smiling, Marge looked in the old grocery bag she was using as a beach bag, but came up empty.

"Sure, but I don't see the stuff in here."

Brigette sat up and pulled her beach bag, covered with tropical flowers, toward her and reached in.

"It fell out of your bag in the trunk, so I stuck it in mine."

She pulled out the bottle and took off the cap.

"Well, thank you so much dear."

"Brigette," she corrected Marge, "since I've got the oil right here, I'll give him a coating."

"With your ragged nails, you'll draw blood," Marge said responding to Brigette's attitude of triumph over her.

"My nails," she said checking out her bright red nails. "Darling, you have steel wool pads for hands that would…"

There was the patting and rustle of feet on the sand and they looked up to see a young woman, perhaps eighteen, with dark hair and a winning smile, pass by in an orange swimming suit. A big brimmed straw hat obscured much of her face, but she looked up, and with her dark eyes looked straight at Greg. The next thing that Brigette and Marge knew, they were still arguing and Greg had gotten up and left.

As the day went on, more people began to dot the beach, men and some women were scattered about. Some had come in groups, others simply sat and stared at each other, wanting and wondering what to say to a stranger.

Mary was getting in the water when a young man, probably Mary's age of twenty, came up to her. He had a silly smile and sandy blonde hair that fell over his forehead. He had a cowlick which looked incurable. He was in shape and Mary figured that like many men he must have already gone through boot camp.

"Just move in slowly and shuffle your feet. It's easier to stand up then," he said extending a hand in case Mary was just about to fall.

"I've never gotten in the ocean before."

"I can tell," he laughed. "I'm from way back in San Diego and grew up by the Pacific Ocean."

"Are you stationed out here?"

"Yes. Now, go slowly."

Mary shuffled into the water as it came and went around her ankles.

"It's kind of scary, you think you're on something solid then the sand shifts under your feet!" Mary stopped, unsure what to do next. Out on the horizon she saw the gray of a ship.

"Good, no let's go out together."

Together they made it out until they were waist deep. He kept his hand out in case she needed it but Mary didn't. She might be a river rat but she was getting the hang of walking in the ocean.

"Now dive in! Ride the waves!"

Mary looked at him as a wave approached then they both dove into the swirling water.

Blue soaked into the ground as the clouds surrounding them turned to a hot gold. The air had begun to cool and Mary and the man were out of the water on the blanket. Marge and Brigette played in the water with Greg, who seemed to be enjoying being the center of attention. Laughter sounded between the crashing of the waves. Most of the people that had been on the beach had left.

"Sam, that's a nice name. I have an uncle named Sam," said Mary taking down her hair and shaking it out. The salt water had matted it together and she thought it must look a mess, but she really didn't care, she was having a good time.

"Uncle Sam, huh?"

"I never thought about that. War makes you think of things in a different way." Mary instantly regretted she had brought up the war. Where was the war now? They were on the beach having one of the best times of her life. She needed to enjoy it.

"And your name is…?"

"Oh, I never said my name, it's Mary."

"That's a nice name. I have an Aunt Mary…"

"Oh, stop, you're making fun of me," she laughed.

"I'm just messing with you, Mary."

Sam reached over and pulled Mary close to him and tried to put his lips on hers. She struggled; he was getting a bit rough, and then pushed him away.

"What's the matter?" Sam was genuinely confused.

"You're too rough and way too fast." Mary said realizing that he had not really meant any harm.

"I just thought…That's how they do it in the movies."

"That's how men who make the movies think women like it."

A small fire crackled in the drift wood they had found on the beach. Their group had grown larger as Sam's buddy, Chris, a guy with a happy-go-lucky smile and mischievous eyes had joined them. Brigette and Marge sat with marshmallows on sticks holding them in the fire, each one trying to be the one not to burn them.

"Ah," said Marge, "this is a good one!" She pulled it delicately off the stick and then placed it in Greg's mouth. "Watch it, it's still hot."

Brigette looked on. She took her marshmallow out of the fire. It was dripping off the stick so she quickly let it drop onto her tongue. She burned herself.

Mary lay back on the blanket and looked at the sky above her. There was the crackling of the fire joined with the soft voices of the others, but she spoke to no one in particular.

"The sound of the ocean, it's the whispering of my mother in my ear when I am asleep. Her breath blows my hair, gently. And this sky, no matter how far from home I am when I look up I see stars and feel at home again. I just have to take the time to look up." One tear formed in her eye and reflected the light from the stars.

Greg had been watching Mary as she lay back, and between the crashing of the waves he heard her.

"I've got something for us to look at." He grabbed the old brown grocery bag he had brought and wouldn't let anyone look in. They had all been curious but were about to see what was in the bag.

"I wondered what was in that," said Brigette moving closer to him. Mary rolled over and sat up. Greg took the bag and ran beyond the wavering orange light of the campfire and into the darkness.

Through the darkness, they saw Greg seeming to float above the sand as he struck a match and leaned down. In a few seconds he ran into the circle of light and plunked down on the blanket.

"Watch…" But before he could finish his sentence, there was a shrill scream ascending into the sky over the ocean and the fireworks exploded in a tangle of white light above the sparkling waves.

"It's the Fourth of July!" Sam said as the others let out their breath with an "Ahhhhhh…"

Suddenly, there was the white hot of an explosion on the horizon.

"It's the tanker!" yelled Sam and all eyes were focused on the glow like a sunrise on the horizon.

"They got one!" said Greg with an angry tone in his voice and he hit the blanket hard with his fist.

"What was that?" Marge asked concerned.

"They blew up the tanker," Sam said with softness in his voice Mary had not heard before.

"It's a Gerry sub. We keep it quiet that they are off our coast."

"That's how you knew," said Brigette turning to Sam concerned about him, "You're a sailor, aren't you?"

"The men on board…" And Marge put her hand on top of Greg's which felt cold.

With tears in her eyes, Mary pulled her gaze from the disaster and lay back on the blanket and looked at the sky above while whispering a prayer.

Chapter 14

Brigette could never make a choice between her art and her writing. They were both places she could go when as a child she found that tears would not come. The fear abounded as she walked through their large house filled with silence. Sometimes she felt she was walking on cellophane and it stretched beneath her feet to an uncertain darkness below.

It was out of this darkness that she had reached out to her poetry and written poem after poem in her diary. She couldn't write the truth, for who knew who might pick up her diary, and then their secret would be revealed, the Snow White bandage off the bloody wound.

When she was twelve, she wrote a poem titled, 'Silent Snow, Secret Snow', about a boy who doesn't realize that he is slowly dying, and snow that begins to fill his vision is a clue to the end. Her teacher had entered it into a contest and she won. She was filled with pride, like a balloon about to burst with pride, and waited for her parents to say something. But they only said, that's nice, and went about their business.

It was about this time in her life when she found she had a knack for realism in her art and she began to turn out water colors. The faces of slaves behind bars from an article she had found in National Geographic, a dog pointing at nothing in a field filled only with dry grass, a vase of roses that were about to wilt. The portraits of people that lived around her, the women with the smooth skin who did their laundry, the old man with time etched into his face who came by with his wagon to sharpen knifes and sell pots. She began to do portraits of the other girls in her girl's school, up the street from her house. She sold them to their parents. Her parents were not especially pleased she was wasting time on art but expressed approval when they saw she was actually making some money. Their plans for her were not to make money, but to marry money when she went to college in New York City.

The city was only forty-five minutes by train from her home town but it felt like an eternity away. She had escaped the silence of the house, the tears she could not cry.

She worked on her art.

Brigette put down her brush with the yellow ocher on it on the table she used as a palette. She stood back from the easel. The painting of the nude man was coming along quite nice, but enough for today. She wiped her hands off on the old shirt and put the brush with the others in a jar of turpentine. Yes, she was done for the day.

"Steven, darling, I'm bored. Put your uniform back on and climb back down the trellis."

"Love, I hate to leave you but I have to get back too," he said sounding disappointed. He got up from the chair where he had sitting. It creaked.

Brigette had turned the other way and was leafing through one of her sketch books. Steven picked up his clothes and went across the studio, through a door, into a small room where Brigette stored even more paintings. When she was done with him, she was done with him and he was done with her. He put his uniform back on, collected his army issued shoulder bag with an object the size of a bread box, was out of the window.

There was something calming to Brigette about cleaning her paint brushes. She even liked the smell of the turpentine and felt a tiny sense of accomplishment when she put a clean brush back down beside her palette. It was always her nerves that seemed to be jangling around inside her, but now she felt more at ease.

She had been humming a song, its title she couldn't remember, when she stopped to take a drink of water. There was a voice from behind the door. Unable to imagine who Steven might be talking to or even why he was still there, she called out.

"Steven, is that you singing or something?"

There was no answer; she went and opened the door. He was going out the window and then climbed down the trellis and was gone.

Brigette didn't like anything out of the ordinary, she felt uneasy and decided to walk down the hall and maybe out to the garden if no one was about.

Marge came out of the bathroom wearing her blue fuzzy bathrobe and a white towel wrapped around her wet hair.

"Oh, you scared me!" she said when she almost bumped into Brigette. "I thought you were the ghost."

"As if you didn't look scary with your prune skin from…"

"Look, let's drop all the smart remarks. We don't really dislike each other."

"Well you should speak for…"

"We just don't like that we like the same man, that's all, Truce?" Marge extended her hand to Brigette.

Brigette had to consider what Marge had just said. She was always catty with other women whether it was about a man or not. That's just the way she was. She never had any girlfriends, only men. Her mother hadn't had any friends at all that she could remember, which was probably the way her father liked it. She had seen Marge and Mary together, speaking in a common language known only to each other, sharing clothes, laughing with each other. She envied their friendship. Maybe she could learn to have a best girlfriend too.

"Truce," and she shook Marge's hand.

The door to her room was right there; Marge opened the door and motioned for Brigette to follow. Inside the room Mary sat before the small oak vanity table with a round mirror above it. She had found it in the back of the garage and asked if she could use it. She had placed a statue of Saint Theresa holding a bouquet of red roses on it. She had found the statue in a junk shop. In front of it was a small votive candle that she had just lit. The dim yellow light flickered across Mary's pale skin.

When Brigette entered she thought she smelled roses. Mary quickly crossed herself whispering, "Father, Son, and Holy Ghost."

"Oh, how nice you're here," said Mary. Brigette knew that she genuinely meant it. She smiled. Mary smiled back.

Mary went over and sat on the bed and motioned for Brigette to do the same while Marge dried her hair with the towel.

"Darling," Brigette began then suddenly felt that was not really the way to address Mary, "how are things with you and Sam?"

"Fine I suppose. Why are men so…? Like men?"

"Men don't have feelings the way we do. They will say they love you but all they really want is something else if you know what I mean. Oh, I might as well say it, they just want to have sex with you." She spoke with her contempt for men barely hidden. "Do I shock you?"

"No, not much shocks me anymore. What could be more shocking than a war going on?"

"My advice is: so-called love is a weapon men will use against you. So, use it against them. Forget these soldier boys and get yourself a professional man."

Mary looked dismayed. She didn't want to believe what Brigette was saying about men. She had never thought anything like that, but had war changed men that much? Would it change her into some cynical woman? She said a silent prayer that she could keep her faith in people, that there were good people out there, people who kept their hearts and souls intact, despite what was happening or what might happen in the future.

Brigette felt the need to lighten the tone of the conversation when she saw Marge give her a dismissive glance and shake of the head.

"Were you praying for a good man?" Brigette said and laughed.

"Aren't we all!" said Marge and they all laughed.

"I'm praying you're not right, Brigette, but I'm afraid I'm beginning to think you are," Mary whispered to herself.

Brigette stood up. "I think I'll go down to the garden and sit for a while. See if I can get my creative juices flowing again."

Mary stood up too. "I'll go down with you. I wanted to go out to the barn."

Brigette looked confused but didn't say anything.

Mary slid open the heavy wooden door to the building where the car, and also the cow was kept. She had never asked if the cow had a name. Surely she had a name, didn't everyone name their cows? Lucy was the name she had decided to give to her friend out here in the barn/garage. Somehow, perhaps the large sad eyes, the cow reminded her of a neighbor down the hill from her family's house, the little white house with shiny red trim and flower boxes filled with red geraniums. The town often talked about Lucy as though she was crazy, talking to herself as she walked down to the post office to get the mail that never came. Her husband had been killed in the last World War and she had never remarried. She had money from some source no one could figure out so she never went out to work. She wasn't crazy Mary thought, she just had large lonely eyes. That's why Mary used to stop by when she could get away from school or her chores and say hello. Little more than that was said, but somehow she knew it helped.

And now the cow named Lucy listened to her as the swing music Dotty was listening to on the radio came through the ceiling above; it was Cab Calloway.

"Good evening, Lucy," Mary said stroking the animal's muzzle. "I need to read you a letter that I've been writing to mom. And you are such a good listener."

Out of the pocket of her dress, she pulled a sheet of stationery with lilacs around the edges of the paper. She unfolded it and leaned back against the car.

"It's been so long, Ma, so long since I had your meatloaf with ketchup on top, so long since I felt the cool mud of the river bottom between my toes, so long since I attempted to cool myself with a paper fan from Bandell's store down the street. And it's been very long since I have seen you. We talk on the phone every week, but there is always a line of anxious people behind me and I always feel that what they have to say in their phone calls is more important than what I have to say. But it's important to tell you about my life her in the city so I'm writing you."

"It's been so long since I've hugged you and Pa and the kids. I know they thought I was strict with them, but I hope they miss me. I miss them. I wish you all could come here and see this amazing place. Even though I've been here so long, every day it terrifies me, excites me and challenges me. I'm not as afraid as I used to be here, but still not really strong, although I have learned to act that way, except when I'm with Marge. She's the only one, who sees me with tears in my eyes after a long and tedious day at work."

"Do I sound sad? No, I hope not. I'm just as sad as everyone is when a war is going on. I do get a chance to have fun. We have gone to movies, sat and watched while sucking on a giant dill pickle. I even go to see and swim in the ocean. It was scary at first, but then loads of fun. It was on the beach that I met a boy, a man really, they aren't boys any more once they became a GI. He is stationed in Delaware, but is from there and has a car. He comes to visit me when we are both able to get the time off. He stays at the hotel down the hill but is getting transferred to the naval headquarters here in Washington, DC soon. He's some sort of person who works with maps, I can't remember what that is called. It is fun seeing him from time to time, but I'm really not sure it would be so much fun if he lived so close by. I think he likes me too much. His name is Sam and…"

With a sigh, Mary looked up into the sad eyes and thought for a minute that Lucy had really been listening to her.

"Should I put in the part about Sam?" she asked the cow. "My folks never seemed to like the boys who were interested in me, and neither did I much. I've always felt that I somehow for some reason (I could always come up with one) wasn't good enough for them, no that's not quite it but I really couldn't understand why they would be interested in me. I'm kind of a mess, Lucy. Maybe, I should leave out the part about Sam. Anyway, I want to finish the letter."

"It's been so long, since last spring, since I've been back there, but as soon as I got the job I put in a request to come home for Christmas, so I will get to see you then. The trees haven't even started to change yet, but I'm planning my trip already. Let me know when the kids start to make up a Christmas list. They have everything here."

"So long for now, love to you and all the family, Mary."

Mary could hear the music coming from Dotty's room louder now, and the sound of clacking on the floor. She smiled. Dotty was dancing by herself.

Chapter 15

Trees of hazy greens, buildings of gray and white, and steam rose from a bubbling and boiling ground. The city crackled and hissed, Washington, DC in August.

Humidity hung like smoke in the air and the women always felt damp, in need of a cool shower. Offices filled with sighs and sweat slid and burned eyes like tears.

In movie theaters, soldiers and government girls touched briefly in the darkness as the film was about to begin.

Marge thought about changing her name to Madge; she felt so different.

Boxes of prints towered over their desks, and Mary found herself smoking more than ever before. She and Roz spoke with silence then went back to their desks.

Brigette had been letting the paint drip on her canvases of flowers.

Greg let Marge lean against him as they rode the trolley on M Street in Georgetown in search of a bar and a drink.

When the elevator door opened and Dotty stepped out, she felt the stares of the women in her offices crawling across her skin. And she tried to ignore what haunted her at night as she lay in a bed of heat and damp sheets, trying to hide in sleep.

Despite or to spite the heat, clubs were filled with music and dancing, picnics were held down by the Potomac, and people laughed as the war with August marched on.

One day toward the end of the month, when there was hope that fall would be just around the corner, the door to Dotty's office slowly opened and a black woman stepped in holding a folder. She was in her mid-twenties, but looked much younger because she looked so shy.

Everyone in the room was quiet. The woman looked at the front of her folder, then the brass numbers on the door. She was in the right place, as right as it could ever be. The women in the room seemed so white. Trying to smile, she said a weak hello and was met by silence until from the back of the room, near another door she heard, "Well, come in, sister."

That was how Candy met Dotty.

Day lingered but dark was fast approaching so Harry turned on the light in the basement room where they ate and were now playing cards. Marge, Mary, Dotty, Harry, and Mr. Barille sat around the table looking at their cards as Brigette drifted elegantly around the table. She seemed like the familiar of some witch.

Dotty let her eyes roll as she studied her cards and continued talking only losing a beat.

"…so then they all treat me like it was my fault that only me and ten other women in Washington can type."

They had smelled them for the past hour and now Elaine entered carrying the white plate of cookies. The aroma of cookie spices, cinnamon, cardamom, and ginger filled the room. As she placed them on the table and sat down in the empty chair, they each quickly took one except Mr. Barille took two.

Out of her pocket, Elaine pulled a yellowed piece of paper and held it up.

"I've told you I think that both our children are in the service, Patty in the WACS in England and Bobby in the Pacific. I got a letter today from him and I can read it to you if…"

Marge folded her cards together and slapped them down on the table.

"They aren't there on vacation, why would we want to read about the war?"

"Marge!" said Mary startled by Marge's rudeness.

"I fold, lousy cards. I think I'll go upstairs and see if I can catch a glimpse of the ghost."

As Marge rose to leave, Brigette said, "Oh, I'll go with you. I'd love to paint a real ghost."

Mary grabbed Brigette's hand as Marge left the room.

"Brigette, stay with us."

Dotty tried to explain to everyone at the table except Mr. Barille, who seemed so absorbed in his cookies and his cards, he hadn't heard a thing.

"Marge is just upset. She was telling me her brother is fighting in Europe. He usually writes her regularly but she hasn't heard from him in a while."

"We all worry," Elaine said in an understanding tone.

"And we all pray," Mr. Barille said softly.

It was now late in the evening and the game seemed to be going Mary's way. She had a large pile of pennies in front of her.

"Lord knows I'm crazy as a buck naked fella standing in a field during a lightning storm," Dotty said, "but I raise you." She pushed five pennies from her meager pile to the center of the table.

"Now is she telling the truth or is she…" Brigette drifted toward Dotty.

Harry pushed some pennies to the center. "All is fair in love, war, and poker. I'll raise you."

In a whisper that everyone could hear, Brigette said, "I don't see how you could keep a poker face with…"

"Hush your mouth, Miss Artist," Dotty said frowning.

"Well," said Elaine putting down her cards and grabbing a cookie, "I fold too."

"I'm already out," said Mary.

"Me too," said Mr. Barille. "I need to go to bed. It's nearly eleven." With a screech, he pushed back his chair and said, "Buenos noches."

Dotty acted surprised. "He's not even going to see what I have!"

"Well, Dotty, the pot is yours, so let's see if you had that ace I wanted," Elaine said.

Dotty laid her cards out on the table and spread them out. All she had was a pair of Jacks.

Mary turned over her cards to reveal three of a kind. "One pair! I thought you had at least…"

Laughing Harry said, "I smell a skunk here wearing Chanel number 5. Brigette, you let that slip on purpose."

Brigette gave a coy look, but before she could say anything, there was a scream from the kitchen.

Everyone ran into the kitchen where two Asian men were standing beside a spilled pot of hot tomato soup. The taller of the two men was holding his left arm and whimpering. They were talking rapidly in their native language which no one could understand.

For a long moment, everyone stood transfixed by the scene: the steaming red liquid on the tile floor with a large metal pot next to it. The taller of the two men seemed to be named Pock from what they could discern.

Obviously in pain, he bowed. "I am so sorry, Mr. Goldman."

"It's only soup. But how are you?"

Turning to Brigette, Dotty said in a hushed voice, "I didn't know they worked here."

Brigette answered a bit louder, "They could be spies. Why aren't they in one of the camps?"

Harry turned around. "They aren't spies." He sounded like he had explained this before. "They have been working for me, with me for years and…" His voice had grown louder.

Everyone had turned to Brigette. She paused, assessing the situation. "All this beautiful yellow skin is nothing unusual."

Mary pushed her way forward and took Pock's arm. "All I see is a man with a burned arm. When my brother Bud burned his arm on a hot pan, we ran cold water over it. Turn on the faucet," she said to the other Asian man.

Before Elaine could move forward to help, Brigette looked at her. "Think I should be an actress the way I helped Dotty?"

Chapter 16

A city is a beast whose weight bends its inhabitants to its personality. Washington, DC was a beast rushing toward something unknown, and the people there were always rushing. No moment was unspoken for; there was always something to be done and busy people to do it and so it was with Marge and Mary, rushing to work, working hard identifying and filing prints, rushing to have as much fun as they could, until they were exhausted.

They were rushing for a train in Union Station. They were going to Philadelphia, well sort of. They weren't planning to get off there but to take a train right back home. But Libby, one of the women in their office had told them a secret.

"And don't tell anyone else," she said. Marge had been complaining about how hard it was to meet a man here in a city where there were so many girls with sore fingers and roaming eyes. Libby sympathized with her. "But there are always men, GI's, government workers and other guys traveling back and forth to Philly and they go by train."

"So, you meet men on the train?" Mary asked. Marge had caught on.

"Yes, you meet, you chat, and then you get to your destination and get off the train only to go back home and meet more men. It's great because they aren't going to try to grab you in public. If you like them, or they are a hot prospect, you give them your number and you can go out on a real date. It's like a series of mini dates aboard the train."

And there were men on the train, talking, laughing, bumping into each other, and all with their eyes on any dame who was on the train. For them, it was a way to meet women too, being away from the barracks or an office, not having to spend a precious dollar on a drink, only a smile and a cheery hello.

With a lurch, the train rolled out of Union Station and Libby was already headed back to the bar car, her sights set on a soldier who seemed to be walking that way. Marge watched her sashaying down the aisle in her white dress with small red polka dots, and realized that this was a game to be played by every woman on the train. She supposed if she wanted, she could make it a competition.

Her father was German and her mother was too, and they were never ones to compliment their daughter. While other girls wore their compliments to school in the confidence of their walk or a flip of their hair, Marge had never heard, "You're so pretty," when she wore her communion dress or new Easter outfit. It was on her first day of school, as her mother stood beside her on the sidewalk outside the school, that she heard, "You look beautiful," not from her mother who remained silently surveying the crowd of mothers and children, but from a woman nearby as she bent down and ran her finger through her daughter's hair. "You look beautiful today." She had looked up at her mother waiting to be told the same thing or something similar, suspecting this is what every child was told on their first day of school. But her mother only said, "Now you behave," and that was all. It made Marge hurt and want to misbehave just to get back at her mother.

"You look pretty today," she heard the voice of a man next to her say. She and Mary were sitting facing each other, with a soldier beside each of them in the seat. They had not planned this seating arrangement, but it had worked out that way. And the man beside Marge was rather attractive, with wide eyes, a strong chin, and a dark five o'clock shadow.

"Thank you," she said meaning it. "Train travel does take its toll though. It's sort of hot in here, Indian summer."

"I can fix that," he said snapping the clamps and pulling down the widow half way. "And you are…"

She thought he was going to use the new term she had been hearing around town recently, you're so hot. But he did not.

"…Nice to talk to me. Seems since I'm a big guy, girls don't want to just talk with me." He had a shy smile that Marge had not expected. She could see starting up a conversation was difficult for him, but he was forging ahead.

"And you seem like a nice guy. You must be from the south? I think I hear an accent."

"Virginia, south, but not Deep South."

As Marge and her seat companion began a conversation, the GI next to Mary, a boy of about nineteen, in a recently pressed uniform sat silent staring out the window.

He's just been drafted, she thought, *and doesn't know what lies ahead.* Her heart went out to him.

She tapped him on the shoulder. "Where are you headed to?"

Turning to her, Mary could see that he was handsome in a wholesome way. Yet there was a hint of something in his eyes she could not place.

He ran his long fingers across his government issued haircut. "That, I can't say."

"Oh, it's a secret?"

He laughed. "No, I have to report to the base and then I don't know where they are sending me. Someplace in Europe, I suppose."

That was what all the soldiers on the train were really thinking about, where were they going, and what would they find there. Her heart went out to him and she thought of her brothers who were already in Europe. Life was fragile and time might be short. There was a distance out there and it was rushing up on all of them.

They began to chat in an easy way, without silent moments, with a flow to the conversation that was about next to nothing. He was from Maine, the youngest boy of three, the other two had both ended up somewhere in the Pacific, where they were was blacked out in their letters. Then they talked about movies they had seen, neither had seen many, but they had seen different ones, so they told each other the story-lines. He liked a good gangster movie, she one with some romance.

As she was telling him about a romantic scene in 'For Whom the Bell Tolls', he suddenly interrupted her.

"You look like you need to go powder your nose."

Mary was startled, but he didn't seem to be trying to offend her. She was about to ask Marge to go the restroom with her, but she looked over and saw she was laughing with her soldier.

"I'll take care of that," Mary said smiling. Getting up. She began squeezing through the aisle which after a few stops was now filled with soldiers and sailors in uniform, men in brown and gray suits, and women with dresses that were tight at the waist.

She finally reached the door of the restroom. She hated train toilets, when you lifted the lid, you could see the tracks below. Why her brother's friends played on the tracks across the river, she could never understand. But she was only using the mirror so pushed open the door and was stepping in when she was shoved from behind, almost falling against the metal sink.

"Well, this is more private, isn't it?" A man's voice said and she turned around to see her seat mate behind her, snaking his arms around her waist.

"Too private, private," Mary said trying to sound like she was joking, but actually taking the time to try to figure out what to do.

"There's not much time before we reach the station, so we better be quick."

With a quick thrust up of her knee, Mary hit him in his crotch. Groaning, he doubled over. But he landed against her, trapping her from getting to the door. She shoved him as hard as she could and he fell face first toward the toilet. Yanking the door open, she didn't wait to see how he was. In minutes, she was out in the aisle again. Looking at her hands, she saw they were shaking.

When Mary and Marge walked in the bureau the next day, they were stopped in their tracks. Somehow during the night, more boxes of fingerprints had been brought in and were packed so high that you could not see from one desk to another.

Marge said trying to lighten the burden she felt, "Why do I suddenly feel I'm in the trenches?"

Roz saw them standing there staring and came up. She whispered, "Don't tell anyone, but I have it from one of my spies that this afternoon Lansburgs is getting in some real silk stockings."

Mary was thrilled. "They called me in yesterday to tell me that I had a run and I was a disgrace to the bureau. What if I lose my job?"

"From the rumors I hear, they should make Mr. Hoover wear silk stockings," Marge quipped.

"Maybe he does," Roz said smiling like she knew something no one else did.

"I've been drawing a seam up the back of my leg so long, I think I've tattooed myself," Marge muttered as she walked toward her desk.

Across town, Dotty was just arriving at work for her shift. She was lucky that she could sleep in a bit and she knew the other girls were jealous of it, but she didn't care. It felt so good lying in bed listening to the songs of birds and the rattling of voices echoed in the alley below.

As she opened the door, she knew something was up because the girls had all stopped their incessant chatting and had become silent. Dotty quietly closed the door behind her. Lelia sat at her desk in the corner and looked down at a desk that had nothing on it.

"Don't stop the gab on my account. Colored women gab just as much as white folk. We gab about ourselves and about you."

Some of the women smiled at the remark and a few even chuckled under their breath. But Susan, looking like a high strung child said, "We had a maid once like you before the depression, thought she was clever, meddled in things not hers. I told you about her, Barb."

"I think you did, she was the one that had her eyes on your father."

Time and again, Dotty had heard such nonsense and was adept at ignoring what was being implied. She squeezed between the desks toward hers, by the door to Mr. Beam's office. She pulled out her chair then suddenly stood there in shock.

"Someone took my typewriter last night, some thief!" She had considered taking it home each day but had thought nothing like this could ever happen. Then looking around she saw that the few other typewriters were still there. And there was a guilty look on the women's faces. Lelia covered her face with her hands.

Susan pursed her lips and flipped her hair. "Must have been that Negro night janitor."

"Can't trust their kind," Barb added.

Dotty was mad but tried to keep herself under control as she said softly, but firmly, "I'm your kind too, an American, a colored one who is trying to serve my country the best way I can which is with my fingers." She sat down hard on her chair and hoped no one would notice the tears in her eyes.

Patty looked around the room angrily and decided she was going to speak up. "Oh look, Dotty, over behind that old desk, isn't that your typewriter?" even though it couldn't be seen from where she was.

Standing up Dotty looked straight at Susan. "Oh, maybe I left it there last night."

Patty quickly went to the desk and pulled Dotty's typewriter out from underneath it. She took it over to Dotty's desk.

She whispered in Dotty's ear. "Today at noon, Lansburgs is getting in some silk stockings, only you and I and one other person knows."

You would have thought it was Frank Sinatra singing. Women pushed through the doors, down past the cosmetics, and into the lingerie section of

Lansburgs. It seemed every government girl was there climbing over each other to reach the counter where a shocked and fearful saleswoman stood beside a cardboard box filled with stockings, hurrying to get it open. Even though she knew it wouldn't work, habit took over and she tried to lay them out in an orderly display. It didn't work.

"Only two pairs per person!" yelled the saleslady now frightened by all the hands grabbing up the stockings.

Marge, Mary and Roz stood at the back of the crowd trying to be orderly and figure out where the line to get the stockings was, if there was a line. There wasn't.

"How do I know when I'll be able to get a pair of stockings again?" Marge said suddenly feeling frantic.

"Two pairs, war time rules," the saleswoman yelled.

Marge yelled back, "You made that up!"

"I know what to do," said Roz, "I came combat ready." She held up an umbrella.

Looking behind her toward the doors, Mary saw a new crowd of women trying to make their way in.

"Oh no, it's lunch time."

Marge said, "Troops advance!"

Roz turned the umbrella side-ways and leading, began to push through the crowd.

Roz and Marge reached the counter while Mary was caught up in the crowd. She had started out trying to be polite, but then saw that it was useless.

Grabbing up stockings, Roz and Marge began throwing them back to Mary who managed to catch them. Mary heard a familiar voice a ways behind her and looked back to see Dotty and another woman. She tossed them some stockings.

"Dotty, are you coming to the dance tonight? The bus is picking up the girls at 7:30 in front of the post office and then…"

"It's not quite my group," Dotty answered as she and her friend came up by Mary.

"Oh. I'm sorry…" Mary caught another pair of stockings.

Dotty smiled slyly, "But I've been keeping a secret, a big secret of a man, named Billy Joe Royal."

"I suspected something was up. Does he work with you?"

“Over at the War College.”

Marge and Roz appeared from out of the crowd holding up packs of stockings.

“Whoopee! That was fun,” exclaimed Roz shaking the umbrella.

“About as fun as chasing the hogs for slaughter. Except the pigs had better manners,” said Marge.

Mary turned to Roz. “Going with us to the dance tonight?”

“No, I’ve got someone at home.”

“Nice to meet you finally,” Dotty said extending her hand. They introduced themselves all around. Patty was thrilled to meet everyone.

“I got me someone, and you can bet in this town with all these girls, I’m going to try to keep him,” laughed Dotty. “Girl, it’s been too long.”

Chapter 17

Brigette was listening to Glen Miller on the radio when her inspiration began to seep from her. She was wearing a peacock blue silk lounging robe with the top sagging open to expose her breasts. Who cares who sees my body was her attitude; it was just a body, not the real her, not her heart and her soul. She kept those close and invisible to others.

She pulled the brush away from the canvas pulling a dab of yellow ocher from the painting. Rubbing her brush against an old towel, she dropped it in the jar of turpentine on the table. She glanced up and saw Steven, sitting naked across the room. It was like seeing him for the first time she had been so in the clutches of her muse. He was a good model for her painting. He knew how to sit still and keep his mouth shut.

"You can get dressed, Steven."

As he picked up his socks from the floor where he had tossed them, as they quickly got undressed and made love, he said, "Why don't you go out on a date with me? Down to the National Theater to see that play with Lucille Ball."

Brigette was silent as she watched him get dressed. It was strange watching him getting dressed. He usually climbed up the trellis to the balcony to the little room off her studio and got undressed in there. However, today he had run in, in the heat of passion.

"I can treat you real good."

"Not good enough."

"You wouldn't say that in bed."

"Sorry, but I'm not getting involved with a soldier. I'm letting a lawyer marry me. They are the wave of the future, my naked friend."

"Then maybe we could be friends?"

"Just an expression. I'm not into being friends with you." And in fact, she wasn't about to be friends with anyone. She couldn't. Friends shared secrets and she had ones she could never share.

Walking over to the rear window, she saw Pock coming out into the walled garden to get some air.

"You'll have to wait a minute before you climb down. There is someone in the garden," she said, finding herself more worried about Pock being seen than herself being caught with a man climbing out of her room.

"When the war is over, I'm moving to Europe and you could…"

"Steven, I think I'm tired of painting you. An artist needs something new and you…"

"You break my heart," Steven said picking up his rucksack.

"You really have a heart to break?"

"Of course, I do."

Pock had walked back into the kitchen.

"You can leave now; I'm going to lie down."

The darkness that had been insipid now gathered around the city. Steven, with nothing more he could think of to say, went into the little room and climbed out the window and onto the small balcony. He opened his rucksack and pulled out a transmitter.

Brigette went to her window that faced the front of the house to look out and see if she could see Steven going down the street. Instead she saw a strange woman with a veil over her face climb the steps to the building.

Getting dressed quickly, Brigette left her room and went down the stairs passing Michael, the reporter that lived on the second floor.

Reaching the foyer, she could see the restaurant was starting to get busy. It seemed that since the war had started people were laughing loud, trying so hard to have a good time in such a terrible time. She came down another set of stairs and walked through the room where they residents ate and into the kitchen.

The warm air thick with the smells of food drifted over her. Near the stove, Pock and Peter sat on low stools talking. Of course, she couldn't understand them, which annoyed her. They saw her when she came over to the cutting board, picked up a carrot, and took a bite out of it. Suddenly, they were silent leaving only the hiss of something on the griddle and the boiling of water.

"Please go on. I just came down to say hello."

Peter rose and started to bow, but thought better of it and stood straight. "Is there something that we can get you? Mr. G is out right now trying to track down some more beef for dinner."

"One time a year ago," said Pock also rising, "right after we entered the war, he brought back a whole cow in the back seat of his convertible."

They all laughed, especially Peter. "The Polish ambassador smuggled it in for him from his farm in Virginia."

"Did you eat the poor thing?" Brigette asked chewing on the carrot.

"He didn't have the heart. It has such big sad eyes."

The door to the cellar creaked open and an Asian woman wearing an old blue cotton dress and a stained apron came up the stairs carrying a basket of potatoes. Pock hurried over to her and took the basket from her.

"My little blossom, please, I must carry this for you."

The woman was young and seemed capable of carrying it to Brigette. There was no reason a woman couldn't do work too.

"Things have to get done, while you sit here and talk…"

Pock put down the basket.

"I have not made formal introductions. This is Pock and his wife Cynthia. And I don't know if I introduced myself before. I am Peter."

Brigette bowed Asian style while the others held out their hands to shake. There was a second of awkwardness, and then they all smiled.

All of a sudden, Brigette realized something.

"Cynthia, you're pregnant!"

Cynthia smiled. "Clever Americans. Our baby isn't due for a while yet."

"My parents write to me what it is like in the internment camps and it is no place for a baby." Pock motioned for his wife to sit on one of the stools.

"The internment camps are for your protection from angry mobs." Brigette couldn't stop looking at Cynthia's stomach.

"Or your protection from us," Pock said emphatically. "Pregnant women are especially prone to commit violence and espionage."

Cynthia knew that any minute Pock would go into his tirade about the camps. She had heard him tell it to Peter many times before and wasn't about to hear it again.

"Husband, come help me bring the potatoes up from the cellar."

"Yes, my little slave driver," then turning to Brigette, "and nice talking with you."

"Nice to talk to you too," Cynthia said, then very seriously, "and please don't mention to anyone about us being here."

Peter motioned for Brigette to take a seat on the stool and after she sat took the other one.

"I noticed you speak English so well."

"It's the only language I know. I was born in Phoenix, my parents in China. But they never spoke their language around the house. And you?" Peter sounded defensive.

"My family is from Italy, ah, Sicily actually. I was born in New Jersey."

"Do they round up Italians?" He still sounded defensive to Brigette.

She tried to lighten the mood. "Only when they think they are gangsters. But the Mafia is really a social organization that helps their own people."

"We have some groups here that help other Chinese here in the United States..."

"Then why is your family..."

"To some people, all of us Orientals look alike."

Sensing that he was getting defensive again she said, "Oh, but I am an artist and of course, I knew that you were Chinese. And I would love it if you would come up and let me paint you. Oriental men are so different from our rude Americans."

"We don't go out of the kitchen or the old servants rooms down here. We do go out in the garden though."

"You could take the back stairs."

They paused when they heard someone coming down the stairs.

With the rustle of paper packages, Harry came down the stairs carrying large wrapped bundles. He looked exhausted and Peter ran over to help him unload the packages onto the counter in the kitchen. Each one landed with a thud.

"Buffalo again?" Peter asked.

"Beef! I stopped at the reservation desk and it seems half the Senate already knows I have beef for dinner tonight."

Harry untied the string around one of the brown paper packages and opened it up to reveal a fine cut of beef, marbled just right.

"Maybe we can make some beef stew for the boarders," Harry said proudly holding up the meat. "You down here to help do some peeling, Miss Perino?"

"No, just stopping through for a carrot."

It may seem awful when you think about it, but the toilet does flush and the water is clean, Mary thought as she dunked her dainties in the soapy water in the toilet. Marge was washing her things out in the sink.

"I have to take special care with these stockings," Marge said proudly.

Dotty stood at the mirror looking at her hair. It was straightened but not what she really wanted.

"I wish I could have hair like yours, Marge, and Mary's breasts. I wonder what my hair would turn out like if I just let it…"

Brigette, dressed in a long, elegant red satin dress, off the shoulder, peered in the door. She almost felt like one of the girls these days, almost felt like she had girlfriends, which was something new for her. Still, she had things best kept to herself and knew she could never get really close to them.

"You wowed me, now who's the man?" Dotty asked running her hand along the smooth cool fabric.

"I heard you have a secret love, Dotty," Brigette replied. The girls sensed that she was avoiding the question, but felt they couldn't press her to divulge who the man was that they had noticed she had been seeing.

Mr. Barille, dressed in his blue terry cloth robe came up behind Brigette wanting to take a bath, but no one seemed to take heed of him. He cleared his throat loudly, but got no response. Turning around and grumbling in Spanish, he headed back to his room.

"Well," Dotty began with a big smile on her face, "he makes my pores spread wide open just thinking about him. He's from South Carolina."

"Isn't that a bit unsophisticated for a New York City dame?" Brigette said in a joking manner.

"Oh, I'm sure, she can teach him a thing or two or three," Mary said standing up and wringing out her underwear.

"You bet I can."

Brigette squeezed herself into the bathroom, her high heels tapping loudly on the tile.

"Is it true what they say about Negro men?" The women looked at Brigette not knowing what Dotty could possibly say. "What? I mean that those from the south have the best manners."

Mary interrupted the silence as Brigette tried to pry her foot from her mouth.

"I know you've probably got a date, Brigette, but how about you come with us to the dance this time. Hundreds of lonely men in uniform."

Under her breath Marge said, "What I wouldn't do to find a husband. Greg is driving me crazy."

Brigette ran her fingers along her dark hair which she had pinned up with silver combs for the occasion. "Sorry, dolls, but I've got a bigger fish on the line."

"Dotty, teach us to dance?" Marge asked.

"Sure, we all got rhythm. Next, I'll show you how to spit watermelon seeds," Dotty said all in good fun. She loved being able to joke with these women. It reminded her of the friendships that she had formed with the band members.

Marge grabbed Dotty's hands. "One of those swinging New York City steps, so I don't feel like such a hick form the Midwest."

"Which we are," laughed Mary.

The limo was a long black Chrysler. Brigette ran down the steps toward it, her red dress glowing in the light from the street lamp. The chauffeur emerged and moved swiftly around to the rear passenger door to open it for her. Inside sat an older man with an impressive head of white hair. He smiled and motioned for her to come in.

Around the corner of the building, Steven had watched the limo pull up. He was observant and knew Brigette's habits. Friday night at eight, the limo was always there to pick her up. He picked up his rucksack and went to climb over the garden wall.

Chapter 18

Leaves of autumn, wet with the previous night's rain, covered the shiny black asphalt with golds and reds. Leaves shimmied through the crisp air, other leaves tried desperately to hold onto the branches that had given them life. With leaves sliding down around them, the women, close to a dozen, stood at the appointed corner, Fourteenth and Constitution, at the appointed time, eight sharp, to meet the bus. It rumbled through the traffic with the screams and laughter of young women coming out the windows. The yellow bus had arrived with banners hanging on the sides of that said, 'WOMEN'S BATTALION'.

The group rushed in the door and up the steps crowding the aisle with excitement. They were going to the dance!

"Whoo-ee!" Dotty was totally surprised. She had been looking up and down the street for her date Billy, she didn't know which way he would come from. It was when she had been looking the other way that the car pulled up behind her. She spun around and there was a beautiful black Pontiac with the chrome glistening in streetlight.

The driver's door flew open and out stepped Billy Joe Royal with every button on his khaki uniform shining.

"Holy smokes, where did you steal that from?" Dotty immediately regretted that she had said that and waited for Billy to look offended. He didn't.

"Good friend in the motor pool lent it to me." Dotty stepped to the car where Billy held the door open for her. "You look really sharp, I mean beautiful as a cool glass of iced tea on a hot summer's day."

And she did, in the burnt orange suit she had bought when the band played Cincinnati. The color of the smooth fabric and the cream color of the blouse, gave a soft glow to her skin color.

"Thank you."

She jumped in the car and he closed the door. When he got in, he put his arm up on the seat almost touching her shoulder.

"Where shall we go? I thought maybe down by the river and out toward Chain Bridge. I've never been out of this city and I could use a dose of country."

Dotty didn't answer, just smiled and enjoyed the way he looked directly into her eyes.

Sweetheart of mine, I've sent you a valentine.
Sweetheart of mine, it's more than a valentine.
Be careful it's my heart.

The singer stroked her fingers slowly up the microphone stand and let out a clean, pure note. She was dressed in a long white off one shoulder gown. The band members all wore identical black tuxedos with white ties, and Mary thought they must be a big name to be dressed so well. Obviously the USO had money to try and make the soldiers happy. And the tall not so handsome soldier she was dancing with swung her around. She had been a quick learner and the steps that Dotty had taught them had paid off.

Marge had things under control. As usual. The sailor with the goofy smile walked away quickly as Mary came up exhausted but exhilarated.

"You sent him away. He wasn't that bad looking."

"Yes, in a cartoonish sort of way. I sent him to get me a soda."

"But they have punch," Mary said feeling her hair to see if it was still in place.

"Honey, punch is too close; the soda machine I hear is across the parade ground. I've got two boys running over there. I hope they forget who they are getting them for."

Mary straightened her dress. "That one was fun but a bit fast for me. But there will be others."

"Well listen to you! Line 'em up, Mary."

"They're boys going off to war. It's kind of our duty to entertain them."

"Well, not one decent-looking guy has offered to step on my toes."

"No wonder. Put your arm in a salute and you'll look as friendly as Hitler. Look, over there, it's Greg."

Greg felt haggard. His job tonight was to blend in, be inconspicuous although he was one of only a few men wearing a suit and a depressing gray at that. But that was what he had been told to wear. At least he got to pick his own tie, a dark red silk with a yellow elk on it. He was carrying a glass of punch. As Mary was dragged off with a good looking soldier with slicked black hair, Greg came up and handed the punch to Marge. She was startled, pleased, but for some reason she could not figure out, still sarcastic.

"Want me to hold this for you while you look for a date?"

Greg smiled. "A date with General Marshall. Supposed to show up tonight or so we heard."

"Don't they have some sort of security to look after him, Secret Service or something?"

"He's important enough that we look after whoever is looking after him. Mr. Hoover likes to know what everyone is doing."

"Maybe we could…"

"There he is. Gotta go," Greg said before Marge could ask him to dance.

Marge had just finished her punch when Mary came back. She could see Marge looked irritated. And she knew why.

"Do I look as dumb as a hog in a new hat at a church social?" Marge lamented.

"See that woman over there in the smart looking blue dress?" Marge winced, it was the same color as hers, but not nearly as stylish looking. "I was chatting with her during a cigarette break. She works a filing job for some agency. But before that she used to live on a pig farm."

"How does she slop a pig with those nails?"

"Oh, come on grumpy, practice one of the steps Dotty taught us with me."

As they were dancing, Sam walked up in his pressed sailor whites holding a small bunch of flowers. The women didn't notice him until he said, "Excuse me."

"I remember you, the movie star!" Mary said stopping their practice.

"I recognize those flowers. They were on the table with the punch," Marge said almost laughing.

"I just wanted to be a bit more…Well, last time, Mary, I…"

But Marge didn't hear any more of the conversation; she had walked off as Mary accepted the flowers.

In the corner of the large hall stood three soldiers smoking and laughing at nothing in particular; it was a loud, rolling laugh with a hint of desperation. Making buddies from all around the country was great. Too bad they knew the next step was Europe.

The tallest of the three, fair haired from Wisconsin, let out a sound like a siren.

"Dame alert!"

"Sh-h-h! You'll scare her away," said the one with the part in the middle and a cowlick.

Marge heard the noise and knew what it meant. These guys, not especially handsome but not as homely as some, were actually interested in her. She debated what to do. The inner struggle took only minutes and she was left with a modicum of courage and a bit of daring. She liked the way she felt.

"Hello, boys. You look as bored as I feel."

"You can say that again," said the tall one, "I'm Hank."

"Nice to meet you."

The shortest of the three extended his hand. "I'm Bud and I'm ready and willing." He pulled his hand away as Marge was about to touch it and ran his palm along the side of his head, smoothing his hair. And laughed at what he thought was a funny joke. However, Marge turned to the third man, the only nearly normal one of the group. She did not extend her hand.

"Marge," she said.

"Carlos. They're playing my favorite song. Wanna dance?"

It was rare for Mary to hear live music and she found the swing, hop, and sway was intensified on the dance floor. There were excellent dancers around her, but it was Sam she concentrated on as they practiced the swing steps Dotty had taught her. Marge came up behind Mary and bumped into her on purpose and when she caught her attention, nodded her head toward Carlos. He was lost in his own world with his own unique dance steps. Mary wasn't sure if she should be impressed or think it was funny. Marge smiled. She didn't know either.

After the music had skidded to a halt, and the clapping died out, the band began to play 'Happy Days and Lonely Nights', a slow song. Mary and Sam hesitated, then decided to dance again. Marge however looked at her partner and decided that enough was enough. No slow dance with him and left the dance floor.

"I'm real sorry about that at the beach. How you gonna know how to act around dames, I mean women unless you got an older brother or go to the movies? It's just that's how the guys act and I thought since I was attracted to you…" Sam said wondering if he could dip Mary.

"So, like a turkey you opened your mouth, looked up, and went out in the rain with the rest."

"Gobble, gobble."

"Don't feel bad. Lots of girls think they are supposed to act like girls in the movies. Lots of girls think they are supposed to like men acting like that. I guess that means…"

"That I liked you, right away."

Mary smiled softly and just as softly kissed him on the cheek.

The fireflies were the stars that were washed out by the glowing moonlight. It was like a sin, that's how beautiful the night was and they drifted in the empty boat across the rich dark waters of the Potomac River. Billy had surprised Dotty, driving across the bridge into Virginia to an old boat house.

But the night had become bittersweet as reality crept into the moment.

Billy leaned back into the boat, his uniform a soft green/brown in the night's light.

"I joined up to fight not to clean toilets. I don't wanna be Jim Crowed. It makes me crazy. Everything makes me crazy lately, even when I think of home."

"Why?"

"I don't know. I used to think I had the world figured out, but now…I was young and stupid."

Dotty laughed softly. "Don't try to figure the world out. The most you can ever understand about this world is that you can never understand it."

"You know what used to scare me? Snakes, white folk with baseball bats, TB. Now I'm scared, but I don't know of what."

He remembered those days before he had signed up, when despite the comfortable groove he had found his life in, something was wrong. He felt like he was kicking his tires, spinning his wheels and spitting in the dust because he wasn't getting anywhere. That was why he had signed up even before he could get drafted now. Now, he was still trying to shift that old car his father had given him before he died of TB. He didn't know where he was, even if he was going to get a chance to fight the Germans.

The silence was like glass between them, but Dotty broke through it and kissed him heavily on the lips.

The corner of the dance hall had become theirs, Marge and the three soldiers laughed, at this point they didn't know at what. They now passed around Bud's flask, each soldier had one and his was the last. With a gulp, Marge took a big swig and felt the whisky slide down her throat.

Hank staggered toward the door and motioned for the others to follow. They all ended up under the trees alongside the parade ground. Marge felt good, felt doubts about the things in her past slip away. It was slippery under foot and she almost fell, but Hank caught her in time.

"Whoa there, girly," Hank said as Marge pulled away from him and walked further down the line of trees with the others following.

They stopped when Carlos said, "Look here!" He pulled a second flask out of his pocket.

"Want some?" Hank said, grabbing the flask from his buddy and offering it to Marge.

When Marge seemed reluctant to take it, Bud said, "Can't handle it?"

"It's nothing compared to the homemade hooch back home down by the river. You boys think you know it all." She took the flask.

As the moon hid behind a gray cloud, two of the soldiers began to pull their shirts out.

"Let's dance," said Carlos motioning to the flask. Marge took a gulp.

"You try dancing out here in heels."

"Take them off then," said Carlos moving closer stepping through a shadow.

"Take it all off," said Hank with a grin on his wet lips.

Hank quickly stepped forward and grabbed Marge by the arm, while Carlos moved even closer. She could hear the sound of his zipper. She tried to push him off, but she was too weak, too drunk. Panic began to inch under her skin.

She could hardly concentrate, but she thought it was Hank who said, "You wanted a good time, didn't you?"

The movement of Bud stepping backward into what little light there was sparked her as if from a sleep.

"Can it," she said struggling to get free, "I'm going back inside."

"Oh," said Bud grabbing her other arm, "A tease."

Now she realized she was in nothing but danger and her mind began to race to try and think of a way out. A scream was incapacitated by a hand over her mouth.

Mary and Sam, holding hands, stepped outside. They had planned to kiss but saw the crowd of soldiers around someone in the distance.

"It's Marge!" Mary yelled putting her hands over her mouth.

Sam was ready to run to the rescue when she held him back. He was one against three. Instead she ran over to a group of sailors who were standing nearby.

"I thought you ought to know. Those GIs over there just now laughed at you and told me that men go into the navy because they are too yellow to fight eye to eye."

"The bastards!" one of the sailors yelled and instantly, the six of them headed toward the soldiers.

Within seconds, Marge was free as Hank was grabbed from behind. Fists, blood, a fight ensued while Marge ran past Mary and Sam, not seeing them, only stopping when she got back in the dance hall running right into Greg who grabbed her. Something was very wrong.

"What's going on?"

"Oh, I did a stupid thing, I lead them on…I'm not some V girl…"

"Of course not."

As Mary and Sam followed Marge into the hall, two MP's with their sticks in their hands ran out past them.

A toot—a toot
Unless a bass and guitar
Is playin' with 'im

Dotty and Billy sang as they drove along the canal separating Washington from Virginia on the Virginia side. Just outside the city but still in the south, a south that to some extent they both feared.

"Gotta lose some weight, too many donuts and too much sugar in my coffee," said Officer Doyle. He actually did wish he could lose some weight, he said it to his partner all the time. Maybe if he had been thinner his wife wouldn't have taken up with that smarmy salesman down at the appliance shop and wouldn't have left him.

Officer Parker flicked his ash out the window and stretched his back by pushing against the steering wheel and arching back. He was tired of hearing

Doyle go on and on about his weight. Sitting by the side of the road waiting to catch a speeder was bad enough without his partner complaining again.

"You're good at stopping eating donuts but then we drive by the shop and you want me to pull in every time."

"Maybe, we could take another route."

"You know that's part of our territory and we have to go that way. Besides Gary expects us to drive by to make sure he is alright. He is open all night and there are some crazy niggers out there who would cut his throat and rob the register."

"Hey, look at that, we done got ourselves a speeder. Put on the siren and let's have us some fun."

They heard the siren rushing around them before they saw the flashing light behind them.

Billy's hands gripped the steering wheel tight and his stomach felt like it had just fallen into a hole.

"The fuzz. This black ass is in trouble now." He slowed down and looked for a place to pull over without sliding into the canal.

"I thought you took this car out—"

"I got permission from my buddy, but you think he's going to fess up for me when—And who's going to get me out of jail? Us out of jail?"

Swinging her legs up, Dotty jumped into the back seat.

"Whatever you do, don't open the door so the light goes on," she yelled above the sound of the siren which was now right behind him.

He didn't think to ask why; he was good at taking orders as he and the police car both pulled over. On one side of him ran the black of the canal with trees on the other side. On his left across the road were more trees. No witness to what they might do, was the first thought he had as the red light seared its way through the air around them turning everything crimson then black again in the darkness.

Before he could think about what was going on, the officer was at the window. He rolled it down. He was trembling.

"Hello, Officer. What can I do for you? We were just out for a little drive."

"Now were you. You army boys think you can get away with anything and maybe you can for a while. Not with me."

Then Officer Doyle said the words Billy did not want to hear, "Get out."

Dotty cleared her throat loudly. Then she said, "Is there something wrong, driver?"

Right away, he recognized the voice of Mrs. Roosevelt and realized what the game was.

"Just a little delay, Ma'am."

Doyle leaned down by Billy trying to see in the back seat. For once Dotty thought, it's an advantage being black. He can't see me back here.

"That sounds a lot like…"

Dotty cleared her throat again and 'Mrs. Roosevelt' said, "If there is a problem, driver, why don't you get my husband on the radio. It's a shame to have to wake the president after such a tough day."

"Oh, there is no problem, Ma'am, Mrs. Roosevelt," he yelled into the back seat.

"Driver, perhaps we should get the officer's badge number."

Doyle squirmed and shook his head. "Oh, that won't be necessary."

"Then let's get back to town, driver."

"Ah yes, we'll give you an escort."

The large black car pulled away quickly as Doyle ran back to his car and jumped in.

"Put down the donut and let's get going. We're giving Mrs. Roosevelt an escort back to DC."

"Mrs. Roosevelt? I read in the *Post* this morning that she's out of town on a USO tour," Parker said as he turned on the car.

"I thought something looked suspicious. Catch them!"

With the siren screaming and the red light flashing ahead of them, the police cruiser tried to catch up to Billy who was going like a bat out of hell. Dotty was thrown back against the seat. She regretted her ploy, but what else could she have done? Now, they were in big trouble, very big trouble. Billy couldn't say a word; he was concentrating on the road, if he could only make it to Chain Bridge…

And the cops knew that too. They wanted his ass and sped up again, the engine roaring. But Billy knew this was a powerful engine, he could feel it beneath him and he accelerated too. The cruiser was closing in just when Billy saw it.

"There it is!" yelled Dotty.

With tires squealing as they made the turn onto the bridge and the DC line, they kept going, too frightened still to slow down.

The cruiser screeched to a halt.

"Shit!" said Doyle, "We can't follow them!"

"Goddamn! But maybe at that speed, they'll get caught on the other side and the MPs will have his nigger ass!"

Another car, less conspicuous than the shiny black ones that slid down the streets and avenues of Washington; this one was a dull brown 1937 Ford that had seen much better days. In it sat two men in suits, bored, but keeping watch. One wore headphones while the other fiddled with the dial on a radio. He shook his head.

Chapter 19

Late at night, the Golden Parrot spoke in many voices: rattling, creaking, wood moaning, the bare trees clattering against the windows. It was all Marge's head could do to endure the sounds as they crashed and clanged around in her head. God, was she going to have a hangover! If she lay down anymore, she was going to hurl all over the room, while Mary slept. She walked out the door and into the dark hallway. Bella came tip-toeing across the floor in front of her wearing a pink fuzzy robe with red flowers woven into it.

"You girls are back early, oh, well, I guess it is late after all. What I shouldn't give to be your age in this town. Feet sore?"

"No just tired, good night," said Marge heading toward the bathroom quickly.

"Night," Bella called after her.

When Marge got to the bathroom, the door was closed and there was a light under the door. In the dim light she leaned against the wall and yawned. What was she going to do if she hurled in the hallway?

Marge turned suddenly to her left. Hadn't she seen someone coming up the stairs? There it was again like a shadow moving in the shadows. But when she looked directly at it, it wasn't there, yet…With control, she looked ahead and managed to just see out of the corner of her eyes. A figure, pale as smoke, the long white gown whispering up the stairs. In its hand was a rope. Then it was gone, vanished like an illusion of the shadows and alcohol fumes.

The bathroom door swung open and light flooded the hallway. Mr. Barille in a gray robe holding a towel jumped startled when he saw Marge.

"I, ah, thought you were the," he hesitated, not wanting to sound silly, but it came out anyway, "the ghost. How could I be so silly…?"

"How could you be so silly?"

It was late and the bar downstairs was empty except for one of the older waiters with a bad knee hobbling around picking up glasses and plates. Marge sat at the grand piano letting her fingers ramble over the keys and humming softly,

You left me sad and lonely;
Why did you leave me lonely?
For here's a heart that's only
For nobody, but you!

She didn't see a man sitting on the stairs in the darkness, listening. Exhausted, but feeling better now, she rose and walked to the French doors in the large stained glass bay window overlooking the dark garden. She opened them and walked down the stairs into the cool moonless night. She was still feeling jumpy from what she thought, but wasn't sure she had seen, out of the corner of her eyes, when she felt a touch on her shoulder and spun around.

"Sorry, I didn't mean to startle you," Greg said holding out a porcelain cup of coffee, "I got off after the dance and thought…It's chilly out here."

"I think the coffee needs a shot of whiskey. Or just forget the coffee. I'm just a little jumpy tonight."

"I can understand that. I thought you might be up and need a little company."

Marge walked over to a stone bench held up by swans and sat down. Greg followed and sat down beside her.

"Oh, I was just feeling guilty about the GI's, leading them on."

"That wasn't your fault," Greg said gently.

"I worked through that finally, so then I started feeling guilty about feeling so stupid."

"You just wanted to have fun."

"Got to that too. Then I started feeling guilty about feeling guilty about leading them on and feeling guilty about feeling guilty about feeling stupid."

"Wow."

"The princess of guilt here raised by an expert, my good Catholic mother. So, what are you doing up so late? Go anywhere after the dance? Maybe the one from the OPA?"

"Oh, you heard about that?"

"From the girl with the red hair at the bureau, who heard about her from the one over at the WPB, who heard about her from the one at the OSS, who talked to the girls at the OPA…?"

"Things do get around."

"You get around. Having fun learning the alphabet?"

"So, what if I go out with a lot of different women? Now you're trying to make me feel guilty! I did show up here to see you."

Feeling guilty about what she had seemed to accuse Greg of Marge got up and walked toward the small backdoor that went into the kitchen. The room was dark and still inside. The stainless steel trim on the old iron oven and stove was glowing with a gray light that came in the windows above the sink. In front of her was a table that was covered with a white cloth. She pulled it aside and saw a tray of deserts either prepared ahead for tomorrow or left over from tonight's dinner hour.

She could hear Greg enter behind her and turned.

"I'm sorry I got on your case, Greg, really."

"Now you're feeling guilty about…"

But before he could finish his sentence she twirled around, grabbed up a tart and spun back and threw it at him. He was too surprised to move and it hit him square in the chest.

"I will not feel guilty about throwing this at you!" And she picked up another tart and threw it, Greg expecting this one, catching it though it burst and blueberry jam dripped out of his hand.

Mary walked in the kitchen, looking sleepy and wanting a glass of milk, but she saw the scene before her and couldn't figure out what was going on.

"What are you doing down here, Marge? Greg, you're a mess," she said then turned to Marge who threw a piece of cheesecake at Greg which he ducked and it splatted on the wall. "Marge!"

"I'm down here feeling guilty about feeling guilty. I'm tired of feeling guilty. I'm tired of feeling guilty about being forward." She looked at the tray deciding what to pick up next. She quickly decided on another tart which she threw at Greg, this time at his back as he turned around.

"I'm tired of feeling guilty about being a woman who doesn't want to act like men want me to." Tears were forming in her eyes.

Mary saw the tears. "I'm tired of feeling guilty about being a woman at the FBI and all the men looking at me!" She picked up some gooey desert and threw it at Marge. The tears of frustration turned to tears of laughter. Greg started to laugh too as Marge threw one of the gooey deserts at him and hit him square in the face.

"I'm tired of feeling guilty about being away from home and trying to have a career." The tears were about to turn back to frustration when Mary lifted up another piece of cheese cake and stuffed it in her mouth.

"I'm tired of feeling guilty about my boobs." They all began to belly laugh. Marge stuffed a tart in her mouth.

"I'm tired of feeling guilty about eating so much."

With bedroom eyes and a black silk robe around her, Brigette walked in hoping to find someone alone and late.

With eyes wide, she was about to ask what was going on, when Marge tossed a gooey desert at her and she screamed.

Then Greg, under his breath said, "I'm tired of feeling guilty about not fighting in the war."

Later, when Mary and Brigette had left to go clean up, Marge wiped herself off with a napkin then went over to the shelf and pulled down a large bowl and a bottle of corn syrup.

"What are you doing?"

"We have to replace all these desserts, so help me get started baking."

Greg took off his coat dripping with all kinds of sticky things and laid it on a stool in the corner. He took off his tie, which was a mess and put it on top of it.

"Grab the sack of flour."

"Got it, I actually used to help in my uncle's bakery before the war, so this should be a breeze."

Marge turned to Greg, "It's too bad we can't find a way to get Mr. Hitler to feel guilty."

Greg walked toward Marge with a serious look on his face, then put his finger down between her breasts and came up with some of the gooey dessert. He put his finger in his mouth and smiled like a little boy who had just been caught doing something bad, but something he didn't feel guilty about. Marge returned his smile and soon their lips met. The sweetest kisses, the passion rising, they made love in the kitchen that night. Afterward, Marge tried not to feel guilty and found there was no guilt there to worry about.

Chapter 20

Whispers echoed against the stone walls and light of many colors slid through the air, dust spinning in it. Saints stood silent in alcoves while candles flickered and gently rattled in their red glass votives. The way of the cross around the sanctuary reminded parishioners of the passion of Christ. The mass, as usual was long, and the pews as usual were hard. What had once been silence with only the Latin mumbling of the priest and the creaking of pews as they squirmed was now filled with the fervent whispers of prayers and the sound of crying.

Finishing her prayers Mary crossed herself. Her lips moved to, "The Father, Son, and Holy Ghost." Then she sat back from the kneeler into the pew beside Marge who was fiddling with the veil on her hat.

Marge leaned over and said softly in Mary's ear, "You're so good, Mary, and I'm so…"

"It's our French Catholic upbringing. My Catholic upbringing was so strict that when I had my first period, I thought it was the Stigmata."

Marge began to laugh then heard something being rolled up the center aisle on the stone floor. She turned around and saw a woman, younger than her, bent over pushing a wheel chair. In the chair sat a soldier in uniform with no legs. Her heart was filled with anger, uncertainty, and doubt in her God. It made her afraid that her faith might be broken, dissolved and she would be left stranded hanging above the abyss of disbelief, of nothing. She began to feel panicky as thoughts of all the wounded soldiers, of her brother.

"I have to go," she said to Mary and fled the church.

"Mail!" Harry called up the staircase to anyone who might be at home.

It was so quick, Harry hardly knew he had it in his hand. Marge grabbed the letter and headed up the stairs, two at a time. Harry knew who it must be from, the person she talked about all the time: her brother.

She got a paper cut opening the brown envelope with her name and address, but no return name and address. There it was a letter from him. She ran her fingers over the letter like she was touching his face. She closed her eyes; yes she could remember how little stubble he could grow on his face. The letter even felt warm, but that of course was from Harry carrying it in.

She opened her eyes and began to read, mouthing the words that meant so much to her. Of course, he couldn't say much about what he was doing or where the troops were in Europe. He had already complained about how tight his boots were, the bad rations, and the great buddies he had made, in previous letters. So, he wrote of the past.

"We were staying in an old mansion in a place the censors would black out if I said it. With the tall windows and flaking white paint; it reminded me of the one across the river in Prairie."

She remembered it, the haunted mansion and the burning lady. And she had seen her. She was fourteen and her brother had just turned thirteen.

Across the Mississippi River from McGregor, Iowa was the small town of Prairie du Chien. The town had now spread inland, but once was mostly on St. Feriole Island. There atop an Indian mound stood the yellow and white Victorian Villa Louie, house of the Dousman family. As the story goes (told on dark nights without a moon), the daughter of the Dousman's, a young teenager, was using the curling iron one moonless night to curl her long blonde hair. The iron was heated over a device that contained kerosene. It was a silly little accident. Knocking the device over, the kerosene spilled on to her dress igniting it. She screamed and before anyone in the house could get to her, she ran burning and screaming down to the river and jumped in. But it was too late. She died a few days later.

On nights where the moon was gone from the sky, townspeople claimed to have heard the screams and some had even seen the ghost in flames running from the house to the river. And this ghost is what Marge and her brother Dick were waiting for one dark night. They had taken a row boat from down by the dock and crossed the still water until they were not thirty feet from the shore. Another thirty feet was the house and its massive darkness against a sky wiped clean of stars.

They lay side by side in the boat waiting, not knowing what time of night the spirit might appear. Soon their eyes grew weary and closed and they fell asleep. They slept peacefully until across the land and across the water came shrill, terrified screams. Marge heard them first and woke her brother as the burning young lady came through the closed door of the house. Her body burned with a hot orange flame which was extinguished as she reached the water's edge. And it was gone. Out of fear, they dove into sleep in each other's arms.

But Marge had always believed it had been a dream, one that they both had with their eyes wide open. They had fallen asleep until morning came creeping in around them. But it was one of the stories they shared now.

"I don't know if I dreamed the whole thing but this place made me think of it and I wouldn't be surprised if there wasn't some ghost story about this place too."

Marge found tears rolling down her checks knowing they were because that night had been one of the most important of her life.

"I thought I heard crying," Brigette said tentatively as she pushed open the door which had been left open a crack. It was a silly thing to do, to think she could comfort someone; she was not good at motherly or sisterly things like that, having grown up with a cold mother and no other siblings. But it was wise cracking Marge, and this was so un-Marge that she had felt compelled to make her presence known.

"Well, I guess it wasn't laughing. Come on in and we can cry together, heaven knows there sure is a lot to cry about with this war going on."

Brigette came in and sat down on the bed beside Marge. She looked down at the letter and Marge quickly folded it together. "My brother, he's alive over there in some mansion if you can believe that. I can't believe that I'm living in some mansion."

"I can't believe that I used to live in some big old monstrosity of a house."

"Where was that?"

"In a town too little, just outside a city too big, New York."

"Someday I want to see that city, get swallowed up by it then spit out again, better off for the whole wild experience."

"Oh, it will spit you out but you land with wounds."

"You had a hard time in the city?"

"Yes, too many men and too many sad dreams. I was good at finding boyfriends, but only the ones who lost that sweetness young men have, and turned into louses who screamed and belittled me. I wasn't good at making friends and I could sell my work anywhere so I left the city, and the pain it had caused me behind. Then I came here." Brigette was amazed; she was telling someone about herself, her real self. But there was something about Marge that she could identify with even though they were both so different.

"Not home?"

"I can never go home." Brigette was silent and so was Marge who was noticing how there was a sense of tragedy Brigette carried in her green eyes. Had they wept too?

"Home is never going to be the same after this war is over." But she knew that wasn't what Brigette was talking about.

"My home, so much as it is, is here in Washington. I just got on a train and headed south. There is something about the south, where men are gentlemen, that appealed to me, but I never made it further south than here. Then the war came and Washington was filled with men from all over and dreams from all over."

"I dreamed about going east and finding a new world, but I miss my old one."

"I bet you miss your family."

"I don't miss using an outhouse, but I do miss my folks and especially my brother."

There it was, Brigette noticed that hesitation in Marge and that look when she mentioned her brother. What was it?

"I should get dressed for my date." It shook Brigette up a bit; they had been talking like friends. But just what did they or could they ever have in common.

"Oh, a date! I remember what those were. Some boob looks at your boobs the whole time, although you have to use a magnifying glass to get a glance at mine."

They both laughed and Brigette stood up to go.

"It was nice talking to you. We could be friends." But were there too many secrets between them? Is that what they shared?

"I can't believe how crowded this city is. I thought New York was filled to the bulging seams with people, but this place is like being on the subway during rush hour, Mama," Dotty said exasperated into the phone. "But in all this hustle and bustle, with all these GIs hitting on anything with breasts, I found me a guy. Now, don't flip your wig, Mama. He's not some fathead talking gobbledygook to all the girls. He's real nice, kind of naive, but I like that. Not some jaded New Yorker."

Mary came up the stairs planning to use the phone, but Dotty seemed to be just chatting away and she had a stack of nickels so she could keep talking. She went into her room, got her stationery and a pen and headed out to the old carriage house. Dotty's radio upstairs that always seemed to be on was off, so the only sound in the building was of the cow munching on some feed. Mary patted the cow on the head and smiled to herself. She had become Mary's friend. She sat down on the running board of Harry's old black car.

"I thought you might be lonely. It's funny how sometimes you can be lonely in a city with so many people. Thank god, Marge is here and you. So many men here, Sam seems nice, but most men are interested in just one thing. Well, two," she said looking down. "Ever notice how some guys talk bull to you all the time?"

She laughed at her own joke then got out a piece of the stationery and began to write.

"I miss you all, but I think I'm making this place a home. The folks here are friendly, we're all thrown in this together, away from home. I have friends here and I'm happy with where I'm living, even if it is kind of crowded. I felt like I was walking over a sheet of glass and it might crack under me at any time for so long, but I'm getting my footing. I'm not so overwhelmed by my job. I've even made a friend at work. How's the kids? And how are you? I'll call but I also like to write. I know you're like me, it's nice to get a letter sometimes, to hold it, to put it in a drawer and take it out when you need to read it again.

But I'll be seeing you at Christmas.

Love you, Mary."

Chapter 21

The sleet had turned to solid ice that slid from the gray sky and down the branches of trees, the sides of buildings and glazed grass and cement and asphalt. The few people who were out slipped along, one occasionally falling, more embarrassed than hurt. One of the women took off her shoes and held them while she walked tenderly in her stocking feet. It would soon be night and the ice storm would make the city shimmer when the street lights came on.

The ice slapped against the wide windows of the Golden Parrot, but inside it was warm as fires blazed in the two fireplaces at each end of the large dining room.

The restaurant was closed but it was hustling and busting as Harry and the boarders pushed three tables together into one long table. Michael, the reporter who roomed on the second floor, was ready with white starched table cloths which he let fly into the air and settle down slowly. Other boarders were going to the dumb waiter and pulling out the food that had been loaded in the kitchen below. It was a celebration of Thanksgiving, but also sadness for those who couldn't be with their loved ones.

What was there to be thankful for, thought Marge. These people, from all over the world, had come together, much like a big family would do on the holidays. She laughed to herself. But without, thankfully, some of the family squabbles. She was thankful for Mary being there. For the smells of pies and turkey. She was most of all thankful that at least for now, her brother seemed to be safe.

Ben and Bella passed in front of Marge, who nearly bumped into them lost in thought. Bella carried a dish of pickles and Ben carried a dish of cranberry sauce. He reached over and took one of the pickles from her dish and started to munch on it. Bella gave him 'the look'.

"What," he said, swallowing, "pickles are good for the circulation."

"They are bad for your heart, your stomach, and your breath."

They lay the dishes down on the table as Debby and Mr. Barille put out the good silverware that Elaine kept hidden up in her apartment. Marge was on her way to the dumb waiter when she saw Brigette saunter into the dining room. She was dressed in a pale pink dress with a beige shawl. Around her long neck was a string of pearls, and pearl and gold earrings hung from her ears.

"Honey," Marge went over and addressed Brigette, "are you still here? I thought Mr. Importance was supposed to pick you up hours ago."

"Would you like some egg nog?" Harry said as he rushed by, "It's spiked with bourbon."

"No, thanks," she replied as Harry put a crystal punch glass in her hand and hurried off.

Brigette looked around as the table was nearly set for the dinner and some of the boarders had already sat down. "Of course, I would rather have Thanksgiving here with you and the others, Marge, since I can't be with my own family. Thank God," she laughed uneasily, "I thought I should go out to dinner with my boyfriend. But he seems to have important government business holding him up."

"So, he got a paper cut shuffling forms in triplicate and he can't dial the phone? Well your middle finger looks fine so when you see him just give it to him."

Brigette laughed, a cruel laugh filled with disappointment. "His wife probably came into town."

"Well, give him a call later."

"Yes much later, after he divorces his wife."

"Marge," Harry called over, "can you go up and get Mary, and my wife? Dinner is ready."

When Marge came lunging up the stairs, Mary was on the phone, crying softly.

"Ma, they made us all kinds of food, but it just doesn't smell the same as your pies. It's just not the same. It's horrible being away at Thanksgiving, but it must be worse for you with me being away and the boys…"

Marge gave Mary a hug. "It's time to gobble the gobbler," she whispered.

"Dinner is ready, Ma, I gotta go. My love to everyone there."

"Now we gotta find Elaine."

"I saw her going into the room downstairs when you came in. I think she is with someone," Mary said sniffing and hanging up the phone.

They went down to find Elaine. She was there in the little room off the entryway with the door closed. Marge knocked on the door and it swung open slightly.

"Your husband says dinner is ready, Elaine."

As Elaine said, "I'll be right there," the person dressed in black who sat before her turned slightly and Marge could see who it was. Mr. Hoover. Somehow it scared her and she turned to Mary and motioned to her that they better go. But Mary had to take a peek too.

Thanksgiving dinner at Dotty's family's in New York City was over, the hustle and bustle, all the fussing, all the family chatter and minor drama was over. Her two sisters, two of her aunts, three of her uncles and various cousins had shown up, each carrying a dish of their favorite comfort food: mashed potatoes made with heavy cream, green beans in a mushroom cream sauce, cranberry sauce, and sweet potato casserole with marshmallows on top. All the traditional foods but then with the addition of items indispensable to any family gathering, fried chicken, buttermilk biscuits and Aunt Florence's mincemeat pies. Dotty's mother had supplied the turkey, corn meal stuffing, and gravy.

While the others drank beer and wine, laughed and smoked cigarettes (except Uncle Phil who smoked a pipe), Dotty was doing what she loved to do the most at these family gatherings, washing dishes with her mother. There was a rhythm to it, the dunking of the dirty plate in the warm soapy water, the rinsing in hot water, handing the plate over to Dotty who wiped it dry and with a clatter put it on the pile of their good dishes. Sometimes her mother hummed to herself, sometimes there was idle chatting between them. Sometimes, Dotty listened to her father talking to her in her imagination.

Her father had always been a musician, playing the trumpet, the saxophone, and the clarinet. Music was his life and livelihood. He played for Dotty and her two sisters, and he played for the patrons of the smoky joints around Harlem and clubs downtown, where the white people came to hear 'Negro music'. It was he who had taught all the girls piano and when Dotty had expressed an interest in the sax, he had taught her how to play with great pride. On Sundays, the day of the week he always took off, they would throw open the high windows of the apartment and play till dusk. Her mother was a dancer at one of the clubs, and she and one of her sisters would dance with her and sing, while her other sister played a mean piano. She and her dad played the sax and the trumpet. Neighbors and strangers, kids, teens, and adults, would gather on the sidewalk below and dance and laugh and have a great time until the light faded, and exhausted they went back to their apartments.

She and her sisters went down to the club and watched as their mother and the girls put on their make-up. They sat backstage and watched her mother dance in glittering costumes. Her father began to take Dotty along to his gigs and let her play for the folks who received the young girl with applause and cheers, she was that good. Occasionally, her father's band even let her do a solo. The gigs were a thrill to her, with blue smoke, mirrors, clinking glasses, and the smell of whiskey. Then the music stopped. Her father went off with a unit of Negro soldiers to fight the Great War in Europe. They still played out of the windows on Sunday but of course it was never quite the same. Dotty began to play in a band at school. Her father came back from the war, and once again took Dotty to the clubs and for a time it seemed that the time of music and joy she had known would return.

But one day, her dad found he could hardly blow his horn. Dotty was there and took over for him. His breath had failed him and over the next year his breathing got more and more labored. During the war, he had been gassed. It seemed to be a thing of the past, but now the ghost came to haunt him and his family. War is never over. By the end of the year he was dead. It hit them all hard, but especially Dotty, she found that she could not play her sax for every note came out as a moan, a sad crying.

Her sisters were still young, and though mother still worked, money was becoming scarce. They had never owned much, but the apartment was big and the rent was high. Mom couldn't seem to move to a smaller place though, this apartment still echoed with her father's music and they all thought they could hear him playing at night. Dotty took a job with an all-girl band and began to travel, sending home what money she could.

And now, while drying the dishes, she heard her father playing his trumpet. Or was it just because of the song her mother was humming? Then she heard him clearly say, "I'm proud of you, pigeon, for helping to take care of my family and proud of you, working to help out with this war." It was not the first time she had heard her father's voice. In fact, from time to time, they had conversations. But only rarely and she never told anyone about them.

Dotty's sister Trouble came rushing into the kitchen and skidded in her stocking feet across the floor and ended up stopping by holding on to Dotty.

"Come hear this song on the radio, its killer-diller!"

"Later, mom and I are having a talk," said Dotty patting her sister, who seemed to have grown five inches since she had seen her last.

"Oh, you're just being a fuddy-duddy," she said and was off and out the kitchen door.

"You could have gone, honey, we're not talking about anything. Just chit-chat," her mother said running the wet dish rag over the dirty plate.

"But I want to talk."

"Is this about your job? You miss your band?"

"I miss the band, but for now I'm doing what I should be doing for the war effort. But it's not about that."

"Then it must be about a boy. You know Joey Roth is back from the war. He was wounded in the leg. I don't think he is seeing anybody."

"No, I don't want to even think about that arrogant idiot. This is about someone special."

"How special?"

"That's what I'm trying to figure out. His name is Billy, Billy Joe."

"Double name, he must be from the south. You know they aren't like us down there. It's a whole different way of life; I wouldn't go down there for the life of me."

"I like that he's different. He's just not so full of himself. He got drafted into the army, but wants to get transferred over to the Air Force. He flew a crop duster back home in South Carolina for a small company down there."

"He hasn't been breathing that stuff has he?"

"No, his lunges are just fine. He's just fine by me. He's a real gentleman with beautiful big eyes. And he really likes me. But do I like him as much as he likes me? That's what I'm trying to figure out."

"Well, if you don't know I can't figure it out for you. Just go with your heart. Does he have a good heart?"

"He does, he really does. I can just tell."

"What's most important in a person is to have a good heart. Like your daddy had. All the rest is just frosting on the cake. Is he tall and handsome? Does he get your blood flowing?"

"Mom!"

"That's important too. Why your daddy and I we just…"

"Mom!"

"Just saying," And she went back to soaping up a plate.

Chapter 22

Even though it was winter, the office was hot, too hot as the radiators under the windows hissed and clanged.

As Dotty came out of Mr. Hobson's office, Susan turned to Barb at the desk next to her, leaned over and in a loud whisper said, "He likes those uppity women of color."

"They come down here not realizing that we southerners know just what they are like."

The two women looked up at Dotty with disdain on their faces. Dotty ignored them as she knew she had to every day. They were just trying to start a fight and she would be the one to get in trouble.

"You may not want to be taught by a Negro," Dotty said pulling up her chair and sitting down at her desk, "but for the others here in the office, the first class will be tomorrow right after work." She spoke in a matter of fact tone and everyone suspected what she might be talking about. There had been a rumor around the office for a couple of weeks that their boss had managed to get some typewriters for the office, not realizing the women couldn't type. Some had begun to worry that other women who could type would be hired and they would be fired.

Everyone was silent when Lelia asked, naively, "What class?"

With a smile on her lips and in her voice Dotty said, "Typing."

Patty turned around to Dotty and said, "I heard months ago the big wigs were going to hire someone to teach us to type, but nothing ever came of it."

"Not someone else, me, I've got mock ups I made and I'm ready to start." Dotty looked around the room at the startled faces.

"He's giving you a chance to earn a little extra money, huh," Susan said slyly. "What else does he have you do?"

"I get paid zilch. I thought since I knew how to type I might as well share my knowledge, my war effort. I'll see the rest of you girls at my desk tomorrow night."

The river shifted and the trees moved their branches away. There, on the wet sand of the river bank she lay with her brother. They talked about silly things, things that didn't matter because nothing did, except this moment under the sun on the cool sand. They touched and laughed and the longing for this dream woke Marge up, just as Elaine knocked at her door.

It was the middle of the afternoon and Marge lay in her clothes across the made bedspread of white and pink flowers. She shook herself like a dog shaking off water and said, "Come in." How long had she slept?

"Oh dear, I didn't want to wake you." She could tell by Marge's disheveled hair she had just woken up. Marge always kept her hair perfect.

"I had to work a double shift and then run home during an air raid drill." She got up from the bed and went to the mirror.

"I knocked earlier, but I thought there was no one in here when I didn't get an answer."

Marge picked up a comb and ran it through her hair. "I guess I must have been really knocked out."

"You got a phone call, I wrote down the message. Here it is, that brown spot is just coffee."

"Thanks for trying to wake me again. Can you read it too me? My eyes are filled with sand."

"So, the message says, 'Please meet me at the Park Street Bridge over Rock Creek tonight at dusk'. He said you would know who it was from."

That afternoon, Mary was bent over a stack of finger prints, labeling them and putting them in a pile to file later. Roz walked by with a stack of files and when she came up beside Mary bent over and whispered, "I saw Sam outside hoping you were coming out for lunch. He said to meet him tonight on top of the Justice Department Building!"

"Ladies," came a loud male voice from somewhere in the room, "serious work here! Reviewing prints for security clearances!"

The bare tree branches resonated with the sound of a saxophone, a slow lovely melody echoed by the running water in Rock Creek. The man was in the dark beneath the bridge, the only light the glint of the moon on his instrument from time to time. He was good, he was very good, why did he need to practice Marge thought. But perhaps he was playing for himself.

The street was dark with the woods on one side of the road and on the other row houses whose gray paint seemed to glow in the moonlight. The street lights were capped so the Japs couldn't see them from above in case of an air attack, even though they threw puddles of light on the sidewalk below.

She was nervous, conflicted because she didn't know what to do. Greg had been sweet to her, a strong male presence in this sometimes scary city. And she liked him, she really liked him. But did she love him? That was part of the problem, the other part was more complicated. Could she love anyone other than her brother and if she could, if she did love Greg, would it betray her brother? Between street lights, the darkness was thick and the moonlight was thin. She couldn't think any more or she felt like she would break down crying, losing control of her actions.

So, her heart kicked into the space that her thoughts left empty. He was there, a tall silhouette leaning under a street lamp, smoking a cigarette, the blue smoke rising above him.

"You came," he said throwing the butt to the ground and crushing it under his foot. He held out his hand and took hers. It was warm in the chill air.

"Of course, I did," she said wishing she could think of some clever thing to say. There was intensity to their words.

"I'm glad. Sometimes I think you like me and sometimes I think you don't."

Being honest, she said, "Sometimes I like and sometimes I don't."

"And what about now, gorgeous?"

That word made her heart jump a beat. "I think I'm liking you quite a lot." And she laughed. He did too.

"Well, I guess we're on the same page here."

With that something broke loose in him. Any feelings he had had for other women vanished like his breath in the cold air.

With that something broke loose in her and there was no past, no future to fear, only the present. She stepped closer to him and found him stepping closer to her. Their lips touched, and all was lost to this moment of passion and love.

Why they put him there, he didn't know. Being on top of some government building didn't make sense to Sam. What was he supposed to see that the radar or some trained eye wouldn't notice coming from the skies? It was damn cold but it was also beautiful. With so many lights out or covered in blackout curtains, the stars shone brighter and the moon revealed each crater on its surface. It reminded him of being back home in Snow Shoe, Pennsylvania. When he was too anxious to sleep, wanting to grow up, he would climb out on the roof at night and look at the stars and imagine what he would do with the future, perhaps be an archaeologist. Even though he was ten, he had heard of the discovery of the lost city of Troy and the treasure of the Egyptian Pharaohs. He didn't know what he would discover, but knew it would shake up the world and probably make him rich. Maybe he would even find Atlantis.

But the war got in the way. College, exploring; they were for after the war was over. For now he was cold and waiting as he heard a distant saxophone playing.

Suddenly, everything went black. There were hands over his eyes.

"Hitler or Hirohito?"

"The woman who won the war for my heart."

The hands dropped and Mary came around in front of him.

"You mean there were others?" she asked sitting down on the roof beside him. He put his arm around her.

"No, there haven't been any others now or in the past, a least not that I was serious about."

He unfolded a brown military issue wool blanket and threw it around the two of them. Mary felt warm, but uneasy.

"You've never been with a woman before?" Mary couldn't decide why she was asking this? Did she really like him? Love him?

"Don't tell the guys back at the barracks, but nope. They probably lie as much about it as I do."

"Do you tell them stories about me…?"

"Never! I swear by this fake gun," Sam said motioning his free hand over to plywood painted to look like an artillery gun to fool the Germans should they attack. "I wish they put fake soldiers up here too."

"That one over there is real. Would you have to fire it if…?"

"Somehow I don't think the Krauts are going to fly across the Atlantic and bomb us tonight," he paused. "Do you tell the other girls things?"

"About us," she said with a smile, "of course, they are my girlfriends."

That seemed to make sense to Sam, women talked about personal things, all guys did with each other was brag.

"So, Sam, why did you want me to meet you here tonight? I had to put up with some snickers from the guard down below when I told him I was coming up to see you."

"I had to see you. I'm getting shipped out in a few days." There was a trembling in his voice and Mary could sense his fear. GI's got so wrapped up in the hectic, almost party atmosphere in Washington that they felt they would never have to deal with the reality of the situation: War. Sam drew her closer.

She didn't know how to say how she felt, so she just blurted it out. "I'm sorry, Sam, I can't do more for you. I really do like you, but I don't love you. And now you're going away." Her guilt welled up in her and she began to cry softly.

Sam's heart fell and his stomach gripped around it. Had he really expected more? He was just hoping, needing, someone to think about when he was over there, someone to write to and get letters from.

"Will you write me?"

"Yes, Sam, I promise I will," she said wiping away tears with the back of her hand.

"Being liked and being able to hold someone when I'm so scared is enough for now."

Chapter 23

The heaving of the covers in the dark of the room, glowing with the ghostly smoke of cigarettes, the sounds of breathing like a train in the far distance and the lonely tones of an alto sax. Marge drifted in and out of sleep next to Greg. She dreamed, or was she awake, of being an FBI agent, like him. It was not so much that there was a certain glamour to the job, or an excitement looking for Nazi spies. It was a job with purpose, a high and noble one that could give meaning to a life that just rambled on through the forest of days otherwise. She had asked Greg how he liked his job and he laughed. She wasn't sure what that meant, was it boring, did it mean of course he liked it? And what he actually did from day to day he wouldn't say. But she knew she would never be bored, just being the first woman to spy for the FBI would be excitement in itself. She rolled over and said to herself, "One day…"

Marge hadn't seen or heard from Greg in days, but she was not really disturbed. She imagined him on some secret mission hunting down spies. He was unable to call her or maybe he had, and one of the girls, probably dizzy Lois, had answered the phone in the hall and once again forgotten to give her the message. She wasn't worried. To her, he was obviously a man who could handle himself.

What upset her now was her stomach. Having promised she would call her folks every Friday, she was on the phone though she would rather be in bed. Carrying an armful of sheets, Ben came up the stairs and was surprised to see her.

"Marge, playing hooky from Mr. Hoover?"

"I got food poisoning I think. I ate lunch over at that little…" she was interrupted by the operator. "Yes, my folks are older and sometimes don't hear the phone, yes okay, I'll wait."

"Aren't you afraid he'll send his spies checking just to see how sick you are?" Ben chuckled in his deep baritone voice.

"I nearly threw up chicken ala king all over some prints." She felt like she would gag thinking about it so decided to think of something pleasant, like being with Greg.

"Well, hope you feel better," Ben said walking toward the linen closet.

A minute later, she heard her mother's voice on the line and let out a sigh of relief. She didn't realize she had tensed up.

"Now, aren't you glad you got a phone?" Marge knew that her parents couldn't just get a phone; they had to have a line strung from the road to their house and pay for it themselves. With no one, but dad working the farm now, she knew money must be scarce. What little she could send them helped some, but not like having her brother there on the farm.

"Yes, I just wish your brother had one over there too. Have you heard from him?"

"Not a letter in so long and it's getting me worried, he used to write regularly."

Marge felt tears welling up in her eyes and her cheeks flush. She must not think of all the horrible things that could happen to him. She had to think positive like everyone on the home front was trying to do.

"All we can do is pray for him."

Marge felt a flash of anger run along her spine and quickly dissipate. Why pray to a God who had let all this happen anyway.

"Are you going to be able to come home for Christmas? I mean we will understand if you can't get away, you are doing important work."

"Not for Christmas Day, but shortly after. They are trying to let us get off some time for the holiday though most of it is taken up in traveling."

"If it's too much, you just stay there, I'm sure that you have…"

"Mom, stop being a saint. I'll be there just not on the very day."

"Good. Do you live near Great Falls, Virginia?"

That struck Marge as an extremely odd question to ask. "Sort of, Mary, and I went out there by bus for a picnic last summer. Why would you ask that?"

"We'll talk about that when you get here."

The sky was thick with gray which sucked up the energy of the city and spit it back down as an ice storm. Sleet slapped against the window pane and slid slowly down. By tomorrow, the city would be spectacular with every building, sidewalk and branch coated with crystal. Brigette looked away from the window with a long sigh. She put the photograph of a young man she held back in the box with the others. She should have kept the box closed. It was a Pandora's Box of memories that flew like moths around her and felt they might choke her. She had rambled through the past and now had stumbled into a dark place. She was familiar with the constrictions of this place on her soul which began to fill with the darkness. It was not that this was something new. This dark night of her soul had afflicted her through her whole life it seemed.

Had it crept around her crib, a dark shape waiting to pounce on her? Had it stalked her as a tot? Or had it all begun one night when she was six and the dark beast slid into her room and around her almost smothering her? Perhaps it was the reason that one day between Christmas and New Year's she had smashed in the head of her new doll. She had taken it to her father to see if he would replace it for her and all he had done was scold her for having flown into a rage. The next day, she had put the doll in a box that she had painted the inside black. She put another doll she had gotten from her grandmother one birthday, in a box she had painted black all over and tied shut with wilted roses. But what if the beast came in and found the boxes? She felt she must hide them, so crawled under the front porch and buried them, then spent the night crying because she had lost her babies.

Below the porch became the burial ground for her dolls and toys which she would have claimed to have lost if there was anyone to listen to her. And still the dark beast came at night when the house was dangerously still and the clouds refused to move. The creaking of boards told her it was coming and would consume here to the bile of its belly. Even after the tears and the beast were gone, she could taste the salt of them in her mouth and she found she couldn't eat. Food tasted like despair. And despair became her companion. She began to feel comfortable in its arms.

Not in their arms, but in the arms of the despair she ran to after another man had disappointed her, did she find comfort? Why was it that the beast, though far away, seemed to lift the covers so gently and crawl in bed with her at night, she asked herself as she lay in its warmth, its heat. With lovers or without, her nights soaked the sheets with her sweat.

There was a knock at her door. She quickly ran to her easel and picked up a brush. She wiped away a tear that had streaked her cheek and left a smear of blue paint in its place. Her serious smile crawled across her lips and she said, "Entree!"

The stairs ran up from the kitchen, to the second, third and finally the floor with the old servant's quarters. They wound from floor to floor through the dim light from bare bulbs, most with broken filaments that no longer gave out light. It seemed they were stairs to nowhere. Peter knew where he wanted to go yet he hesitated. Who was he? A castaway from his heritage, hunted by the society he had trusted in for freedom and opportunity with little to offer. But his heart, a feeble heart that had never felt like this before, like a morning glory that had just opened for the first time.

He climbed the stairs.

Peter swung the door open and its creaking was electricity to his nerves. What do you say to one such as this?

"I hope I'm not disturbing your work…"

The despair drained away and the thoughts of the beast fled. "No, no come in, Peter," Brigette found herself saying with more excitement that she could have anticipated.

"I mean if you are in some kind of artistic ecstasy…"

She couldn't help, but laugh. Did they all think every artist was mad? "I wasn't about to cut off my ear. I hate to admit it, but you'd be surprised how much artists are just like normal people. Well, sort of."

"You'd be surprised how many people think all Orientals are all Samurai and Geisha girls." They both laughed at the same time.

"Come in and close the door." Peter closed the door and stood there not knowing what to do next. "You can take a seat over in the window seat." She motioned with her brush.

Peter settled himself in near the cold glass. "Why did you become an artist?"

"Why did you become an oriental?" Brigette smiled and put the end of her brush between her lips.

"I was born that…Oh, I see what you mean, artists are born that way."

"In a way being born with talent is like being born with a big nose. It sort of informs who you are and what other people think of you."

They both laughed as Brigette dropped her brush in a jar. She sat down on the stool behind her easel and picked up her sketch book. She opened it to a blank page and paused before the blank page. As always, she felt she had to produce something someone in the future would see, when she was famous. Even though she could always tear out a lousy sketch and throw it away. After those thoughts and feelings had run their course, she picked up a charcoal pencil and began to loosely draw lines that would form into Peter sitting there on the window seat.

"You must be grateful Harry hides you and lets you keep your job in the kitchen."

Peter sighed. "He is a very kind man. Pock and I came out east to go to medical school at Georgetown. That is where he met Cynthia. Harry came into the clinic to get his ulcers treated and we began to talk."

"Oh, I thought…"

"You thought we worked in a laundry. Anyway, we needed jobs here and he offered us jobs in the kitchen. Whoever he hired seemed to keep getting drafted."

"But why didn't one of the waiters inform on you, thinking you were Japanese?"

"I know, we all look alike. So, do you Caucasians, except you of course." They both laughed at the ignorance of society. "But with your artistic eye, I'm sure you would never think that."

"We send the food up through a dumbwaiter and the man who is the expediter, Paul, who is in the kitchen calling out the orders, is German and seems to understand our predicament."

"I suppose we all have our predicaments. At first, my parents were supportive of my art, though they would have preferred to have a son. I was an only child. You could paint as a hobby, something to do with your time since my parents weren't hard up for money. But then you were expected to get married, settle down and have kids, many kids, and be satisfied with doing little watercolors you could give as gifts to relatives who were obliged to keep them. I took the other route. I 'ran' away to New York City and got rejected by the critics and galleries again and again. So, I came here to Washington and have found my niche doing realistic (I say that with disgust) paintings for the embassy officials and the rich."

"That's why I am dropping my painting and going into a field where I think I can really make it: screenwriting. Sure there aren't many women, but I'm determined to be one of them."

"How could anyone reject you?"

There was a tapping at the door that grew louder.

"Hey, Mrs. Rembrandt in there. It's Mr. Federal Importance on the phone," came Marge's voice through the door.

Brigette had forgotten that she had told Marge about her boyfriend or whatever he was to her. That was one thing she had yet to figure out.

Brigette shifted her weight uneasily and called out with annoyance in her voice, "Tell him I'll call back later, I'm resting."

"That never worked before, and he sounds real insistent."

"Well, if you can't act like a friend…" Yeah, Marge thought, *that's what friends are for, to do your dirty laundry.*

"Well, pardon me for pardoning myself, babe. I'm going back to my room and feel nauseous. It's more fun than talking to you."

Brigette turned to Peter, angry at him for a moment for having seen her get angry. It was not in the image she wanted him to see.

She hesitated, both afraid and anxious to talk to her Mr. Smith. His voice was deep and always reminded her of someone's voice that haunted her although she could not think of who.

"Hello, honey," she said as though licking the drips on the side of a jar of honey, "Why yes, no I wasn't busy at all. If you can get away for a couple of hours, I can meet you there. You'll send a car for me? Why isn't that sweet of you!"

A black wool dress with a blue silk scarf looked very slimming on her and her dark hair was gathered at the back of her neck with a silver comb. She knew she looked like the bees knees, the way he liked her to look. She smiled in the mirror. It was too bad she had to tell Peter she had something come up and she had to go out. He was so…She couldn't think of words to describe him. Perhaps loving, a person she could trust with her secrets and he would hold her anyway.

But Mr. Smith was more of a man with presence and authority on him. He held her hard against him and she liked that, there was a thrill in being with him she couldn't explain. Sure, he was as old as her father, but her father had been so young when she was born, so the age difference really didn't bother her.

Excited, she ran down the stairs when she saw the black Chrysler pull up in front of the building. Harry was just walking up the stairs with a new light bulb, like everything else, difficult to find.

"Dropping in to see the president?" He said as she passed him not hearing a word. The chauffeur with skin black as night in a black suit got out of the car and came around to open Brigette's door. She dove into the darkness of the automobile.

In the dark, she could feel his lips and the smoothness of his cheeks. He had just shaved. She turned just before the door was closed and saw Mary looking a bit frazzled from work, walk up and stand beside Harry. Mary said something she couldn't hear; Mary had a soft voice, then heard Harry say pointing to the rear of the car, "Maybe she is going to see Mr. Roosevelt, that car has company plates."

The door closed. Then something happened that upset Brigette, though she could not put her finger on why. Mr. Smith leaned across, rolled down the window and winked at Mary.

Evening had fallen like a head on a soft blue pillow. There was a sigh to the world, a whir of slight wind, and a temperature that thrilled a beating heart. Dusk had fallen like ash and the sky was still lighter, a relaxed deep blue while below, like below the surface of water, the city was dark. Headlights were shaded with cardboard as their light skidded across the asphalt; light seeped out between the parting of blackout curtains. The Greek columns of the Lincoln Memorial stood in silence. There was only the sound of Dotty and Billy Joe's footsteps echoing stone as they stepped into the 'sanctuary' where the huge statue of the former president was in a mighty chair.

Billy Joe stopped. "So, it's Mr. Lincoln, a great white man, who freed us. Like we hadn't been fighting for our freedom already? Caused more trouble than Daniel in the lion's den. It was slavery, but we had jobs. What was this past ten years with so many of us without work, being a day laborer trying to keep food on the table?"

Dotty turned around and slapped Billy Joe but with her gloved hand, it only made a soft thud. So, she took off her glove and this time the slap echoed off the walls. They both looked at each other startled. Then they both laughed.

"You know I wasn't being serious. I'd die for this country."

"Give me a gun and I would too."

"You'd slap the Germans, silly. So, what's up? You tell me to look real nice and you look like Buster Keaton, but all we do is come here?"

"The last time I came here was for a concert," Dotty said walking out toward the mall, where the Washington Monument held up the sky and the Capitol Building was on the hill in the distance. She sat down on a step and motioned for Billy Joe to sit beside her. "Have you heard of Marian Anderson?"

"Pa listened to her on the radio on Sundays sometimes."

"She's one of the greatest opera singers in the world damn it and the snooty Daughters of the American Revolution denied her use of Constitution Hall for a concert. What did their fathers fight for?"

"So, what did she do? She up and decided to have a concert right here on the steps of the Lincoln Memorial on Easter Sunday. This was back in 1939. Our whole family came down from New York City for the event. Mrs. Roosevelt, Katherine Hepburn, everyone was here, white folks and colored folks, thousands. The papers said there were seventy-five thousand, but they lied. There was more down the mall and spilling into the side streets."

"Every Negro in America was listening to her that day singing 'America the Beautiful'. Her voice could sound like a clear blue sky, or go down to the heart so your whole body, your whole soul vibrated. For one magic moment we were whole, one nation. Then she sang 'Nobody Knows the Trouble I've Seen' just for her people.

"Then we all rambled back to our lives, knowing this nation could be something beautiful and that we belonged."

"Do you feel you belong?"

"Mama has told the story many times about how excited papa was to go to war. Fight the Germans in the war to end all wars. Because even if he died in battle, he felt that white America could not deny Negro blood was being shed for their country. And they would open up their jobs, their hearts to us."

"And when he came back?"

"Almost nothing had changed." Dotty quickly stood up and brushed old memories from her dress. She extended her hand to him. He smiled, took it, and let her pull him up. "Now for the reason I asked you to get dressed up."

Billy Joe had never seen a play before let alone a musical. He had heard singing in church of course, gospel songs that gave him tingling down to his toes, and the songs that were sung around town by the men and women and children. Silly songs, beautiful song too but the best singing he had heard was on the radio when they would sit around the old mahogany box in the living room, mama knitting, papa smoking his pipe and Billy Joe lying on the floor with Blue, their hound dog, listening intently. Billy Joe knew he could sing with a trembling baritone that set the church windows to rattling, but he wished he could sing the songs on the radio.

Dotty took the pins out of her hat with the pheasant feathers and put it in her lap. She had on her best green dress with the padded shoulders. Staring at Billy Joe, she wondered what he was thinking, looking around the theater, taking in all the white folk dressed to the hilt. He looked grand and handsome in his uniform, no one could deny that. Dotty looked around too and up in one of the boxes. *How could you see well from there?* she thought. She saw Brigette dressed in black with a blue scarf around her shoulders.

She was talking to two men, one older, probably fifty or so with lots of graying hair slicked back over a high brow. He vaguely looked like Clark Gable, though an older version and with darker eyes. This, Dotty assumed was the mysterious Mr. Smith, if that was his name, for he had his arm around Brigette's shoulder, almost down to touching her breast. The other man by contrast was completely bald and the yellow light from the chandelier shone off his head that was probably waxed. He was younger than Mr. Smith by at least a decade, and his face a bit gaunt. Even from where Dotty sat she could see his teeth had yellowed from chain smoking.

With a bit of a flourish, he always had a sense of the dramatic, Mr. Smith pulled out a cigar (one he had gotten from a humidor on the president's desk), and lit it with a gold and silver cigarette lighter. As it snapped closed, he turned his wandering mind back to Brigette. She had asked him if she could do the talking with Mr. Howcroft, which he really didn't mind. He found these Hollywood types boring and bothersome. He did like the movies Howcroft had directed and that was the reason he had invested in one of them, a spy story set during World War I.

"It's really not that different," Brigette said in her serious voice, "painting and films are both visual arts and I can see by the framing of your shots you must believe it too."

"Why, of course," Howcroft said, "I carefully plan out each shot. Sometimes I draw it out on paper so the camera man will know what I want." Although his voice was naturally rather high, it deepened as he leaned toward Brigette and touched her hand.

"I've always thought that being a rather well know artist Hollywood and directing would be the next step." A look of humor passed by his face when she said director, a woman director, but she wasn't about to let that stop her. "I've even written a screenplay."

"You have?" Mr. Smith said as Brigette gave a tug to the back of his hair. "I mean, yes she has. I should know," he laughed, "I am head of intelligence gathering for, well, I can't say. Of course, after this stinking war is over, I can go back to my drugstore empire and won't be working for the government for one dollar. Why that is…"

Brigette gave Mr. Smith a quick look and then turned back to Mr. Howcroft. "Perhaps I could bring you a treatment. How long are you going to be here?"

"Well, I have to do a training film on venereal diseases to show our boys, and then back to Hollywood. I'll be back in a month or two and I am eager to get back together again." He looked over at Smith. He seemed to be lost in thought again.

Chapter 24

Clouds whispered by in a solemn silver sky. Ice streaked through the air and slid around the dome of the Capitol Building. *When will this ice end*? Mary thought as she stood on the platform where a river of people passed her by. When will it turn to snow, spread like a bandage over the city to heal it? But I'll soon be where there is snow, I'll soon be home.

"Ticket?" Marge, ever the organized one asked Mary.

A moment of panic before she realized she had not put her ticket in her purse, which she frantically searched, but in her coat pocket. "Yes, got it. I scared myself."

"Well, you are so anxious to get home I thought you might have forgotten it."

"What about the goodies Elaine packed for you?" Dotty said pulling her coat close around her. It was damn cold, and colder when wind and a train slid into the station platform.

"Yes, that too," Mary said as she bent over to pick up a Christmas package wrapped in silver paper with a red bow that she had dropped. A woman handed it to Mary and ran for the train.

The three women, in threadbare winter wool coats, stood in silence. *It's exciting, heading for home*, Mary thought, *but I will miss my family here.*

As if reading her thoughts, Marge said, "I'll be heading back in a couple of days."

Dotty was silent. She couldn't get any time off from work, but somehow she didn't care all that much. It meant that she could spend more time with Billy Joe who would also be in town.

The conductor, looking a bit frazzled around the edges, hurried up to the women. "Ladies, if you are going to get on the train, I would advise you to go to the end. All the other cars are full, so we're going to add on some additional cars." The last words drifted behind him as he hurried away.

Mary yelled Merry Christmas to him and the three ran to the end of the train.

Mary found the train was already beginning to fill up as people crowded the isles trying to get suitcases and presents on the upper shelves. Finally, she saw a seat that had remained empty. Beside the empty seat sat an overly large man in a stained brown suit eating a sandwich with the mayonnaise dripping from it.

"Is this seat taken?" He only grunted back at Mary and tilted his head to the seat as Mary heaved up her suitcase onto the rack. She thought of trying to make conversation when he finished his sandwich but then he pulled another one from his pocket.

The train pulled from the station and sleet fell like slug trails from the sky. But the ice-covered landscape soon turned to snow as the train headed west and north. The glare of the snow slowly turned to blue and the earth became dark and the sky lighter as often happens at dusk. As the sky gave up all light and turned to black the stars came out, hovering, and waiting. The slow way of the train over the rolling hills brought sleep to many of the passengers, but not Mary.

The rotund man next to her snored like he was drowning in a vat of mud. She looked around for another seat, but there were none. He reeked of sour pipe smoke and sweat. Then it got worse. His head nodded forward, then to the side, and landed heavily on Mary's shoulder. She imagined she could feel his sweaty face through her shoulder pads. She began to squirm and cough trying to wake him up. The situation became almost unbearable when he started to snuggle up to her. She was about ready to try to pull herself out from under him when a drop of water fell on his fat cheek and rolled down the folds in his neck. Drip-drip. She strained to look behind her to see where it was coming from but could hardly move.

Then, out of the corner of her eye, she saw it, a man's hand holding an ice cube from his pop over the fat man's head, letting the melting ice drip, drip onto his bald head and down his face. As each drop plopped on the bare scalp, the fat man began to squirm around, mumbling something to himself. With a jerk, he awoke and wiped the water from his face. Looking up, he could not see where it might have been coming from. Grumbling, he realized he had to use the restroom and hauled his body out of the seat and headed down the aisle.

No sooner had he left than Frank Sinatra sat down in the seat beside Mary. At least that was who he looked like at first glance, tall and lean in his tight-fitting army dress uniform, gold spectacles over kind eyes. His voice had a certain sway to it as the train moved along.

"Hi, hope you don't mind me moving up here but you looked like maybe you could use a rescue from him," he said and immediately saw the relief and smile in Mary's eyes. "My name is Bill."

"Mary, nice to meet you, Bill, and nice to be rescued from that blob." They both laughed and were still laughing when the blob showed up.

He grumbled again when he saw it was a soldier in his seat. He looked around and could see that those close by watching were waiting to see what he would do. There was not much he could do, this was wartime and this was a soldier. Grunting, he moved on.

"Rescue complete," Bill said leaning back and making himself comfortable. As the train raced forward, they began to talk, easily, sometimes even excitedly.

"Are you headed home for the holidays?" Mary asked.

"Yes, a ways to go, North Dakota. It's cold here in DC but it's really going to be cold back home."

"I know what you mean, I'm headed for Iowa. Along the Mississippi, and when the wind comes off the river, it will rattle your bones. So, you were lucky enough to get leave for Christmas?"

"Yes. It's going to be so good being home. I've been out in the Pacific, then in Washington. And I don't know where next. But right now, I'm sitting beside a beautiful lady and not a care in the world."

Mary had heard men talk, especially the soldiers who were trying to make the best use of their time with a woman, and it could drive her crazy. But somehow it didn't with Bill. Somehow she didn't feel she had been thrust out in a strange and wild world away from Iowa and all it held for her: friends, family, and the song of the world beneath the bluffs along a rambling river. She felt suddenly secure in herself, able to do things and meet new challenges. Suddenly, she realized, she was feeling like an adult. And it felt good. And she liked Bill.

"Do you like DC?" Bill asked wiping his glasses with a hanky from his back pocket.

"Actually, I do. It was scary at first, just all the…well everything," she laughed to herself. "But now it makes sense to me somehow, the men, the women, the war effort. It's what we have to do to keep our country free."

Bill nodded, knowing what had seemed chaos was actually an ordered chaos because there was meaning and purpose to it. He had let himself dream he might have a purpose one day and now he had realized he had one, working for and serving his country. All the rest were islands and rocks in the giant stream of war. He looked up and their eyes met.

"Oh my!" gasped Mary.

"What? Oh," Bill put his glasses back on. "You noticed my left eye."

"Yes, oh I don't mean to be rude. But it is unusual to have two pupils together in one eye."

"It's an injury…" Bill saw Mary looking at him sympathetically. "No not combat, my brother shot me in the eye with his BB gun. Not on purpose, at least, I think so."

"How many brothers do you have?"

"Ah, one, I mean two. One is a half-brother."

"Are they in the service?"

"No," then he paused for a long time. "My brother Brian is only twelve, and like, a child, he wishes he were. My other brother, Dee is older than me."

There was a silence again, the one that most every family has in its past or growing in the present. With Mary he felt something different that he could not identify, not something that made him uneasy, but something that made him feel he could tell her whatever was in his heart. It startled him such as when he began his story, he almost felt outside of himself watching the two of them.

He told her how his father had worked on the Annenberg estate when prohibition was at its peak and North Dakota was an entry way from Canadian booze into the United States. It sounded more glamorous than it had actually been, but then as a child, he never attended the wild parties held at the estate or rarely met the rich and the famous that came to stay there. He told her how he and his big brother Dee, his brother with the blackest hair he had ever seen, jumped over fences, rode the horses from the stables, and did all the things boys do. How he had looked up to Dee! But things had turned sour and memories curdled like sour milk. It was that day when he found Dee, almost a man, playing in the stable with his little brother, nine at the time, in a way that made Bill's stomach tighten, though he wasn't sure exactly what had happened. It was that night that Dee and Bill had fought around the kitchen table. Dad had taken some of the guests out on a sunset ride in the hills, while his mother was at the main house helping with dinner. What words were said? Bill couldn't remember, only how they filled him with anger and he had lunged at Dee, who didn't fight back as Bill punched him again and again. Brian began to cry and ran from the room. Dee stood up with very sad eyes. He seemed resigned to some fate Bill did not understand. Then Dee left by the kitchen door, closing it carefully, silently as the sunset. That was the last they had heard from Dee.

The story almost made her wish she had a secret so she could share it with Bill. The ice that had collected on the roof of the train in the station had been dripping, but now with a series of snaps, began to fall past the window.

When she left the train at her stop, Mary smiled. She had Bill's telephone number in her hand and he had hers in his pocket.

Chapter 25

The snow and ice creaked and cracked and crunched under foot as Pa had walked down to the river, frozen over clean, white, and smooth with the snow that had fallen last night, Christmas Eve. He was tired from being up late putting together a tin gas station for Mickey and Paul while Ma finished the hem on a doll she had made for Kathy, and wrapped the dresses she had made for Tessy and Mary in the comic pages from the newspaper with red ribbon. She curled the ends of the ribbon and looked up pleased at Pa. Now was his favorite time at Christmas. He took his nightly walk then arriving home he and Ma went into their bedroom, always on the chilly side, and crawled under the layers of quilts and snuggled. They would drift in and out of sleep. They were waiting for everyone to wake up and knowing Mickey, who probably hadn't slept at all, it would be soon.

After opening presents, there was their traditional breakfast of hot coco with a peppermint stick and 'Snow Buns', a warm bread and frosting concoction that was the first thing Mary had asked about when she had arrived at the train station late yesterday afternoon.

Mass at St. Rita's. Almost everyone in the town would be there, except Pa. He always went down to the river, winter spring summer or fall to talk to God. He knew that Ma thought he might be Jewish and had just said he was Catholic for her. But he never let on, saying his relationship with God was personal. And who could argue with that?

The homily that Christmas Day was on love and judgment of how we God's children could not judge others because we were never capable of knowing enough about another person. Only God could know all there was to know about one of his children and judgment should be left up to him.

Father Arthur's words were almost a whisper, which made everyone listen harder. *And what could be a better thing to hear about on Christmas Day than love,* Mary thought, and she knew she had more blessings than she could count.

She knew from the looks and whispers around her that some were thinking about the war and they had every right to judge the 'Huns'. She prayed for all of them, for everyone, and felt God whispering understanding to her and she was comforted.

Sometimes the winter wind was all about you, invisible, like ghosts frightening the leaves left on the trees, sending the white/gray clouds rushing by. Other times, it was soft, like cool breath whispering against your cheek, with words you cannot quite hear, and are unable to understand. But the wind that came to the tiny town of Harper's Ferry, Iowa that Christmas afternoon arrived like a train. First in the distance rustling branches on the Wisconsin side of the Mississippi River, then silent as it slid over the surface of the ice with slow-moving water beneath it. Arriving at the edge of town, it had suddenly gained strength, become more frantic as the dry leaves pulled on their stems and old branches creaked. Dogs began to bark and a loose shutter slammed against a clapboard, a woman's cry.

"Hear it, it's getting closer!" Bud said standing perfectly still as only a kid can and still looking like he was moving. He thought about taking a lunge toward the porch of the house.

"Yes!" Mary said to the sky where a bird had suddenly taken flight. She loved the wind, the exhilaration of this invisible force like God without an image but whose effects humbled her. She could tell her brother Paul, twelve, was scared but why? He was the brother who walked out of the house at night without fear, went down in the cellar alone, walked the train trestle over the river, talked back to Pete Desisto when he got drunk.

After a big Christmas dinner, the whole family went down to the gas station that Pa owned. Tessy, seventeen, wearing her new blue and green summer dress below her wool coat, Kathy, six, carrying her new doll, and Mary wishing she had brought some more sensible shoes. Mickey and Paul seemed to be conspiring together about something to do with snow balls. And Ma, as always was singing to herself some song she had made up.

Ma and Pa went into the station acting very mysteriously while the others made snow angels. The wind was approaching with a giant yawn and little snow devils whirled around them. The swings in the school yard across the way were suddenly ridden by gremlins who rattled the chains. As the roar of the wind arrived, snow was flung in their faces and a shingle blew off the station.

"Let's amscray!" Paul yelled and they all ran toward the gas station office, throwing powdery snow balls at each other as they went.

"It's about time you came in. You must be freezing," Ma said, pushing Mickey's hair back in order when he took off his blue knit cap. "But you had fun, didn't you?"

"We sure did since Mary is here," Kathy said climbing up on a chair to try and open the soda machine and get herself one. Kathy stopped and listened. The train was approaching. As it rattled by, "Is that the phone ringing?" Ma yelled above the din at Pa, who stood beside where it sat on a shelf like a frightened black cat.

"What?" Pa shouted back as a glass thermometer fell from the enameled Pepsi sign by the door and broke on the floor. Kathy ran after the mercury that slid across the floor as Mary tried to stop her.

It was Paul who answered the phone. He smiled and started talking so fast that no one could understand him.

"Who is it?" Tessy asked.

"Onytay," Paul answered holding tightly on to the phone. "Yes, well, basically good. I didn't get a lump of coal in my stocking. Yep, I hold Kathy's hand when she crosses the street, but she bites it sometimes. Can I come fight with you? But...Bye! Here's the phone."

The phone went round the room with tears and laughter till it finally was handed from Kathy to Mary. But what could she say? She missed her brother so much. The receiver was warm against her ear after she had pulled her hair aside. She had been trying to remember, as she prayed for his safety at church that morning, what his voice sounded like. And here he was sounding so far away when he said to his sister only a year older than him, "I miss you and all the brats." They laughed. They had always called the younger kids in the family the brats. They really weren't brats except maybe Bud who was off in the service too, someplace that letters could never say.

Time was precious on the phone, Mary knew that. There was probably a line of sailors waiting behind him to call their loved ones at home. She tried to be brief, but really all she wanted to hear was the sound of his voice. "It's nice to hear the sound of your voice," Tony said. Mary chuckled.

"Are you lonely?" she asked running her hand up and down the phone cord.

"Lonely! I've got guys around me all day and all night. They are great guys, but we're all lonely for our families."

"I know what you mean, being off in Washington. But I've been making some friends that I think I will have forever. Please come home soon. All my love."

Pa was quick on the phone. "We're all proud of you and your brother. Keep yourself safe," and he opened the door and spat a wad of tobacco out in the snow, but the wind blew it back against the pane of glass and Kathy gagged. He then handed the phone to Ma who was already crying. She began to whisper into the phone.

Mary ushered everyone outside with promises of more snow angels to give Ma some time to talk with Tony. As the sun hung low in the west and was almost snuffed out by the bluffs, Pa opened the door and nodded. Everyone filled back in, banging snow off their shoes and onto the floor. Ma stood by the phone with her back to them, took a Kleenex out of her pocket, and wiped her eyes before she turned back again.

The phone rang again. Ma jumped and stared at the phone. Pa picked it up off the counter.

"Who?" Pa said loudly, but then he began to whisper. After he put the phone back in its cradle, he turned to Mary and Paul. "I've got a mission for you two."

The wind seemed to blow away the white of the snow turning it a deepening blue, as the sun was sucked up on the horizon. Snow, shaken off the trees and bushes swirled in the air as Mary and Paul walked down the snow-covered road toward the Desisto house. They came to the creek and crossed the small wooden bridge. They passed a shack where Mr. Desisto had the still that brewed up his special hooch, which he sold throughout most of the county.

At sad and sagging shingled house with fake plastic flowers drooping in crumbling flower boxes, Mary and Paul stood.

The shades were worn and torn and the blue light seeped into the gray darkness of the room.

"How come they don't have a telephone?" Paul asked preferring to stand than sit on the couch where flowers faded into the smudges of dirt.

"They can't afford one. Now quiet," Mary said listening to the whispers in the next room. Paul shifted his weight as he looked at Leona, about his age, but with a tired and aged look in her eyes. She stared into the shadows of the room as she faded into the old brown chair in her brown and pink dress.

Then rising above the whispers in the next room came the voice of Mrs. Desisto, "I have to go, my mother hasn't spoken to me in years and now she's…" and then whispers again.

Finally, Mrs. Desisto appeared, buttoning a Swiss-dotted blue dress over her slip.

"Will you two stay here with Leona while I go up and use the phone?" she asked with a trembling voice.

"Tell them run along home. I'll entertain Leona," Mr. Desisto called out, startling Mary.

Mary saw the look on Mrs. Desisto's face, the pleading eyes and lips that wanted to say something. "I'd like to stay and visit with Leona. I haven't seen her in ages."

Leona opened her immense dark eyes and pulled on the dull thin hair that gathered about her face like fragile cobwebs, and smiled. Mary quickly realized that she was not like other girls, giggling and full of energy. It had been years now since Mary had seen her. Once a little chatter box, she was now sullen and not talkative at all. They ended up playing with some paper dolls she had gotten for Christmas, cutting out the clothes and putting them on the paper dolls. Paul even played along, seeming to sense that Leona not only wanted to play with them but that she needed to. Mr. Desisto stayed silent in the back of the house.

The next morning, Leona sat at the Frank's kitchen table watching as Mickey and Paul argued over who got the tin top from the cereal box. Mary had been talked into emptying the entire contents into a large green bowl to get the prize which was always at the bottom. Tessy had driven Mrs. Desisto to the bus station over in Waukon so that she could go see her mother in the hospital. It was Ma who had insisted that Leona stay with them and not be left alone with her father. At first, Mary couldn't understand why. She and Ma had ridden with Tessy to the house to give Mrs. Desisto her ride. It was then she saw how angry he was, almost in a rage, and she began to understand something. Something dark that disturbed her sleep that night when she heard Leona quietly sobbing in Kathy's room. When Mary went in to comfort her, Leona dried her eyes and rolled over.

The next afternoon, they all sat in the kitchen eating small pieces of minced meat pie that Ma had just made when the howling wind leaked between the cracks around the window in the pantry and sent something crashing. As Pa went to investigate, Mary picked up Leona and put her in her lap. "Don't be afraid," Mary said, but Leona could not hear her, she had covered her ears.

"You never hang anything on the hooks that I put up. You're always stacking things up." Pa came grumbling back into the room.

Ma was ready to launch into an attack she had saved away for a time such as this when there was a knock at the door. Mrs. Desisto stood there with her suitcase, snow on her shoulders and looking tired. She had walked all the way from Waukon. Leona launched into her arms and was crying she was so happy to see her mother.

"I've had a little talk with Leona this morning before everyone got up," Ma said as the children went out to play in the snow, "and Pa and I would like to have a talk with you," she said looking at Mrs. Desisto.

In the kitchen which was just off their parent's bedroom, Tess and Mary sat drinking coffee in silence hoping to catch the whispers behind the door.

"Tessy, Mrs. Desisto, and Leona will be staying with us. Can you take her suitcase up and put it in Kathy's room?" Ma said and Pa nodded as if to say, "It's the best thing."

It was that afternoon, when the sun was high enough for the icicles to start dripping that Mr. Desisto came trudging up the road to the house. Mary and the kids were making snowmen and women when she saw him. "Paul, take Leona and your brother inside," Mary said slapping her gloved hands together. It had been a long time since Mary had actually seen Mr. Desisto; he had never shown his face the day before. She didn't remember that he looked so frightening. His blue/black hair was disheveled, not like he had just gotten out of bed and not combed it, but like he had been running his hands through it. Heavy lidded eyes were perched over dark bags, while a sharp nose dripped from the cold. He had not shaven in days and his beard which grew up to his cheeks, gave them a hollow look. His thin lips were firmly pressed together.

He didn't even say hi, but demanded, "Tell your father to open the gas station so I can use the phone. I haven't heard from my wife, and I want Leona back now."

Mary was startled, but she knew all he really cared about was getting Leona back, and all to himself. "She's not going home until her mother says it's all right to head home."

Mr. Desisto got too close to Mary and was about to say something to her when he looked over her shoulder. Mary turned and looked that way only to see the curtain on the upstairs window close quickly. He had caught his wife staring out the window to see what was going on. That could only mean trouble.

"She's back. I want them both out here now." He made an attempt to walk toward the house when Mary stepped in his way. He looked like he was about to knock her aside when she heard the screen door slam.

"They are staying here as long as they want," Ma said, "dressed only in her house dress and an apron."

Walking around Mary, he said, "She doesn't know what she wants, just what you are telling her she wants. Send Leona back. She wants to be with her papa."

"Now, you listen here, I'm not going to let a man like you tell me what to do."

It was at that point that Mr. Desisto started to step around Mary. She could see that his intention was to run up on the porch toward Ma. She stuck out her foot. She caught him in mid-step and he went straight down, head first into the snow. Cursing, he pulled himself up, snow on his face and blood dripping from his nose.

"They are mine now…"

"They are not your property and I know what kind of devil you are."

"You can't stop me," but Mary still stood in his way.

"Mary, go inside, get Pa and…"

The screen door slammed again and out hobbled Pa, his old hunting gun tucked under his arm. "I think you better get along now," was all he said. Mary turned and saw the determination in Pa's eyes. He looked larger than life holding the rifle. When Mary turned back to Mr. Desisto, he was already headed back down the road cursing. But Mary wasn't looking at him, she was looking at the blood in the snow.

Evening sprung up around them and they began to turn on lights and set a fire in the parlor fireplace while Pa and Ma went about their business. Pa sat reading the newspaper and listening to the radio, spitting tobacco in the can he kept 'hidden' under his chair, and Ma was in the kitchen sewing a patch on a shirt for Pa. The rest of the family had laid out the Monopoly board and were getting ready to play. Mrs. Desisto sat next to Leona, Paul, who seemed to have taken a fancy to her, sat next to Leona. Mickey sat between his two uncles. Only one of the men was actually his uncle, Shane, and Irwin was his honorary uncle. The two confirmed bachelors lived together on the tiny houseboat they had built to float up and down the river, collecting furs or whatever else they could find to make money. Shane showed his Ojibway blood, with his dark features and long straight black hair, while Irwin was a red-headed Irishman with a thick red beard.

Kathy sat on Mary's lap and Mary had a sudden rush of longing realizing how much she missed nights such as this. She was Kathy's favorite and while too young to actually play the game, she kept urging Mary to buy hotels so she could place them on the properties. Money exchanged, arguments arose, and there was laughter. Mary noticed that Mrs. Desisto was laughing along with or at the others. Most of all she noticed that for the first time since she had been there, she saw Leona laugh. She realized that there was something so wrong about the girl's situation that she must do something. He would be back, she was sure of that. And maybe next time, he wouldn't be scared away by Pa's gun and he might have one of his own. Fear tightened her stomach and her mouth went dry as the others laughed on.

There were dreams that Mary couldn't remember, but they seemed to leave the taste of metal in her mouth. There was the stillness in the house. Then she heard Ma downstairs humming to herself a new song that she had made up. Mary couldn't face things returning to how they had once been for Leona and her mother. She pulled the blankets up around her. She whispered prayers into her pillow until she knew what she must do.

Dressing in her warmest clothes, throwing on her coat and scarf, she went downstairs. Ma looked up from the pie dough she was rolling out and stopped humming. Mary said nothing but an understanding passed between the two women. And Mary went out the door.

It was a long walk but with each cold breath, Mary became more and more determined that she had to do something, say something. He would be back, and the worst might happen, his wife and daughter might go back with him. Maybe Mrs. Desisto was too ignorant about what was going on between her husband and Leona. Maybe she was so frightened, she didn't know what to do, how to escape. Maybe she now felt so safe in the house in Harper's Ferry that she didn't realize that he would be back. But Mary knew something had to be done.

The gray and peeling house seemed to frown as snow weighed it down at the corners. The torn blinds were pulled down. The stairs hadn't been swept since the last snow, but she couldn't see footprints. The house was in a solid block of shadow and silence; Mary knocked on Mr. Desisto's door. There wasn't an echo to her knocking only a dull thud. Or was that the sound of her heart?

"What is it you want?" The inner door swung open, but the screen only showed a shadow of a man. "Is Leona with you?"

"Let me come in and we can talk about it," Mary said trying to sound as determined as she had felt earlier.

He stood aside and she entered the living room, filled with deep shadows. She noticed that he was in a stained white t-shirt and white underwear, but made no effort to cover himself. They stood in the center of the room staring at each other, saying much without words.

"You can't keep her from me. I'm her papa," he snarled.

"You don't act like a father, you act like a devil."

"I give her everything I can and more. I work hard for her and treat her like she is my little princess."

"I found out how you treat her, and I'm not going to allow you to have her." As she said this, she could see by the curl of his mouth, the raising of his eyebrows, that she had misjudged all of this. He wasn't going to listen to a threat from her, or perhaps anybody.

"You just keep to your own business, who do you think you are anyway?"

Grabbing her arm, he squeezed tightly and drew her toward him. She was held up against his body, smelling smoke and alcohol on his breath. She was so tight against him she could feel him getting hard. Her mind raced and she realized she should never have come here alone. With a great effort summoned up from she knew not where, she shoved him back. The rag rug his wife had made slid from under his feet. His grip loosened and his fingers slid down her arms scratching them. He sailed away from her, through the buttery winter light and down into the shadows. She heard a thud, felt a knot in her stomach. She was no longer in her world but in a black-and-white movie, although mostly gray. Black began to surround his head like a halo. She knelt into the shadows and put her ear to his chest. How could someone die so completely, so quickly? His head had hit the radiator.

As memory will do in traumatic incidents, her mind fell into confusion. And her memory from that moment on was confused. She knew only that she had been looking down and saw his mud-caked boots slip on the multicolored rug. Then she was running wildly, the wind not flying in her face but carrying her to the next farm down the road.

For some reason, she could not understand, she didn't want anyone to know what she knew he was going to do to her. Would they believe her, had she gotten herself into the situation? Questions sizzled in her brain and she ended up saying she had found him dead on the floor.

Now, she had a secret to share with Bill.

Chapter 26

It was noisy at Marge's house in Waukon, Iowa for a late Christmas dinner. Gathered round the table, they had put together from saw horses and covered with a bed sheet, sat the uncles and aunts and cousins, along with her mom and dad. They laughed and shouted above each other, and being good Germans, they farted at the table to show how much they enjoyed the meal. And as usual, Uncle Kurt had a story to tell that brought everything to a halt.

"Some of us suspected there was a monster loose in Farmville. The signs were there: too many dark clouds, the geese flying in unusual patterns. Strange animal sounds in the night." He paused to wipe his mouth on his tie and make sure everyone was listening to him. He continued, "You can always tell what is going on in people's minds by what is happening around them and there was a very sour apple in the barrel. That's when Jed Turner disappeared. Just up and vanished like he never was. He didn't come home one day and his wife could read the signs too, something was very wrong. It was fall, and remember when we had that Indian summer? Well once he vanished it seemed to get colder by the minute. Everyone in town was out searching, the fields of dry corn stalks, where the dairy cattle grazed and the woods down to the river. Then someone, I don't remember who, but I think it might have been the good minister himself," thought he remembered. "Jed's old Chevy truck back behind Doug Weinstein's feed store, right across the street from your grocery store," Kurt said nodding seriously to Marge's dad who nodded back like he could tell something bad that had been close to them was coming.

"So, we went and asked Doug if Jed had been in that day and he said yes that he had, but that was the last he had seen of him. Then that first snow came, remember all wet and messy. Jed's wife was still out everyday wandering around looking for her husband like a ghost herself. She was a little crazy by then. They weren't one of these husband and wives who just ran the farm together; they actually loved each other. He used to play the violin at dances and she claimed that day she heard his violin playing. So she followed the sound, way out by Doug's house. She knocked at the door but that wasn't where she was hearing the violin coming from, it was in the barn out back. So, she went out there, but the door was padlocked. But like I said she was a bit crazy, so she managed to climb up on one of the sheds and into a window. So, she climbed in the dark loft, I believe she told me it was dusk by then and only a little light seeped through the boards. The first thing she saw was her husband's truck. She said the music was loud by then. And then the next thing she saw was…Now wait and send the little ones into the parlor."

The cousins that were young were hustled about of ear shot. But of course the older ones listened with their ears at the kitchen door.

"There was the most horrible sight anyone could have ever imagined, but I swear it was true and I can even show you the picture of the barn and the headline in the Farmville paper. Her husband, or what was left of him, was hanging on a meat hook. And that wasn't all, there was another hook and on it hung the body of a teenager. She had disappeared the week before from over in Prairie and I guess her parents thought she just up and ran away. But this was a fate that was…Well, it's all too horrible to imagine."

"Did they catch him?" Marge asked thoroughly horrified, but wanting to know more.

"You bet they did. Right at the store waiting on Mrs. Garwood like nothing was wrong. There is an even worse part to the story if all of you want to hear it." As he knew, being a good story teller, they would. "When they took down the bodies, they found that certain organs were missing. They searched the house and found some pickled in a jar on a shelf in the pantry and a kidney in the ice box."

Marge gasped and felt her stomach turn; she could see her uncle was not through yet.

"I heard this from the minister, when we had a few beers in the tavern that Hildy Schaffer had told them that, being Doug's closest neighbor, he had brought down some liver for them to cook up one day. And it was a bit sweet but delicious."

There was total silence at the table, so thick that you could cut it with a carving knife. It would take a while before anyone would be ready for pie for dessert.

A loud crash broke the silence and a brick hurled through the kitchen window. Everyone jumped and looked confused. It landed right near where Marge was sitting. Trembling she picked it up because there was a note tied with string around it. She just stared at it in confusion.

"Take the note off," cried her aunt Gertrude.

Seeing that she was too startled to react, her uncle took it from her. The string was tied like a bow on a Christmas package and he pulled it off. He unfolded the paper and read it to himself, then with an angry face crumpled it up and threw it across the room.

Everyone seemed to be asking what was going on, but he wouldn't say as his face reddened. Marge went over by the stove and picked up the note. Coming back to the table she read it aloud, "Go where you are wanted, Krauts."

"Just because we all came from Germany," Aunt Gertrude said.

Marge's dad was mad. "We are as American as anyone here. Why, our son is even over there fighting for this country."

Uncle Kurt let out a long and audible sigh. "But Rick isn't even German."

"We can't let anyone spoil the holiday," Marge's mother said getting up and clearing the table. "Dad, put something over that window so the cold won't get in and I'll clean up here and then you won't believe what a wonderful pie I've made."

Marge hesitated before she went to her cousin's side to sweep up the glass. Something had been said that she didn't understand.

That night Christmas snow swirled in the search lights cutting through the sky above the Capitol Building. It was the city's first real snow of winter, wild and white, glowing and setting everything it landed on into a glowing white light.

Brigette waited anxiously at the window to her studio dressed to kill in her green satin, low cut dress. Not very bohemian for her, she looked more like a dark haired bit player from a Goldwyn film, somewhere in the background of a night club scene, noticed for her Hollywood glamour. Her deep green eyes flashed with the unusual lightning and thunder that shook the window pane. Her heart raced. She loved giving gifts, to men especially. It was always something unique, unexpected. He had given Mrs. Smith a painting once and he had told his wife that he had bought it for her. Apparently, she loved the scene of the cherry blossoms blooming around the Tidal Basin. But her 'boyfriend' never said that he did.

Brigette shook the hair that she had waved back. She didn't want to be annoyed. Not today, not after the disastrous Christmas Day before with her huge extended family. She had taken the packed train of excited men, women, and children to Pennsylvania station in New York City, then hopped on the Raritan line out to Westfield. She was frightened and excited. She felt like a little girl again, full of hope for a happy Christmas, a Christmas full of shiny paper, bright red ribbons, a fire crackling in the fireplace, throwing cinders onto the old carpet they kept in front of it. Snow, there was snow on the ground with clear skies. She had pulled back her hope and her vision of good cheer when she knew what was about to happen. Her father picked her up at the station alone. Then the darkness fell quickly outside the car window as he kept saying how much he missed her over and over, waiting for her to say the same thing to him. Why had she ever thought coming here would be a happy Christmas, why did she still hope, fool herself, and trick herself? He put her hand on her knee as he spoke words she couldn't hear. Thank God, they only lived five blocks from the station.

She shook her hair again and with it all the words of her father, "Isn't my little girl beautiful?"

Her great Aunt Antonia asked her father, "When is such a pretty girl getting married?"

Her father stared at her and said, "She's in no hurry. I'm the man in her life for now."

"Oh, but I have been seeing someone and we have broached the subject, and well," Brigette said to her father, smiling so big it hurt, "I don't think, it will be long."

She'd be rid of all these annoying people, people who dug down into her childhood and twisted all that was good out of it. When could she trust again? When could she love again? Love had only been damage to her heart. There was this child called Nat who annoyed her mother like a gnat buzzing around her and who she swatted when her father wasn't home. So, Nat turned to her father. He wanted things from her she now understood were part of the sickness he kept hidden, and now Brigette also kept it hidden, ashamed of what she had done. After all, that eight-year-old girl had gone to him for love. He twisted her mind around in circles to squeeze every bit of love out of her.

Looking down to the street below, she saw Mr. Smith's black car slide up, the snow melting on its body, franticly swirling in circles in the headlights. When he was divorced from his wife, he would save her. Or rather she would save herself, she chuckled to herself. She grabbed her old fur coat from the hook beside the door and put it on with a red wool scarf he had given her.

Ah, this felt good, she thought, as the chauffeur opened the door for her and shut behind her after she had gotten in. The car was warm and filled with the scent of spice and oak. She loved his cologne. Maybe she could learn to love him. After all he was giving up everything for her, his marriage and his kids. That meant he loved her. And as he stroked her cheek and lay his other hand on her leg, his eyes spoke of love too.

Out of her pocket, she pulled a small black box tied with a silver ribbon. "I have this for you," she said handing it to him with both hands. He smiled and kissed her on the cheek.

"You don't have to get me gifts, your smile, your presence with me is gift enough." And he kissed her again.

"Open it."

"Oh, yes, your beautiful eyes distracted me." He slid the ribbon off and dropped it to the floor. Opening the box he fingered through the cotton inside until he found it. A gold ring with black onyx and one diamond in the middle. "It's beautiful, it will always remind me of you." He kissed her again.

She pushed the box away and moved right up against him. "Put your finger nail in that little indent on the side of the onyx." When he did, a little door popped open. There was a portrait of Brigette. "I painted it myself. I've never painted anything so small before."

He smiled at her, but instead of putting it on she noticed, he slid it into the pocket of his coat.

Smokey's was down on the river, held up on pylons for some reason he had heard was the law, though he couldn't imagine what law it was, but then all laws about his people made no sense to him. It was a rowdy place, filled with liquor and smoke and aptly named Smokey's. There was always lots of sweat dripping down to the dance floor from the singin' and swayin' bodies of the colored folk. And there was always a band. And that's why Billy Joe Royal would sneak down there after a long day working at the garage. He would change clothes from his back pack behind the gas station. Mama would never know he was going to this place of sin. He'd change back to his greasy overalls before he went home and said he had been working late. He loved the old man, but he had to have a life too. He had tried meeting a girlfriend at church, but he never seemed to click with any of them. Maybe, you weren't supposed to click with someone, just find a good woman and settle down and get married. Have kids, he wanted kids.

The women in Smokey's didn't seem like bad women. They just wanted to have fun too. Some came with their husbands; some didn't have one and left the kids at home to be cared for by a sister. And some were just plain single. But the one that set him in a swoon of cheap whiskey and the sound of the saxophone was Dolores. She sang with the house band in that voice that stirred his soul like honey dripping from a spoon.

Dolores winked at him from time to time; she always sang with a cigarette in her hand and would blow blue smoke his way, then bat those almost black eyes and slip a smile across her face. That is all that happened though, just the fantasies clouding his brain.

But the woman he sat next to now, well, she was even more beautiful, she had a great big heart, and most of all she loved him. Click. It had happened and he loved her too. The club in New York City they had come to, the Red Ribbon, was thick in the trails of cigarettes puffed on by more black faces than he had seen anywhere out of a church social. The notes of the piano vibrated in the air. The glasses rattling, the chatter of men and laughter of women, combined with the music, left him almost breathless. Dotty left him breathless. Out of politeness, they had invited her mother to come with them, but thank God, she had refused with a smile on her face.

The singer with the band, while not as beautiful as Dolores, had a voice that could make him cry or thrill the pants off him. But Dotty, well, nothing could compare. When the set ended and the noise of the crowd grew even louder, the sax player from the band came down and sat beside Dotty. He was older, but not that old. Bald, but not that bald. He wore one of the gray zoot suits that were once so popular. When the war came, how could you waste so much fabric on a suit jacket that hung down to your knees? He had a speaking voice as smooth as he had played his instrument. He pulled up a chair at their table and leaned over and kissed Dotty on the cheek. A new emotion ran through Billy's stomach and he wondered if this is how jealousy felt. He had never had any reason to experience it before.

Dotty laughed and hugged him. "Oh, Barney, I was hoping you would be playing tonight!"

"And I always hope that I will see you here. So, who is this soldier boy you are with?" He waved to the waitress with the sassy attitude and she nodded. Before Dotty could answer, she had a drink on the table for him, it looked like straight whiskey.

Dotty wrapped her arms around Billy, "This is Billy, my soldier boy, and Billy, this is a longtime family friend, Barney, one of the greatest sax players in New York City." Billy felt relief, just a friend.

"So, you two are rationed?" Barney asked with a twinkle in his eye.

"Well yes, we are going steady. That does sound a bit high school though," Dotty said.

"Billy, you met my sweet potato here in New York?"

"No, sir…"

"Wait no reason to say, sir."

"Yes, sir, I mean well, I'm just used to the military. No we met down in DC. But I'm from down south. It's a whole different world here. But I guess I will be seeing a whole lot more when they deploy me to Europe. I'm a mechanic and they really need us over there. I'm glad to be serving my country."

Dotty paused at the thought of Billy in harm's way, but she pushed it aside, that's what all the girls had to do. "I'm still typing away and just trying to get along with the other girls in the office."

"Well, don't hurt those fingers," Barney said downing his drink and waving a finger over theirs. They nodded, no. "After this war, you can go back to playing the sax."

"You played the sax?"

"Yes, that's what I did before this war took over my life. I played with a band."

"I didn't know such a thing. Did you quit to go to DC?"

"No, but it's a long story that I'll get into some other time. Now, it's time to hear some killer-diller music and forget about everything else."

"Did you forget how to play the sax?" Barney laughed and so did Dotty, she knew what was coming next.

"Did you forget how to breathe? Of course not."

Billy didn't know what was happening, but the next thing he knew Dotty was up on stage getting ready to play Barney's sax with the band.

I'm leaning on a lamppost at the corner of the street,
In case a certain little lady come by.
On me, oh my, I hope the little lady goes
do do do dah dah dee dee dee…

There was something so sexy about the alto sax when Dotty played it that Billy knew Dotty was the woman for him.

Stars skidded across the black ice at their feet as they crossed Amsterdam Avenue, arm in arm, laughing about something. They had forgotten what it was. Billy stopped abruptly. Dotty looked at him as if something was wrong. He had a concerned look on his face, the first time she had seen this expression. Ahead of them in the doorway of a bodega, lay a crumpled figure, wrapped in a torn gray/green blanket, on a slab of a cardboard box. Billy looked at Dotty, then at the figure. He reached inside his coat pocket and pulled out a photograph of a tall dark man, dressed in his best go to church clothes. At his feet stood a boy of about twelve looking up at the man.

Billy let go of her arm and walked over to the figure, bent down and tapped it on the shoulder. Dotty felt confused, then pulled a dollar from her purse and walked over to where Billy was showing the scruffy man the photo.

"Do you know him?" Billy asked with a hint of desperation in his voice.

"No, soldier, don't know the fella."

"His name is Joe. He acts kind of strange sometimes, but he's a good man. Have you seen him around?"

The man sat up. His hands were wrapped in rags to keep them warm. His old worn coat didn't look like it would do the job.

"Yeah, now that's a different question. Do think I seen him around. Not lately though."

With his voice getting more excited, Billy said, "Where did you last see him? Where might he hang around?"

"Well, let me see if I can get this old head to remember. Probably over at the shelter the Salvation Army runs over on Seventh Avenue. That would be my best guess, don't quote me or nothin'."

Billy pulled a five out of his wallet and handed it to the man. Dotty bent down and handed him the dollar.

"I come on some hard times, still living in the Great Depression, but it's folks like you that give me hope. God Bless!"

When Billy stood up, Dotty was staring at him.

"Where's Seventh Avenue?"

"Not far at all. I know where the Salvation Army is. Who is this Joe you are looking for?"

"My father."

Walking over to Seventh, huddled together, Billy at first was reluctant, but then told Dotty the story of his father. He was crazy, that's what everyone in their little section of town said about him. But to Billy he was just his father, a father who would play ball with him, pretend he was a fire breathing dragon, and put him to bed with a song he had made up. Mama was always telling him to calm down, and he could get kinda overly excited about little things, like his brother coming over for dinner, even though he lived just down the road and he saw him every day at the garage they owned together. He would cry alligator tears when he saw a dog tied up in someone's yard and looking lonely. It was like being on a swing with his papa pushing him. You never knew how far he would push you away when he was in one of his moods. But then it swung back and he was there for him, grabbing him in his arms.

Then he found God. Not in church where he sang in the choir, but one day while fixing the carburetor on an Oldsmobile. God just slapped him in the face, he said, totally unexpected, and it woke him up. His brother found him under the car talking to God. Angels came to him and brought him messages about demons who would be coming from the north, and that he had to learn to recite certain passages in the Bible over and over again to be ready to use them on the demons when the attack began. Soon he was too busy with his recitations to work on cars. At dinner, he stuffed food in his mouth between words from the Good Book.

One day the archangel Michael came to him and stood by his side. He told him that to protect his family he must go north and fight the demons, destroy them before they could head south and claim his family for the fires of hell. But where north? Michael said he would send a sign. And one arrived. An all-girl band rolled into town on their bus. He knew it was evil for women to play in a band like a man. He heard at diner that they were from New York. And that is where he told his family he was going.

His uncle had made one trip to New York City to look for him, but he wasn't to be found and so for all they knew he was dead. But Billy always believed his father was alive, that someday he would find him.

"What will you do?" Dotty asked as they began to walk over to the Salvation Army.

"When I find him?"

"Yes, do you want to take care of him, give him money…?"

"I don't know if I'll even tell him that I am his son. I can't take care of him, I only have a little money and wouldn't know how to handle him. He's crazy, I know that."

"Do you sometimes worry that you will start seeing visions?"

"I used to but then the fear went away. I used to volunteer at the soup kitchen run by my church and I saw men and women with some of the problems my pop has. I just knew in my gut I wouldn't end up like that. I could never let that happen to my mother again."

"So, what do you want?"

"I just want to see him and know that he is all right. Maybe, the streets are the only place for him. I don't know what I would do."

Dotty stopped in the middle of the cross walk and gave him a big hug, then they walked on.

But he wasn't at the Salvation Army. Dotty and Billy sat through a service of praise the Lord and music, so afterward they could approach the woman who seemed to be in chargé. Of all the men and women working there, she was the one with the immaculately pressed uniform. Her plump feet were stuffed into black polished shoes. There were a dozen men and women who had sat through the service, a few looking as if the service moved them, but most just restless as if enduring until something else happened. That seemed to be dinner for the 'hungry souls', as the man in uniform called them, as he led them into the hall in the next room where a line of tables had been set up with pans and pots of food.

Dotty could see the disappointment in Billy's face as he looked closely at every man who left. They walked up to the leader and introduced themselves.

"I'm looking for my father," Billy burst out even before proper introductions could be made.

The woman who had introduced herself as Miss Simms, straightened her skirt. "We get so many poor souls who are seeking Jesus and something to nourish their bodies."

"I have this picture of him." Billy handed her the photograph. "He would be older now, that was taken over ten years ago. His name is Joe."

"Yes," she paused and Billy held his breath. "I believe I do know him. He comes here every Wednesday and sits during the service talking to Christ. He eats, then leaves."

"Do you know where he goes?"

"They all have their own routines; we all seem to need them. He may travel from soup kitchen to shelters that different churches run around town. But I couldn't tell you where he goes."

"Does he ever talk to anyone? They might know where he goes," Dotty said feeling the discouragement growing in Billy.

"He only talks to himself, I'm afraid. To angels I believe."

So, he'll be here next Wednesday, Billy thought sadly. It was Thursday and he had to go back to Washington.

Chapter 27

The train was squeezed out of the sunrise as it headed for Washington. It rattled and swayed, lurched and trembled, but none of this bothered Marge. She felt a certain peace she would not be able to describe. There had been a darkness lurking inside her. Depression or despair, she knew not which. She felt like she had gone to confession and been told by the priest it was not a sin after all. But it was not what she had said, it was what her mother had said to her.

It was the warm water and the smell of soap that eased her heart and her mind. She would hum softly the last song she had heard on the radio, this time it was 'The White Cliffs of Dover', though if someone asked her what it was she wouldn't have been able to say. Marge took the hot plates and dried them in a red and white towel that had 'Merry Christmas' embroidered on it.

While Marge's mind usually was wandering from fantasy to memory and back, she only had one thought stuck in her mind this time.

"What did aunty mean when she said that my brother wasn't even German? He's as German as I am."

"Marge, get yourself a new towel out of the drawer and hang that one up, it's soaking wet. Now what silly thing were you asking me?"

Marge hung up the towel on the oven's handle and got a new one from the drawer. This one said, 'Happy New Year'.

"I was just wondering why auntie said that my brother was not German like the rest of us."

"Oh, that's a story in itself, one I was meaning to tell the two of you when you grew up, but then you grew up so fast and I never got around to it."

There it was, now it was gone. But it didn't really matter that she couldn't remember what was just happening. It was left in the echo of change. But she did remember it was something funny, something that could still leave her chuckling to herself. Oh, she enjoyed sleeping.

She looked down at the old boots that she had slipped on. Her father's, it was pleasant to be in them.

Mary had kept an old sweater of his, one he was going to throw away after Aunt Holda had knitted a new one, sky blue, for him one Christmas. So, he was discarding the old faded brown one. Worn as a jacket, it reminded her of his hugs. Smiling, then letting it fade away, she realized she could sense beneath the snow something breathing, soft and wet and dark. Was it squirming?

Oh, if the snow would never melt! Pure, glistening white, made up of a rainbow of crystals settled on the ground, gently hissing in the cool windless air.

It was the fire that was hissing inside the dragged stone staked fireplace. She was in the house now, a construction of memories. The warm stroked her cheek. But on other side, she felt a chill and grew apprehensive. Turning that way, a cloud passed over the sun outside. Looking around the room, she saw a long barreled shotgun hung on the wall. On the end of it, a small disheveled doll hung by its brown hair.

She could feel the bluffs outside looming dark over the land and down toward the Mississippi.

Suddenly, a thunderous darkness crashed in the corner of the room. Invisible hands left their impression on her arms. Acid swam around in her stomach as she looked into the shadows luring in front of her, enticing her forward. Something was wet at her feet that were now bare. The slime that had been under the snow was leaking in under the door. From the shadows huddled in the corner, something was skidding across the wooden floor. It was a pool of black growing toward her. No, it was red, a deep red. Blood, she could smell it like her nostrils were coated in copper. Mary ran into the darkness, knowing she needed to find out where it was coming from. It was cold in this darkness. Looking to where the blood was coming from, she saw Bill on the floor, a pool of blood growing around his head like Satan's hallow.

Had she screamed or moaned? Nothing echoed from the walls of her room. She was sitting up on her bed. Looking around she realized that Marge wasn't there. Mary remembered her telling her she was going someplace (a late work shift, a date?) but where?

It may have begun south of Alexandria and along narrow streets which whipped it northward. Rattling windows, swirling around chimneys and pedestrians through garden gates sending crocuses swaying. Up along the George Washington Parkway, rolling over Daingerfield Island where men fished in the murky water that rippled as it headed up the Potomac and across the 14th Street Bridge where it gained strength and men and women held onto their hats lest they lose them. Sifting through the white columns of the Jefferson Memorial blowing them clean of dust. Then with a surge of energy whirling around the Washington Monument after running through the cherry trees which promised pink flowers in the approaching spring, around the Tidal Basin. Up Constitution Ave., where the war's workers typed and filed and fretted in the shaky temporary building.

Then a turn onto Connecticut Ave. blowing up leaves left exposed after snow had turned to puddles. It blew Bill's hair as he sat next to the fountain in Dupont Circle. He took out his black plastic comb and ran it through his thinning (to his dismay, he was only 22) brown hair. Another gust of wind grabbed at the comb and threw it into the fountain.

He didn't care and smoothed down his hair after licking his hand. He had things to think about and this was as good a place as any. When he had first arrived in the capital, he was overwhelmed by the amount of people around him, more in a day than he would see in a year or more back home in North Dakota. But then they sealed their distraction off from him and he could find quiet and to his surprise, sometimes loneliness. It was the sound of the splashing waters of the Dupont Circle fountain. There was a stream near their house that wandered through trees and meadows with cold water from above in the foothills. On the thick fallen branch of one of the large trees, he could sit and listen to the water splashing against the shining rocks as it struggled it's way south. There was silence in this sound, a thick lack of sound, wrapping around him like warm cotton swaddling embracing a baby as it slept. That was the place where whispers and mists of water spoke to him.

Beneath it, he could hear a rambling tune. It was just his father whistling a tune that was no tune, it was not a song. It was something his father found in his joy of silence when he was working or sitting and smoking his pipe, the notes surrounding him like the swirling trails of blue smoke. He missed his father, a person made of rough tanned skin from working outside. The stubble on his check when Bill had kissed him as a child, the movement of his gray eyes as he read the newspaper in the evening, the mellow/harsh sound of his voice, the smell of Old Spice and sweat. And then that something else without a name that emanated from the soul of the people you loved.

He missed his father more than anyone now, for who else could know that sense of excitement and all-consuming fear that was how a man feels things, as he knew that out there just beyond his thoughts, simmering in all his thoughts: War. What would he find there? It was not all confused in images his mind projected on its multifaceted surface.

And what lay beneath the surface, deeper than his imagination and dreams? Father what did grandpa tell you of his war with Germany? Are there secrets that I should be armed with that are more important than a gun?

As a bus rumbled by, a new tune was forming in his heart, one of his own making. Was it a gift from his father, or one he had perhaps softly whistled not so long ago, the day that he had died?

No, this one was unique to him. Then he realized that in all the sounds around him were disparate rumbles, laughter, rattling and a myriad of sounds that were constantly forming music you could hear if you listened. Was this what composers meant when they said they could hear the music around them as they walked through the woods, rustling, crunching, a bird's song and animal's cry?

The world around him was seeping blue and he laughed when he realized he had not even seen the sunset or the sunrise. He knew where ever they sent him; as long as he was alive he would have those with him. That's why he tried to see them each morning and each evening.

"What the hell are you doing, Bill, with all these crazy thoughts?" He almost said aloud. Well, maybe he had. And it was time to get out of these crazy thoughts to pick up Mary. He began to hum a joyful tune, got up, and walked through the crowded sidewalk.

It felt like an omen, the sound of a muted saxophone playing along to the radio. It was a prophesy of a time to come not to be faced without an iron heart, one that could take yet another blow by the hammer of fate. The melody sank to bass notes of a broken piano. Could a voice be discerned through the shadows that dripped down through the cracks of Dotty's apartment above?

Wearing a dress designed like a flower garden in late September, Mary stood in a deep silence listening to the sinking of the notes as they ran down their hearts and dissolved around them. They both reached up to pet the cow at the same time and laughed in little bursts at both needing the comfort of a big ole cow. Mary had finally picked up her pen and stationery box and headed out to the old carriage house/barn. She headed through the rain and was about to pull open the ancient door when she heard a voice. Standing under the overhang she listened and then recognized that it was Mr. G. He was talking to his cow, about what she could not hear. The tone sounded more serious, more longing and loving and even more sad. But the war lingered on bleeding out the citizens of joy and pride and even outrage they had once had. Did she imagine she heard him say, "War changes everything, but will it ever be able to change back to what we knew?"

When she had entered the barn, she thought he may have had the glisten of a tear in the corner of his eye.

"I think even cows enjoy good music and I'm happy she's out here and can listen to it. Well, Miss Frank, I think you might want to talk to our lady here, so I will leave."

"Oh no, you can stay. We can have a little group conversation."

"No, Mrs. G will be waiting for me to plant a kiss on her cheek. She's been doing readings all day."

Dear Ma,

I know I haven't called, I know how that must disappoint you. Believe me that I want to hear your voice too. Whenever I want to use the phone, there seems to be a line of mostly women, women listening to whoever is on the phone trying to convey tears and smiles through the wires. Do smiles and sorrow reveal themselves through our voices? Can you hear a tear sliding down a blushed cheek? A tear of happiness or of sorrow?

I want the smell of vanilla and rose water when I hold you. So, I've sprayed some of my perfume on this stationery, the one I wear most days. Pretend you are holding me. I'm smiling because I can feel you close to me. Sure I've been away from home before: teacher's college, work. This time is different though as everything is soaked in this war, every place you go, every one you meet, every bit of news. Some say it is going good, but is there good if there is a war?

Sometimes love seems like a curse. Is this our punishment for original sin? To love is to be vulnerable, for your heart to be at risk. The pain of loss is just up ahead in the future, waiting to rumble down to crush us. And then when you are in a war? Old age is something that leads us to the Lord. But to love this much, to have risked this much, not willingly but despite my fears. Am I brave to love or a victim of it shot in the heart by Cupid's arrow on some lacy valentine? I hang onto Bill, so strong, and he holds on to me, so strong. But will we smother each other? Everyone needs some room to breathe, but I am so afraid they will send him overseas again. I used to be afraid of everything, but then I felt it lighten from my shoulders. Now it has been replaced by fear of losing Bill. Not that he would run off with someone else, he does love me, but that he will be taken from me. And can love endure when this war seems to be wearing everyone's emotions away? Some have wrapped their hearts in barbed wire, some in a frantic search for escape, and some have escaped and lost sight of their heart in a fog. I can still feel, hope, love but it's a struggle. One I won't give up on.

I couldn't have said any of that over the phone with the others listening but I'm speaking aloud and I'm sure this cow here, with the sad eyes, is listening.

I'm not alone here, I have a new family. Mr. and Mrs. Goldstein, Brigette, a crazy, but kind-hearted artist, the people who work in the kitchen, some at work. We laugh and chat and sometimes we let a tear slide down a cheek not bothering to wipe it away.

And of course, the cow, hidden in the barn. But the immediate family the one that I know I can depend on always and whom I would do anything for, are Dotty and Marge. You know Marge, of course, and I am so glad, so lucky to have her here with me. A life line of home. A garden of sanity, of memories I can stop and pick like flowers, lie on the damp grass in a warm sun with a sweet breeze dancing over me.

Chapter 28

Washington around Dupont Circle rattled with spring. The branches played in the gentle breeze, the clack of high heels and Buster Browns. Change chi-chinging in the pockets of the men. The laughter seemed to joyfully rattle out in the words of everyone. The world rattled with early spring pushing, birthing a new season, the season of war rattled differently overseas, there it clanged. Somewhere Brigette could hear the drip-drip of an icicle melting from a rooftop in the shade.

Bill's hand held the tickets. He had been standing on the street in front of the Golden Parrot watching the blooms on the trees planted in front, sway then shudder in a quick breeze. Just right, the yellow sunlight hit the pink blossoms so they tingled with it. They seemed happy, no, joyous, or was that him that felt this way. But his heart did not beat faster as it once had, from fear or anxiety, when he stood there a year ago. It was happiness he realized. And he looked down at his hands that held the tickets he had been given at the USO. They were not limp from the nervous sweating of his palms, but firm just as when he had picked them up. Not like the time a year earlier when they were chewed around the corners from when he had sat his desk earlier in the day. What had made the difference?

He knew what it was, or at least he thought he did. He didn't have anything to compare it too. It had never happened to him before. Not with Jenny and golden hair that smelled of vanilla and fresh straw, or Becky whose breath just smelled bad or Nora who just smelled. He shuddered and wondered how he had asked her out to begin with.

In a movie, he and Mary had seen, he remembered some sap saying, "I think about it all the time, I can't help myself," but now he understood what it meant because he thought about Mary all the time. And he wished during the day that he could go and sit under the stairs and be left alone to think about her. Because it made him so damn happy! He didn't want anyone to know how he was feeling, not even his closest friend Tony, because they wouldn't understand and think he was some sappy guy. He thought of her hand and warm and soft in his, so small in his. The fall light, winter light, spring and summer light that took her hair in their hands, and ran their fingers through it. A blush on the cheek when he knew she had no make-up on, after they had been at the pool. Not just the caramel color of her eyes but a spark within them.

He was smiling so hard people stopped and smiled and said hello then went on with that smile. Not a sound came out, but his lips said the word Love as if it explained everything in his life.

Brigette lay stretched out on the bed, her brilliant blue robe spread around her as she chewed on the end of a dried up paint brush, as was her habit when she was thinking. Thinking about the rattling in her bones, the electricity in her flesh. It was all too wonderful. She felt she might soar like a helium balloon and burst when she rose above the clouds. It was gone, the sadness and anxiety she always carried with her. Oh! It would come back, but for now, it was gone.

The door cracked part way open and there stood Marge, her yellow and green dress, joyful colors that together contrast with the dark shadows clustered around her eyes. By the way she looked at Brigette, she knew Marge had been stranding there for some time. She seemed frozen as the door swung open wider of its own volition.

Behind her Brigette saw the figure she now had come to acknowledge as the house's ghost, pale, young, empty and carrying a thick rope. Brigette shuddered and then it passed.

"You can come in," she said in an overly happy tone because she could see that Marge was as sad as could be. A sad sack, Brigette's mother would call her angrily when she was genuinely sad. She was not allowed to be sad, she had a wonderful life with loving parents, or so she was told again and again.

Brigette dipped the rag in the turpentine to clean the crimson paint off the handle of her brush. She was in a shallow place of creative muse. Lucy. Since adulthood her childhood invisible friend had become her muse. She whispered, shouted, screamed, and now was silent. But Brigette was certain she would return. She need not become anxious that Lucy was gone for good. Over the years, she had learned she would return fresh and full of spit and vinegar. So until she did come home, it was time to tidy up and clean her brushes.

"I'm not sure if we are friends or not," Marge began as she picked up a brush with green paint on it. She jabbed it into the jar of turpentine and swished it around. "But I need, well not advice but some…"

"Why don't you ask Mary, she's your best friend?" Brigette said wondering why she seemed annoyed that Marge was not asking for advice.

"It's something I couldn't ask Mary about. She wouldn't know how to talk about it and I already know what she would say."

"And I'm the woman of the world who knows the underbelly of DC?"

Brigette was becoming a bit sad that she had a certain reputation among the boarders. But then I am a bad girl and always have been since…

"I've gotten myself into a jam, a real…" Suddenly, Marge felt her dinner coming up, real fast. She knew she wouldn't be able to make it to the bathroom, and what if someone was in there? Looking around, she lunged toward the open window out to the garden, and hoping no one was below, threw up roast chicken and mashed potatoes.

"So, I can guess what kind of mess you've gotten yourself into." It was pretty obvious after that demonstration that it is morning sickness. "And I can guess what it is you want to ask, dear. There's a glass of water over there by the painting I'm working on."

Marge felt her way over to the water, which ended up tasting like the best thing she had ever had. She felt sweat cooling on her forehead. And she felt clean and pure. "I need your help. It's just that this can't happen now, not now when I'm about to move into a career that I think is perfectly suited to my, well, temperament. I've always been for the underdog and that is what the FBI is supposed to be doing, fighting for justice for the underdog."

Brigette lay across her bed, the bright blue swirls of her robe contrasted with the pale blue paisley of the bed spread. Her hair looked so blue/black, her skin with a glow from her heart. Yes, she had a heart. She rarely let it show for it made her feel weak and vulnerable. But with Marge there was something that bonded them together. Did she know what it was? She could guess, as she usually did, guessing and dissecting every feeling she had, every action of everyone around her. But lately she was giving all that up. It had never gotten her anywhere understanding other people. Besides she didn't want to know what others were feeling or thinking, what was motivating them. She couldn't figure out her own motivations, let alone those of others. She was Brigette, and she was begging to understand that. She wanted her life to be like her painting, a smooth slide into her soul. Maybe she could free herself from her mind and go for the guts of her relationship with others.

Marge suddenly discovered she was weeping softly. "It's so hard to know what to do except get rid of it." It? Was it really a soul that she would release from this world?

"There is always another way or so I thought until it was me who had a brat growing inside of me."

"Did you tell the father?"

"As far as I was concerned, there was no father. Not that it was an immaculate conception. But the bastard kept himself deep in shadows. Maybe he even had a dark mask, a black bandanna pulled over his face. But that was a story I try every day to forget. And when I found out I was pregnant, well, there was no question what to do. It was just finding someone who…I hinted around but to no avail until I broke a tooth. I got morning sickness while at the dentist and somehow he knew when I had to run to the bathroom and came back pale and glistening. Women never sweat we glisten."

"I know for sure who the father is, but it's my body. Could you give me the name of the doctor?"

"I'll do better yet for you, dear. I'll call him myself and set things up for you."

"Would you come with me?" Marge wondered if by asking she was over stepping the boundaries of their 'friendship'.

"Of course, we have to stick together, us ladies." But Brigette noticed that Marge did not seem relieved. "Are you sure you want to…"

"I guess so. What else can I do?"

There was a long silence between them, a car honked its horn outside, and another joined in. The honking turned to shouting. The clouds spun circles in the sky. And a stray breeze jumped in the open window and onto the dusty floor.

Brigette could tell Marge hadn't really made up her mind. It showed in the downcast of her eyes, the way she bit her lip as she waited for Brigette to tell her more about this dentist who took care of things for her.

Down the hall, someone flushed the toilet. The door squeaked open and they could hear Mr. Barille with his distinct shuffle going down the hall.

"When something this big weighs on me, I go see Saint Paul and I'm not even a Catholic."

By now, the darkness had sunken like damp blankets over the city where no streetlights dared to burn and only the stars were brave enough to ignore the nightly blackout. They headed down Wisconsin St. past soldiers and more soldiers. Steep steps and tall stone columns met them. When they arrived at the huge door, Marge realized they were at the National Museum of Art, closed to visitors for the duration of the war. A guard stood by the door, an almost handsome young man with a face that seemed to want to grin.

"Sorry, ladies, but the museum is closed. No use going inside anyway, all those paintings are off the walls." This was the most exciting thing that had happened to him since he was assigned to guard the National Gallery.

"Oh, we know where they put all the paintings in case a bomb falls on the dome. Now if you would just…" said Brigette.

"I'm sorry, mam, but…"

Brigette raised one hand and put it on his chest. She pushed him staggering back into a corner too deep in the shadows for Marge to see what was going on. Gradually, the shadows exuded panting and soft moaning. Brigette slipped out of the shadows and opened her purse, pulled out her red lipstick and began reapplying it. The guard came out of the shadows with a huge grin and walked to the door and unlocked it.

"Enjoy yourselves, ladies."

Past sleek pillars and a fountain that was dry, they found more stairs and headed down, slipping through the light from the fixtures that had been left on. When they came to a very solid looking door Brigette did not hesitate to open it.

"You've done this before?" Marge asked.

"Oh, yes. But this was a new guard."

Through a labyrinthine of corridors where paintings were stacked against the walls, they walked as quietly as if they were in a church.

As they turned a corner, it was the Rembrandt painting of St. Paul, the light from a bulb above shining on it. Light seemed to shine from behind the canvas as shadows were cast from the front of the apostle.

Brigette watched Marge's face as she traveled over the image of the man sitting at a table about to write. "But look close at the way his hand holds his pen, the way his head is turned as if waiting. He's not about to write, he's waiting in contemplation of what to write. To me, it always seemed he is not concocting one of his letters but listening to deep voices to tell him what to write."

"He doesn't seem to be anxious but has great faith that if he waits he will receive the answer his soul is asking," Marge said in a whisper.

"And I come here and rest in my waiting when I am troubled or in trouble," she laughed.

Chapter 29

A beautiful white box, it was about as long as her arm, as thick as her two hands, and wide enough to contain something wonderful, something exciting, something just for her. The anticipation on the wrinkled face of her grandmother, the anxiousness on her mother's face, and looking so like her grandmother's. None of the men had been allowed in her bedroom. Just the women, and she felt the bond of generations of women for the first time. They belonged together; these women would always need and support each other.

Marge had been thinking of things to distract her. It wasn't the short attention span of a seven-year-old, which she was, but to delay opening the box, the box with pretty pink bells and ribbons printed on it. She loved this feeling, that something wonderful was about to happen. She couldn't stand it any longer. Then she realized it was pink and white, with pink birds and ribbons and flowers, because it was the kind of box a wedding dress would come in. She had seen one at her aunt's house when she got married. It was a box that size, but the decorations on this box she realized when she took a closer look, had probably been drawn long ago, with a red crayon, now faded to pink.

"Am I gonna have to get married to some boy?" Marge asked with concern, her face curled up like an old apple.

"No, darling," said her mother with a grin that quickly became a chuckle she could just barely contain.

"Well, yes. You are going to marry Jes…Oh that does sound a little strange. Open the box dear, open the box."

And Marge did, struggling to get the top off. And when she did, she saw a cloud of white shimmering before her, satin and lace and real ribbons. It was the most beautiful thing she had ever seen; her first communion dress.

"You sure, Nana, that I don't have to get married?" she asked delicately lifting the dress from the box. "Guess, I would like a baby, but not a husband."

"It was a wedding dress, your great grandmother back in Germany, who gave it to me when I got married. I had it stored away in the attic. I don't know why I tried to save it, the humidity here by the river usually swallows fabric up. But I just had to see. So, I went up in that old place and found it."

Marge looked around St. Paul's Catholic Church, candles flickering, the smell of face powder. And the woody smell coming from the Golden Purse one of the altar boys was swinging over the head of one of his friends, who were sitting in a pew up front. She had the prettiest dress on so she kept twirling, loving the way the material and petty coat swirled around her and watched the candle light flickering through its folds.

She looked over at one of the nuns, dressed all in black like a witch, and she got 'The Look', the most feared weapon the nuns used on little kids. She had been so excited, with her beautiful white dress she could go whirling down the aisle like a princess. But no, it wasn't going to happen, instead putting her in the duty of walking down the aisle with her head bowed and her hands folded, all because of 'The Look'.

Marge got in line with the other boys and girls, trying not to squirm, trying not to laugh. Some thought the sea of women in fancy hats, the men with their hair slicked back, and everyone staring at Father Vader in a long white dress, was funny. But some laughed because they were scared. This was their first communion. The priest had come to the stinky religious education room in the basement of the church to explain what first communion was. But none of the kids could understand him with his thick Belgian accent. She asked her mother when she got home to explain it to her because she couldn't figure out what he was saying.

"Don't worry. None of the congregation can understand him either. The mass is in Latin, and who knows Latin? The rest of the time we just nod politely when he is talking to us. But I'm sure he is a nice man saying holy things."

A Catholic Church was not meant to be just a place to join the congregation with friends and other Catholics; it was mean to be an experience. Not a white thing sitting on the village green, paint peeling, and not a tent out in a field in the baking summer sun. This was not just a fiery sermon (or homily as the Catholics called it). There were prayers, there were hymns sung. But the focus was on the most important moment in the Christian faith: The Last Supper.

There was the scent of woody incense still drifting through the atmosphere, permeating every gap in the stone floors, every crack in the worn oak, the walls, the ceiling, and the statues; the statues of Saints and of the Virgin. The smell of women's sweet and flowery perfume, of men's Old Spice. Warmth had been left by the bodies of the congregants, by the heat of candles. Even though the church was empty, Marge could hear the murmur of prayers echoing from the hearts of the hopeless, the sick, the doubting, and the faithful. In this silence Marge burst out laughing. She was remembering her first communion: trembling as she drew closer to the altar rail, close enough now to smell the cigarette smoke on the holy robes of the priest.

She heard one of kids behind her whimpering in fear. Probably afraid that he was going to breakout sobbing in front of everyone. Marge knelt down on the edge of her dress. She looked down at her hands. From the corner of her eye, she could see the priest giving the wafer (no the body of Christ, how icky was that) to the boy two away. Then she felt and smelled him in front of her and she raised her head and she said out loud: "Oh my! Jesus shaved his arm pits!" And on the cross above the altar was the crucified Jesus, hanging on it with shaved pits.

Marge burst out laughing, the sound echoing off the walls of the church. Then she swallowed her laugh, although it threatened to pop out. Thank God for memories. You could use them to dampen your thoughts or bring you joy. Right now she chose joy. She could hear the angels tapdancing like Fred Astaire and Ginger Rodgers. A cloud that had been stubbornly blocking out the sun slid by like it had been scared off by a devil. Yellow, blue, green, and red light rushed into the church.

Out of the corner of her eye, she saw a shape moving. She turned as a young man with the colors playing on his shoulders, the medals on the front of his army uniform shining, walked up to the alcove where the devotional candles stood. Almost all of them flickered through their red glass holders. She expected him to kneel and light a candle. But he leaned over and row by row blew out all the candles. He turned and disappeared into the shadows which had returned. War had changed everything, even the church, even everyone's view of God.

She knelt on the kneeling pad, looked down and folded her hands and tried to pray. She waited. But no words came to her. Behind her, she heard the squeak of the door, the shuffling of feet and the clicking on the stone floor. Remembering the way her grandmother would click her nails on the table when she told them tales of demons, a chill scampered up her spine.

It had been seeping through the stones of late. It was in the soft smoke that rose from the incense, the old oak pews that now smelled burned, it filled the confessional he was heading toward now. But by God's blessing, most of it had risen toward the wooden rafters, where the angels walked on the roof. It was his word, God's grace. It was a sadness. He could not say: don't worry, trust the Lord. He could only say: I know your suffering, I have seen it, felt it. I have been there, I am there with you now. He had started a tradition in the church: to let his parishioners be sad, to cry, to let the sadness spill from their hearts. Then they rose and he held the hand of the person to the right and left. "This is too…Protestant, Evangelical," some complained, but then they were reminded they were not alone. They had each other, and in each other, there was the prescience of God, The Holy Ghost. Sure the Bishop had complained about how he was tampering with the mass. But finally he came in his dark presence and left with his heart filled with a hope and light presence he had long ago forgotten had existed. The blessing that had risen with the hymn was powerful.

To his right, he heard the deep breath of a shuffling limb and the clack of a crutch. The clattering of the candles in their red glass holders stopped one by one with the hiss of extinguishing the flame, another casualty. That he could understand. An explosion had taken his sight. He had been sent by the Bishop as a chaplain to the battlefield in France, it had never occurred to him that this would happen, he was on a divine mission. Oh but he had gained so much!

As he lay there on the rough surface, the sounds of men groans, howls, screams and broken tears, with the soft desperate whisper of the nurses and nuns beneath them willing themselves to be heard. He could smell the vanilla she wore as perfume, because perhaps she was too poor to afford perfume, or perhaps because it reminded her of cookies baking in the oven at home. He had never seen her of course. That flash on a battlefield in France had taken his sight away. He knew many boys had their lives taken away and he only lost his sight, but he had felt hope. In what? Slipping between the beats of his heart, was his faith in his God dissolving in the deep water of this war?

When he had opened, his eyes in the tent filled with casualties, he felt her hand in his and could smell cookies baking in the parish kitchen. A light shown through the fabric of the despair he had begun to feel ever since his arrival in Europe. It was a risk he knew he was taking, asking to be at the front where he thought he was most needed. The boys needed to have his assurance from The Holy Ghost, the touch of Jesus.

But war was more horrible than he could have imagined. At first, he would lie awake at night under the stars and try to bask in the wonder of God. But his words dwindled the next day as he said mass; his heart felt like maybe he was committing the sin of lying to these brave, shaken boys, who had been so mistaken about how cruel life could be. So had he. And before he could deliver the Eucharist to a line of soldiers, grunts, nurses, and medical staff, that annoying reporter the flash had come, and he woke up miles away in a Red Cross tent tended by Marie.

He thought he had received every blessing through her, this woman he could not see, but who had spoken in lilting words and smelled of home. But there was one more, even greater. She had family back in the states, in Elliot, Maryland, who she said, would come to St. Leo's in Washington, DC, and one day he sat in prayer in the pew Father Negar had led him to, his favorite. Actually, he knew the rooms of this church too well, having grown up in it, but he knew the father needed to feel useful to someone. He heard the tap-tap and click-click above the sound of footfalls on the stone floor. Suddenly, he felt grace descend on his shoulders and sink into his heart. A blessing had arrived. It was Marie's father, the tap-tap click-click growing evermore excited and they approached. The dog jumped on him when he turned and licked his face all over, even his scared and blind eyes. God had come to him in the guise of a dog.

He named him Saint.

And he smelled vanilla. Vanilla and perfume, Taboo, a mixture from someone who missed home and tried to carry it with her. There were no prayers, only silence.

Saint lay down on the floor of the confessional beside him. He knew he could sense the presence of Jesus there and he was sure that Jesus had a dog, which he probably had cleaned up after himself. He chuckled.

The panel was open where the penitent kneeled to give confession and he hoped the woman smelling of vanilla hadn't heard his laughter. He felt Saint shift where he lay on his right foot, telling him this woman was in great distress.

"Bless me Father for I have sinned…" she said and he just had to interrupt.

"Haven't we all."

"Except Jesus."

"He was born with the sin we are all born with, then he was baptized. So, he was free from the propensity to sin for a while, until the devil came to tempt. And Jesus never gave in. Even took on our sins, died for our sins. Well, enough of my little sermon. Everyone says I talk too much."

"It's surprising but I needed to hear that."

"It's called Grace. And you are Grace to me."

"How can I be? We've not ever met." Marge was confused. This was not going as she had expected.

"Because you smell of vanilla."

That really threw Marge. She decided not to ask for an explanation. He had said he was a real jabber mouth. Oops, she shouldn't think that any sermon, no matter what length, should be thought of as jabbering. Was that a sin to think?

"It's been, well quite a while since my last confession."

"You sound distressed. God doesn't blame you, he never does. He is glad you are here." Saint nuzzled his hand as he spoke.

He was nothing like she had expected. But what was there to expect? In a time of war all the expectations she had for her life had fallen away.

"Father, I'm glad I'm here because I am confused. I think I committed a sin. But I'm not sure it is a sin to have seriously considered committing a sin."

"Well, I will do my best to help you sort it out, but this does sound a bit confusing. Go on dear."

"What if you were going to do something that was a sin, a real whopper of a sin. I mean I couldn't see any other way out. I still don't see any way out. All I see is my plans for my future falling apart. I don't know what to do about it."

"Sometimes God's plans and our plans do not align."

"But I don't know what God's plan is. He certainly doesn't make it easy. Why does He have to make it so hard?"

"You do ask the hard questions. I'll give it a try, it usually goes like this: we cannot always know God's plan, His grand plan fits into the puzzle of existence, involving everyone that is alive and the plans He has for them."

"This isn't helping, Father. I am confessing the sin of intending to do something. Isn't that in some way as bad as doing it?"

"It's not a question of how bad it is. Whatever it is, God has forgiven you. God is loving; and knowing what is in our hearts can't help, but forgive us, if only we ask for it."

Chapter 30

Streets without a smear of yellow light as the air raid warning kept the lamps dark, signs that once would have rattled with neon, silent, merely dim shapes. Everything seemed so loud, as it does when it echoes off of silence, the squeal of the church door and the clack-clack of her heels. Always there was a dog barking in the distance, always the sound of laughter or crying in the distance.

Marge stuffed her hands in her pockets and smiled. One never knew God's plan, but she could learn to live with her own plan, the plan she had never expected to be hers. Maybe, maybe, maybe something would be revealed. As the priest had said, he lives by 'one never knows' and that was the way he liked it. It was how he felt most comfortable and the one reason he loved the church, mystery. He was not expected to have all the plans and answers, nor was he meant to, because his faith was wed to mystery. The burden of trying to find the answer to all life's questions was lifted. It was just mystery. And Marge laughed out loud as she was grabbed from behind.

Marge spun round and immediately recognized them, the soldiers who had grabbed at her at the dance.

"She owes us."

"All these dames owe us."

"Hold her tight."

"You sissy, I said grab her!"

"She knocked out my tooth."

"Then knock her out."

"I want her awake and squirming."

"It's only what you asked for."

"We're far enough down the alley now. Take your hand off her mouth." "I want to hear her moan."

"I want to hear her scream."

"If we're going to die for her, the least she could do is give it up."

"Give it up…"

Their eyes were blurry and soggy. The smell of alcohol, bourbon spun around her. Drunken hands waged war with her body. Laughter split the night in pain and sorrow, laughter growling by her ear. They were mad. How could she resist a man who was about to give up his life so others could live? His arms were hairy, breath putrid. The earth reached for her and pulled her down into the gravel. Trees screamed again and again until muffled by dark clouds of fear. Not her fear, their fear. Her resignations as the numbers were against her. As the attack went on and on until she was swallowed up by the mystery of why God would let this happen.

There was smoke. It seemed to permeate the air with smells of sulfur and flesh. People's shouts shot through the smoke and landed around her as a great wind came up. The smoke fled, but the stench remained, lingering, circling her until she felt the urge to gag on it. To her left and behind her, she heard slow unsteady footsteps. Flashes of light and thunder obscured her vision as the figure limped by. She looked down and saw a trail of blood.

"What is it, dear?" Mr. G said as he opened his eyes and saw his wife's night gown glowing in the moonlight that came in the window as she stood in front of it. She didn't respond. He didn't expect her to answer. She wasn't listening to him, but to her voices as she called them. When they were first married, he was careful not to make fun of her voices, visions, and dreams. They were right too much of the time. Before she could answer, Elaine ran to the door and tore it open setting the crystal lamps on the dresser it hit to singing.

She stood on the stairway looking down the steps where she saw a trail of blood and turned around looking up the steps. As she ran up the steps following the drops of blood that quickly became pools glistening red in the dark, she yelled for help. Quickly, doors began to open, the men and women in night gowns and pajamas came running out not even bothering to put on a robe. They saw Mrs. G running up to Mary and Marge's door and flinging it open. Mary heard the shouts and sat up in bed. The bed was wet. She looked over to Marge who lay on the bedspread, her clothes torn and surrounded by blood.

Mary would later curse herself for dancing so hard out with Bill that she slept so soundly she hadn't heard Marge come in.

Atop a hill in Iowa was the Waukon Church, gray weary stone, and stained glass windows of deep blues and rich reds that shimmered from the candles lit inside. The mourners stood outside where the path of mud and wilting grass led to a grave. Tears could not be held back. Hands trembled as they lifted handkerchiefs to their red rimmed eyes. Mr. and Mrs. G had come from back east as had Mary and Brigette. And all were filled with sorrow for Marge.

Time had become a beast, feared not embraced, a beast stalking all joy. A war changes everything and that includes time. Holidays came and went, were celebrated or mourned. Friends were made but then went off to war. Prayers were said and God was cursed. Time meant that terrible things were hiding behind the curtain in the living room, ready to be barked out of the radio. Time went on, but people began to notice that hope hadn't gone on.

But love struggled to exist. Mary had found herself in love with Bill but also afraid of that love. He could be going overseas at any time, any time she would have to begin the unbearable anxiety of worrying about Bill, the thoughts of what might happen to him. Was she strong enough to endure? Should she be fighting to hide away her love for him? But she was in love.

And so was Bill. He feared leaving Mary behind because he knew she would worry with every call, with every dream that turned into a nightmare, waking her sweating and trembling. Could he do that to her? And what if he was shot and killed? What would that do to her? And now her closest friend who would be her solace was gone. Was there a shoulder she could cry on? But what could he do when love seemed to have soaked into his thoughts, ran with his blood through his veins?

Love was its own kind of battle field, where the battle was with yourself.

The day had rambled though the weather, cold morning, a spat of rain in the afternoon, but now there was sun. He felt a bit warm as he climbed the steps and hoped the daisies in his hand didn't wilt before he gave them to Mary. He walked into the lower lobby and turned as Mary came down the stairs, holding hands with a youngish man, probably older than his appearance. His brown suit was wrinkled, but he still looked almost noble in the straightway he carried himself, his handsome way.

And he was holding hands with Mary as they laughed at him.

"Mary, who is this man?" He could tell from the pencil and writing pad sticking out of his pocket that he was probably a reporter.

"This is my new friend Michael. Someone to talk to now that…"

"You can talk to me," Bill said, slowly backing away feeling disoriented and maybe angry. He turned and went to the table where he stuck the flowers he held into a vase of roses. Then he walked down to the lower lobby, swung open the door and left.

"What happened?" Mary asked Michael not having a clue as to what had just happened.

Michael said softly, "He's jealous. Go after him and explain to him we're just friends. If you have to, tell him about me."

Mary ran out the door and was ready to yell down the sidewalk for Bill when she saw him at the bottom of the stairs, leaning against the lamppost about to light a cigarette. He stopped and looked up at her, but then decided he was not going to let himself be hurt again as he had been with Debby back home. So, he went back to lighting his Lucky Strike cigarette with a crack and hiss of the match. He tossed the match in Mary's direction like a flag at a race to begin what they needed.

But Mary didn't want to fight, she wanted to explain. "His name is Michael, he lives a floor below me and works for the *Post* as a reporter." Bill was ready to make some smart remark but decided against it. "He goes out by himself every Saturday night to the park. He told me he wears pink suspenders."

What does that have to do with anything? Bill thought, but then he understood. It was code for looking for men. They used a pink handkerchief in the service to find another man with similar desires. He felt so stupid that all he could think of to say was "The cherry blossoms are blooming around the Tidal Basin. People go to see them before they blow away."

Brigette began to think she might be falling in love. How could she be falling in love when she had never been in love before? How did one know what love felt like, and not just the fascination or desire to be in love. Not just lust or the need to be held, softly. Was she beginning to fall in love with Peter? She had become sad, lonely. There was not a friend to confide with, to weigh her thoughts against her fears; time had overtaken her and her friend Marge was gone. And she realized that she had no other real friends to go to.

For now, she had Steven, with his tired way, he said he loved her, tired of life. Oh he was a good lover, well endowed, and he knew how to use it. He spent most of his time going down on her which she preferred anyway. She had thought of finding another woman to pleasure her, but it just didn't seem right. She knew others in the arts who had taken a lover of the same sex. But even that, though it might offer some fun, would probably wear thin. She needed more, wanted more.

Steven began to stir besides her, twisting the sheet off Brigette and tight on himself. With a groan he turned over and for a second Brigette had a flash of it being Peter beside her. She laughed to herself. Now that will never happen. Then she felt angry and decided that the best person to take it out on was Steven.

"No, not just out of bed but back down the fire escape before someone sees you." Brigette put on her peacock robe and went into the studio leaving Steven time to get back in uniform.

Betty burst into the studio startling Brigette. She knew Betty well enough but not well enough to not knock. Betty looked excited, flustered, and afraid all at once as her checks grew redder as it spread to her neck.

"What's going on?" Brigette said confused.

"You have the radio!" Betty said, taking a frantic look around the cluttered room. Easels, tubes of paint, jars of turpentine and the portrait of a nice young man.

She heard a rustling in the bedroom as Steven ran into the room. "I heard all the hollering, what's going on?"

"Well, you must be a reporter because you ask the best questions," Brigette said heading toward the bedroom behind her. "But I don't have a clue!"

As Betty ran into the bedroom, she saw Steven, pants on but carrying his shirt, going out the window to the fire escape. And on his shoulder was a bag that she was sure had a transmitter in it.

"Stop, you traitor!"

Michael entered the room and pushed in front of Betty and saw Steven scurrying down the fire escape. Some excitement! He jumped after Steven as Betty kept yelling. Michael got to the ground first; he vaulted over the railing and landed on Steven, knocking both of them to the ground. Michael rolled over as he clenched his hand into a fist. But in the middle of his swing at Michael, the reporter took a swing at Steven, and with a crunching sound of teeth, slammed his fist into the traitor's jaw. His head fell back and his eyes rolled back. As Michael stood he dusted off his new tan pants and saw two men in dull gray suits run through the to the back garden. They had a Mutt and Jeff look, one shorter and on the plump side with the other being very tall and thin, with something that looked like grape jelly on his chin.

As Jeff leaned over and cuffed the soldier/spy just coming back to consciousness Mutt looked up to the window above. Brigette and Betty were hanging out the window. He smiled slyly and waved toward Betty.

"What's happening?" Brigette tried to sound annoyed but was actually startled. The annoying look was just a habit by now.

"I'm, well I guess you could say I'm a spy, or not. Depending on how you look at it. Or you could call me snoopy." Betty walked back into Brigette's studio without meeting eyes with Brigette.

"Snoopy for yourself or someone else?" Brigette asked suspiciously.

"Actually for the FBI."

"What? Oh, I get it. You were looking for a spy here in the Golden Parrot. That means you were spying on us?"

"The FBI knew there was a coded radio signal coming from this building but couldn't figure out who it could be. I guess they thought it couldn't be me because they asked me to keep my eyes and ears open. And I am so relieved it wasn't one of my fellow boarders."

As Michael opened the door to the Golden Parrot, the news had spread fast and all the boarders that were home had gathered in the lobby. They let out a cheer as he came in. He looked confused then understood. Mrs. G let out a holler and came running down the steps. Ana threw her arms around Michael, planting a big kiss right on his mouth. Betty came up beside Michael and put her hand on his shoulder.

"No one will know about this though," he whispered to Betty. "The FBI doesn't want anything said about this, after all, this would have been a big story for me to post."

"Well, I can at least make you a drink."

Chapter 31

It was spring but it wasn't spring. It had been like a tardy child who was reluctant about what might blossom in this New Year. Mary had expected explosions of yellow: daffodils swaying in a quiet breeze, crocuses about to drop their purple petals and the fallen leaves, sprays of forsythia like fireworks exploding into the spring air. Instead the grasses were brown and the trees branches were still bare without even the stubble of green buds. The air spoke of dull times ahead, dull with waiting for a wind to bring variety to the days of war. The dead corn stalks knew they had been feeding men who were trying not to die at the hands of the Germans, Italians, and Japanese.

Spring was so late in coming, Mary sighed as the train seemed to tip toe silently through Illinois on her way home. She could have stayed back in DC away from the haunting of Mr. Desisto's ghost. Being a Roman Catholic, she believed in life after death. And that gray land of Purgatory where souls waited out their fate. But couldn't one of those souls waiting in the line to go where Mr. Desisto was going (Hell), slip unnoticed out of line and wander into the world of the living? Journey down the road to her parent's house and peer through the bedroom window and scratch at the screen?

Mary was afraid but her mother was ill and she knew she could help out with the kids, do the things around the house that her crippled father could not. Tess was off working with the Red Cross in Europe and Mary had managed to get some time off from the bureau to come home. Her boss had said no, so she had written a letter to Hoover and actually gotten a reply: permission to go home. Could it be because she had hinted she had seen him around the Golden Parrot?

Washington was yet to waken up spring too and a late snow had left puddles of slush at the street corners. Brigette sat with a drawing pad in her lap and a charcoal pencil between her teeth. Instead of drawing, she was watching the people trying to cross the street at 20th and R without stepping in the mess.

She laughed to herself at the attempts they made jumping and splashing. Then she laughed out loud as one woman in a tight blue suit flew up in the air and landed on her backside in the puddle.

"If I am interrupting your thoughts, I can come back another time," Peter said softly, apologetically.

Brigette turned from the show below. "Please interrupt them. Actually, the problem is there is nothing to interrupt."

"I am certain there is always something going on in your head."

"You mean I'm plotting?"

"I apologize if you thought I was saying. I mean that you are very clever. I like that in American women."

"Well, I don't know where you got that idea from. American men seem to think we are bimbos. I am very clever though and I'm taking advantage of it. Through a friend I have met a very important Hollywood producer who wants to sleep with me."

"What a bastard he must be!"

"No different from all men…present company excluded. Of course, I will only let him touch my story, not me. So, I am writing a treatment, the story line for a screenplay. This is what I've always wanted to do, direct a movie out of beautiful pictures. Since they don't seem to let women behind the camera, and I have no talent for acting, I will write my way to Hollywood."

"A clever woman, would you do anything to get this man to look at your screenplay?" Peter cringed realizing what he said just slipped out and was rude.

But Brigette didn't take it as rude, it gave her thought. "I do have my dignity. The struggle is always to make others believe I have it."

"I believe in you."

"I think you do." She opened up her sketchbook and turned to a page she had written on in big broad strokes. "So, here's the plot so far: a young artist infiltrates Hitler's inner circle and becomes a spy…" She paused, dissatisfied with the beginning of her pitch. "I know it sounds silly when I say it out loud but I have to find something…"

"A plot," Peter wanted to be helpful and even more to be part of anything she was doing. "History is full of plots and intrigues, some so mysterious, so hidden that all we know of history is what we are allowed to know." Then he came on an idea. Of sorts. "A Japanese official comes to the United States on government business. But what he is really doing is searching for his only nephew, who had left the family and come to America, hoping to make him the surrogate son he does not have."

"A spy story?"

"A love story. The official finds that his nephew is working his way through medical school."

Brigette smiled and pulled a cigarette out of the pack, "Working in a restaurant."

Peter began to pace the room, absently touching the paintings as he went by. "And then one day, he sees a beautiful woman, with an air of independence unlike the women he has known. He keeps his eye on her but is unable to approach her."

"And then one day she approaches him, to model for her."

"She is so different, yet so like his heart and soul. He models for her and they chat and reveal much of themselves as he sits and she paints."

"Let me sketch you while you tell this story."

"His uncle tries to persuade him to go back to Japan with him, trying to warn him that soon things will happen and it will not be safe for him to stay in the United States. He cannot leave her behind. He is falling in love. Then one day, his uncle leaves suddenly and goes back to Japan. It is only a week later that everyone is listening to their radio to find out what is happening and what will happen next. Pearl Harbor has been attacked by the Japanese. This is war. There is no time for him to escape being swept up in what he knows will happen: blaming the Japanese that are left in America. He hides out in the house where he has been working, with the consent of the owner, so he can be near her."

Brigette was not watching him but still listening. She was working on her drawing of the two of them in each other's arms.

"But this woman was so much her own person with such high moral standards, he did not know if they could consummate their love…"

Chapter 32

The Casino Royale had become their place to frequent. When they were there, they didn't notice anyone else only each other. The music was brassy, the atmosphere was classy, and because there were now so many places in town competing for the same crowd that swelled the city, the drinks were cheap. Mary was having a whiskey sour and Bill a Manhattan.

"And then we ran right into the water," Bill said with one of those contagious laughs. Mary nearly spewed out her drink as she started to laugh too. Then she swallowed and tried to straighten herself out and act more like a lady but began to laugh again, spilling her drink on her dress. She excused herself and headed to the ladies room, while Bill lit another cigarette and picked the tobacco off of his tongue.

Mary came back looking solemn. She slid in next to Bill and took his hand in hers.

"The war in the Pacific Theater, it couldn't have been so much fun. I mean these stories I hear the GIs tell, it sounds like fun, but it couldn't be. Not all the time."

"Not all the time. Some of it was pretty horrible. I joined up but I never knew what it would be like, one can never imagine how horrible war is. I never saw a man cry or a man scream until…" Bill trailed off, looking around the room which seemed in a fog with blurry color showing through a dirty glass.

Mary wanted to change the subject but she also needed to know. "What was it like coming back?"

"The nightclubs are jammed with laughter, the movie houses are everywhere, shows, and dances. Too much hollow fun, it seems so wrong, but everyone thinks it is so grand that you are a soldier, and they wave their flags, and…It's fine to have support but so unreal…"

The silence only thickened with the clash of glasses, the laughter as the comic on stage seemed to be unable to stop himself.

Mary said, "It's a good thing war is so terrible otherwise we would grow too fond of it."

The club was crowded with women in stylish suits, with padded shoulders of beige and dusty rose or gentle green or elegant evening dresses of silver and red and black, strapless or with spaghetti straps. The men wore dark suits with wide ties of all colors and patterns, or an occasional white jacket with black silk lapels. Every table had a white crisp linen tablecloth and small red candlelight lamps. The tables were dotted with blue Casino Royale ash trays, filled with cigarette butts or a chewed on burned down cigar. Cocktail glasses with ice cubes melting from the heat of a room filled with people, cherries and orange slices, a twist, an olive or onion. Glasses smeared with lipstick clinked and feet on the dance floor clacked on the polished ebony wood. Cologne and perfume mixed with heavy smoke snaked through the room, between the guests. The band stood up and began to play, 'Pennsylvania 6 5000' with a brassy wail.

In the corner of the room, in a bright blue leather booth, sat a man few knew but many used his products often enough to make the family a fortune. And now that there was a war, his fortunes grew. He was Dr. Harold Smith of Smith Family Products. They made bandages, of all sorts for all needs. But as the money rolled in and the demand increased, Dr. Smith began to feel uneasy. He was making money off of people's sorrow. So, he left his son in charge of the company back in Cincinnati and headed to Washington, DC to become one of the businessmen who worked for the government for one dollar. He was the head of distribution of medical supplies, and of course he made sure they were bought from his company.

He ran his hand through his thick white hair, pulled off his glasses and wiped them with his pocket kerchief. He put them back on but the smoke in the air still fogged his vision. His friend, movie mogul Samuel Goldwyn, also known as Samuel Goldfish, was in town to talk over a series of war films, on battle protocol, venereal disease and other things. Though he was at least ten years younger than Dr. Smith, his once thick hair was gone, but he looked dashing in his suit.

Brigette wore a low cut black silk dress with a dragon embroidered on the side, Smith put his arm on her bare shoulders. Her hair was up, her eyeliner was thick, and she looked ravishing.

"So, did I tell you that Brigette has written a story?" Smith said with a puff on his cigar.

Brigette had been waiting for Smith to bring the subject up. "Treatment is the industry term, darling."

"Yes," Smith interrupted her, "I have read it and it looks very romantic to me."

Goldwyn moved closer to Brigette. "I'm sure you are a very romantic lady."

"One who knows what she wants. She asked me to bring it up in case you didn't."

"I haven't forgotten our conversation last fall. You are also a very attractive woman. I had no idea…"

"You two talk business while I excuse myself to get another bourbon."

Goldwyn moved closer to Brigette and looked straight at her, after letting his eyes slide down toward her cleavage. "Is this some little project of Smith's that you helped him with and or is he embarrassed to say he wrote a romance?"

Suppressing her anger, Brigette said, "You underestimate me. I let him read it to please him. He knows I'm the romantic."

"I'm sure you do a lot to please him, a married man."

"A temporary situation, he's planning a divorce."

"And what would you do to please me, if I read your screenplay?"

They saw Smith approaching the table, drink in hand.

"I will be staying at the Madison Hotel for the next two months if you care to personally drop off your screenplay," Goldwyn whispered as Smith sat down.

"So, what do you say when I finish this drink, we head over to the Blue Mirror next?"

"Darling, I love the shows there but I have to go home and pack. I told you, don't look surprised, mom is driving down to my aunt's in Virginia Beach and she is going to pick me up on the way. Will you miss me?"

She kissed Smith on the cheek but winked at Goldwyn.

It was the three of them who walked out of the movie, Betty, Michael, and Earl, the new boarder on the second floor. With his bum leg from a war wound, they watched him slowly struggle up the stairs, but he never complained. He was lucky to get a room at all. He had hobbled in looking for a room just as

Trudy had given up on Washington and gone back to Los Angeles. He seemed a pleasant person at dinner, quick to laugh. And a pleasant looking person with brown wavy hair, a wide forehead above bedroom eyes, and a mouth that always smiled. He was a stocky man which only gave him more weight to carry with his bum leg. He was still in the army but worked in one of the temporary buildings on the Washington Mall. He had been an accountant before the war, a skill that was now invaluable.

They had been chatting about nothing in particular when they came up to the front steps of the Golden Parrot. Mr. and Mrs. Schwietz were just going inside, arguing as usual about the movie they had just seen, a comedy.

"I'm sure glad they don't live on my floor," Michael said quietly to the others.

"Yeah, they live on mine and well…I learned to sleep through bombs falling and even worse snoring in the army."

Betty felt that Earl was about to say something, well, romantic to her. She had to nip that in the bud. She had been dumped recently for a waitress. There were so many women in the city these days that a man, especially a soldier, could have his choice.

"It was nice having you come along with Michael and I. Cary Grant is one of his favorites too."

"It's that accent," Michael said. But feeling he was interrupting something stayed quiet.

"Thanks for the great evening, guys," Earl said. "I have to go back to the office and finish up some work, Betty."

"I'm sorry I spilled the popcorn in your lap," Betty laughed.

"I'll be pulling it out of my pockets for weeks."

Betty watched Earl going down the street realizing there was something unique about him that she liked. But she couldn't quite put her finger on it. Was she feeling sorry for him? She doubted it because he never seemed sorry for himself. Maybe it was that smile that always seemed to linger around the corner of his mouth. Whatever it was it mystified her, and attracted her. So why had she leaned away when he had leaned over to kiss her on the cheek?

When Betty walked by Mary's room, the door was cracked and Mary, looking exhausted, sat on the edge of the bed, staring out into her thoughts.

With a rap on the door, Betty asked if she could come in.

"Of course, come sit down," Mary said pulling bobby pins from her hair, which fell down rich and dark in the dim pink light from the lamp on the bedside table.

The mattress squeaked as Betty sat down. She realized that they were sitting on the side of the bed that Marge had slept on.

"Mary, is something bothering you, dear?"

Mary fell back on the bed and stared at the ceiling. "Love, I never used to think about it, I was afraid. Now it's all I think about and I'm still afraid."

"I don't know what to tell you. I always wanted to get married, but I guess the war changed that. Too scared, besides, I think I want to go to college when this war is over. Be some kind of business executive. Get a career going like a man is able to do."

"You would look good in a gray flannel suit."

In the heat that was beginning to sizzle around the city, rising to the point in the next few months that everyone would remark that you could fry an egg on the sidewalk, the barn smelled like a barn again.

Mary sat on a bale of hay and remembered how she and her sister Tess had tried to fry an egg once on the front stoop of their house, all that happened was they got in trouble with their mother.

The cow turned to Mary as she began to talk, as if listening closely. "So, I wore this new blue dress but of course Bill didn't say anything about it. But he did say that my eyes were lovely. The dress I can change but my eyes I'm stuck with so I'm glad he likes them. Do you get cold out here? It's never sane to love a soldier during a war."

Coming in on a wing and a prayer
Coming in on a wing and a prayers
Tho' there's one motor gone we will still carry on
Coming in on a wing and a prayer

Looking out the window, Brigette saw dark clouds but that didn't matter to her. As a fog rolled up the streets, the air smelled of water, the building was a giant ship she was soon going to abandon and meet her mother downstairs. They would be off to Virginia Beach to visit her crazy Aunt Mel. It had been a long and winding way to let her mother into her heart. She had blamed her mother many times for not protecting her from her father, but then she came to see her mother, with the help of Aunt Mel, as someone who did love her. Her aunt had said about her mother, "She's only a woman, and that isn't fair. So, we do the best we can."

Brigette smiled. She didn't know what had happened, probably when her grandfather died and left money to her mother she felt like she didn't have to put up with his philandering any more, and threw him out. Brigette grabbed her suitcase and ran for the stairs as a car honked below.

Sofia and Carl sat in the shiny blue Pontiac as the fog swirled around it. Carl honked the horn again, impatient.

"My headache," Sofia said rubbing her temples with her pointer fingers. Then she smoothed out the wrinkles in her lime green cotton dress and leaned back against the leather seat.

"I'm anxious to see my baby girl." Carl tossed his cigarette out the window right before it burned his fingers. "…there she is!"

Brigette had been running down the stairs when she saw her father open the door and get out of the car.

"There's my little princess. Come and give me a kiss."

He looked the same as when she was twelve. He always looked the same with his silly smile and sharp green eyes. Sofia sat up.

"Mother," Brigette screamed at her mother who put her face in her hands. "What is he doing here? I thought you threw him out for good!"

"I left, I repented, I asked forgiveness, and I'm back. And I missed my beautiful little girl. Now, come and get in the car with us, Sophia, move your big ass over."

"I forgave your father…"

"But I didn't forgive him and now I don't forgive you mother."

Brigette ran up the stairs two at a time as her father yelled after her, "What was that for? Didn't I give you everything, spoiled you rotten, that's it."

"Please, baby, let's not fight with your father."

"What did I say I ask you? What did I say?"

But Brigette barely heard them as the door swung closed behind her.

They were gone, the fog had stayed. The sun, what there had been of it had gone and the darkness had crawled out of the sewers and languished over the stars. Brigette sat in the window overlooking the back garden, her eyes sore and caked with dried tears. Suddenly, below yellow light pushed through the fog and revealed the shadow of a man. The light slid back in the basement and she could now see it was Peter dressed in his kitchen apron, his shoulders slumping. Brigette grabbed a sheet of paper, wrote a note with a stick of charcoal and folded it into a paper airplane and sailed it out the window. It hit Peter on the back of his head.

It had passed by the dining room window where Mr. Smith sat with Barb his wife.

They had sat at the table by the window because her 'best side' faced the dining room there.

"Did you see a paper airplane?" But Barb wondered if she had just imagined it.

Brigette's heals click as she walked down the staircase to the lobby. It was a typical evening dinner with guests walking in and out, everyone seeming to be relaxed and at ease. Of course, a war is easy to forget when you've had a great meal and lots of cocktails. She was going to go out the door to the garden when she saw him, her hope of getting out of her poverty. She saw herself without the diamonds and mink stoles she saw other women wearing. She would marry someone who loved her and who would let her live in the lifestyle she had grown up with, that she felt she deserved.

Mr. Smith was with his wife, laughing and holding her hand across the table just like he held hers when they went out to a club. A waiter walked by carrying a tray with two steaming meals on it. Brigette stopped him.

"Joey, what table is that for?"

"Table 6, the one by the window, why?"

"That's the table where my friends are sitting. Let me take them their dinner, I'm sure they will appreciate it " Brigette took the tray from the waiter and headed into the dining room.

As she walked over to the table where Mr. Smith sat with a woman in a tight, very expensive looking dress, she swore to herself she could smell his cologne, too much, as usual.

"The flounder for the beautiful woman," she said setting the plate down in front of the woman, then turned to Mr. Smith, "and this is for you, Smitty," she said using her pet name for him. It was then he looked up with a look of recognition on his face and it was then that she dropped his pork chop in his lap.

The door to the men's restroom swung open and Brigette rushed in. There was a man at the urinal and Mr. Smith trying to get the grease off his suit.

"I thought you were out of town!" Smitty said, "So, I took my wife to dinner here…"

"I thought she was another woman, but worse, she's your wife!"

"She insisted on coming here." He was beginning to realize the mess was not going to come out of one of his best suits. "I usually refuse, but she's getting suspicious. We do go our own ways but she afraid we're going too much our own way lately."

"Good. Now is a cozy little time to tell her you want a divorce. I've been waiting for that for some time now."

"I'm afraid it would not be a good thing to do until the war is over. It would compromise my power base here and…"

"Then I'll go tell her you want a divorce."

"The affair is over. Other people, Mr. Hoover, know about us and it could be used against me to…"

"I've given you so much and then you betray me like this!"

Brigette began to storm out, then stopped and put her hand on Smith's chest as he hurriedly tried to leave. "Your zipper is down!" And she reached down and pulled it up to his surprise.

Outside she stood on the sidewalk. She could hear the wind swooshing along the street up from Dupont Circle rattling trash on its way. The wind blew her hair across her face. She pulled it back but a strand stuck to her lip. She did not notice. The song that had been in her heart turned into a scream, settled into a murmur of dark thoughts.

Chapter 33

Mr. G was pulling down the tickets from the shelf where the cooks had used them to fill orders. He would be saving them for toilet paper. Everything was scarce during the war. But then he had saved them during the depression when he needed to save any money he could. He had intended to open a diner with the money he had inherited when his grandfather had died in the 'War to End All Wars'. He and Elaine had plans to have it built in Forward, New York, a small town where the people and even the street signs felt friendly. He had visited there as a child, before his dad died of a heart attack at age 43, when he was aged ten. It was that sweet taste of nostalgia that had him always fantasizing about opening a diner there, with locals meeting, chatting and laughing, sharing and comforting. But before he could even choose a site to build on, the stock market crashed into the Great Depression. He had followed Elaine's advice before the crash, which with her unusual insight she had predicted, and taken the money out of the bank and turned it into gold.

But he could see the writing on the wall: Forward was falling back into despair fast. Still wanting to open a restaurant he realized he could only open one where people had money. With Elaine's help that was Washington, DC, where the government was always paying its employees and where the rich often gathered. So, they bought an old mansion and restored it themselves. Doing it together their marriage had never been closer. Even their son, though young, had helped out. It became 'The Golden Parrot', a name that he had in a crazy dream about a golden eagle, but he decided a parrot sounded less military.

The rich and the famous came, and they survived.

"Well, busy night. I think I'll go up and see if the misses is still awake. Night." Mr. G headed to the stairs as Pock, Peter, and Cynthia all said good night.

Peter pulled a skillet out of the sudsy water and rinsed it off. "Pock, take your wife and rub her back." He worried about Cynthia, she had the miscarriage but seemed to be doing quite well with this pregnancy, although they were all a bit concerned that she was so far overdue.

The couple said good night and headed up the back stairs for the servants. Peter wiped the skillet dry and went over to hang it up in front of the window. The window should have had bars on it after someone had broken in and stolen a chicken, but Mr. G felt sorry for the poor fellow, heading for food and not the silverware. He had put a sign at the back doorstep that said, "If you are hungry, knock on the back door."

Through the pans, he saw something moving in the back garden, white against a bush of white roses. At first he thought it was the ghost that he had heard roamed the halls and now the garden. But it was a real woman, Brigette alone in the dark with light from a sliver of a moon. He headed outside.

Peter stood in the heavy shadow cast by a tree and was silent, waiting. She turned toward him, the gathering mist whirling around her. She saw him. He stepped out of the shadow.

"I wanted to tell you that there is more to the story you are writing," Peter said as the mist was pushed away by his breath.

"Yes. The story we are writing."

"He is the son of a foreign diplomat who when the war came did not leave the city in time so had to flee to a hiding place. He does not want to involve this woman he meets in his intrigue."

"But they are attracted to each other."

"The audience will demand more between them."

"An audience demands lovers, passion. How shall it happen?"

"One night they meet accidentally in the park when the street lamps are dark, when the only light is a sliver of the moon reflecting off the fog. He is thinking about before the war when he could roam the streets freely. Then the moon slips behind a cloud and all he can see is her glowing in her white dress, singing to herself and weaving the fog into patterns. She can't sleep…"

"Because she remembers seeing him in the park before thinking and dreaming of her. But what do they say?"

"There is no need to say anything as they move closer together," Peter said. As he moved closer, Brigette turned, confused and scared. She couldn't allow herself the risk of pain that love might bring. She turned and ran up the garden steps.

At the top of the stairs, her footsteps thundered in her ears. What was wrong, she wondered, why was her heart pounding, why was she beginning to feel moisture on her brow? Entering her rooms, she leaned against the door, suddenly exhausted, although when she went to push the light button she pressed so hard she could have broken her finger.

The room smelled like oil paints and turpentine, old wood and clouds, her perfume, Taboo. But beneath it all she had noticed a smell that came from long ago when her grandmother had died, the rotten smell of rotting skin, the smell of death. Death spoke of loss and fear with its sour breath. Why had this smell followed her for days? When she painted, walked beneath the trees, ate beef stew for dinner as she smoked a cigarette?

Going to a corner of the room, there were a pile a landscape paintings, scenes of Rock Creek Park, the Tidal Basin, the Mall, that she planned to sell in a show in the fall, she moved them aside carefully. She needed the money. But she also needed to find what was happening to her. Behind the paintings was a short door that went under the eaves of the house. It squeezed open as she slowly pulled, then paused. There stood a painting of her first boyfriend, the Jewish one, the one who would not understand when her father had forbidden her to see him. The painting was done in spring colors. Craig. But she had slashed over the paining with an oily black when he refused to run away with her. They were too young, too attached to his parents to leave, too afraid of the world out there. He didn't love her enough. That was when she had put large slashes in the paining, across his face and luminous eyes.

She was confused, with love and hate, with despair and loss. Brigette was feeling too much, too strong, too anxious while she questioned why she feared a relationship with Peter. Canvas after canvas was pulled aside in her life, with men on slashed canvas, obliterated so they couldn't accuse her of being a coward. To love, why?

She came to the last painting she had worked on, although filled with love, it frightened her. Peter. So, she had hidden him in the back of her mind so often but he kept rising unwanted to the surface of her thoughts. Hesitating, she reached behind her to her palette and picked up a sharp palette knife. Could she do it? Could she? She threw down the palette knife as if it was a grenade as her head seemed to explode, and she fainted.

The Blue Plate Special that day at Scholl's was a huge chunk of meatloaf with ketchup on top, mounds of mashed potatoes and gravy, and withered yellowish peas.

Neither Mary, Dotty, nor Roz picked it up. While they were all working together (well they both knew that Roz cheated constantly) at trying to retain their girlish figures, they ate Cobb salads.

Mary picked up a plate of apple pie off the counter. "I would hate to tell my mother that this pie is better than hers."

Roz, who was always dreaming of being back in the Bronx said, "I miss a good bagel."

Mary looked at her salad with a sigh. Whatever a bagel was she was sure it must be good. "What is a bagel?"

"It's like a donut with rigor mortis," Roz explained almost tasting cream cheese in her imagination.

They had reached the end of the cafeteria line and Dotty began reading off her tickets to Betty whose reading skills still weren't that good. When Dotty got up to the cashier, she picked up her tickets, but before reading them asked Betty, "How is that boyfriend?" She seemed so enamored with him lately. Betty began to cry softly, as she leaned over to take the tickets and try to read off the food and prices herself, but as she leaned over a few tears plopped into Dotty's vanilla pudding.

"That's alright," Dotty said knowing what was probably happening, as it was happening to many women in this town, "they water down the pudding anyway."

As lunch wound down, Peg was over at the cafeteria line where she was pulling a piece of cherry pie out of its glass cubicle. She was picking up a cherry that had made its escape when she felt a tap on her shoulder. Turning around she saw a very sad looking Betty.

"I just talked to Jonesy. I feel like a possum that didn't make it across the road. Taking off early. See ya'll tonight."

She walked away knowing she would have to go back home to Alabama in shame, leaving this southern, almost northern town she had come to love.

It was getting hot and moist in the city as if the swamp that the founding fathers had sadly chosen to build on rose from its winter grave and with a sweaty, humid touch wandered about. But in the Golden Parrot, the ceiling fans kept the air moving and with a good sweet iced tea kept you cool.

Michael was treating himself to a steak dinner. He didn't do it often, he hated to dine alone having grown up in a large family of hungry brothers, but today was his birthday. When he looked over at Mr. Hoover, and his friend Tolland, he felt like crying or screaming. Everyone knew Tolland was more than an employee but no one could say anything. Who could threaten the man who kept all of the city's secret liaisons? He wielded his power over the city but there was even more that hung like a sword above his head. He, like Mr. Hoover, was a homosexual. It was lonely not being able to have a permanent relationship like Hoover had. In fact, even in the gay community it was widely accepted that of course men couldn't have a loving relationship. Michael didn't fall for that. Of course, they couldn't when this city wouldn't let them. If the paper he worked for knew, unlike others that would fire him on a morals charge, he would be assigned to 'assistant to the gossip column', (that wouldn't ever dish on Cary Grant and Randolph Scott though they lived together).

He took his knife and stabbed it into his bloody steak.

Mrs. G, dressed in a wine colored dress that barely contained her ample bosom came up to the table where Mr. Hoover, with a tie that matched the dress, sat with the man he dined with every night. She held a huge piece of chocolate cake on a plate with two forks. Mr. Tolland smiled as Hoover rubbed his ample stomach.

"Oh, but my waistline!"

"I'm just glad you didn't go to Harvey's tonight," she winked. "And we got in some real sugar, not saccharin. Besides your companion here could use a little…"

Mrs. G began to stare into space as the two men began to slide into the background, while the wails of a woman climbed to the surface of her thoughts. Everything seemed to be lit by a red light. Then it passed and she rushed out of the room. As best she could with her arthritis, she rushed up the stairs and toward Betty's room. She stopped as the door was a bright red trail of fresh blood leading toward the bathroom. Not stopping to knock on the door, she tore it open. Betty sat curled up beside the toilet softly crying.

"The cramps," she whispered. "I thought something was going on, but I didn't believe I was with child, I didn't want to believe…"

Betty lay sleeping in her bed, restlessly turning and shifting. Mrs. G opened the door and Mary stood there. She knew what had happened and was waiting to find out how Betty was.

"She's sleeping and unfortunately dreaming."

"She should be in the hospital," Mary said.

"It was all I could do to get her to let our doctor in the room. She feels such shame."

"I talked to her earlier. She got a call from a friend of her boyfriend Jonesy that he had been shipped out. She doesn't know when she will hear from him, if ever. I think I'll go in and just sit with her for a while."

Out of sight, the ghost moved toward the cleaning closet door.

And I guess it is all growing up, Ma, that's so hard so sudden and so necessary. I can't rely on your arms to comfort me now. But I have friends, good friends, Ma, whose mothers are far away and they need my arms now for comfort. Love you, Mary.

In the rectangle of sunlight that fell through the window at the end of the hall, Michael and Bill stood as Mary stepped out of the light and went toward Brigette's door. She heard furious typing through the cracked door. She pushed it open cautiously because Brigette could at times be quite touchy and temperamental, something Mary had heard was true of artists.

"Working hard?" Mary said as the door started to squeak.

Brigette continued to type. "I'm nearly done with this screenplay I'm writing."

"Want to come with us to…"

"No. But thanks. I have to work while I'm inspired."

Michael decided to leave Brigette and Betty, his new friends, a note in case she changed her mind. He pulled out the notebook always in his pocket.

"In case you want to join us, come to the amphitheater gate at Arlington Cemetery. Give them my name and they will let you in."

Then he sipped it under the closed door and nodded to Mary.

Chapter 34

The heat of the day had melted the clouds and left a milky film over the sky. Ladies swished their fans through the air and men pulled at their collars and then at their neckties. Everyone was restless on the stone benches as they waited and it seemed, waited some more. In the distance was the sound of shovels digging; another grave for another brave American. It was the Memorial Amphitheater in Arlington National Cemetery. The cemetery was once the plantation of Robert E Lee, overlooking the Potomac River and on across to the Capitol. Green lawns that were once fields with slaves were now fading green lawns studded with glistening white gravestones, like stumps of cut down trees.

Bill, in uniform, and Mary sat with Michael who was writing furiously in his notebook.

"Who is that over there?" Bill pointed to a man in some uniform he didn't recognize with perfect posture.

"That's the deposed ambassador from Norway I think and the woman with him is countess something or other. I'll have to look that up. The men in the black suits are Secret Service but I'll bet there are some here in the crowd who are dressed like civilians."

"Are there going to be many speeches?" Mary asked as she pulled at her skirt that was sticking to her legs.

"No, just one that I thought you might want to hear. I gotta go down and find my photographer then do a few interviews. See you after the speech." Michael jumped down over the empty seats like a mountain goat as he went toward the side of the stage.

"I guess the only man who could impress me if they showed up would be Mr. Roosevelt or Cary Grant."

"I don't think I'd be impressed if God showed up with the Virgin Mary on his arm."

"It's as hot as the other places. It's like being in the Philippines." And he might be there soon he thought which caused him to suddenly be pensive. He could be shot at soon. He could be dead and where would Mary be then? Was it right to put the woman he loved through that or was it better to somehow end the relationship?

"Something is going on," Mary whispered grabbing Bill's arm. The crowd in the oval colonnade all seemed hushed as from behind a curtain came men in full dress uniforms from all of the services. As their medals glistened in the sunlight peeking through the cloud sewn sky, the band raised their instruments and began playing 'Hail to the Chief'. The blue curtain parted slightly and in two steps out came President Roosevelt with Mrs. Roosevelt on his arm, and a Secret Service man on the other side. He grabbed the podium with a firm grip that said strength and confidence in his leadership.

Then Mary fainted on Bill's shoulder.

Would it be in a green field where yellow and white flowers danced in the breeze, the breeze that suddenly was over powered by the metal smell of gunpowder and blood? Perhaps in a swamp of howling and cries, of calls for loved ones? Or in a plane that roared and screeched through the sky as the land came up faster and faster? Would it be the boom of water as a ship slid into oblivion?

Mary woke in Bill's arms which were covered in Old Spice aftershave. They smiled at each other and she could see he had been very worried. But the heat had pressed her down into sleep again; she woke from her dreams terrified that she would never be able to sleep with dreams such as these when Bill left for combat. Could she survive with him in harm's way?

She lay on the stone bench which was somehow cool and looked for Bill. He was down talking to Michael and a man in a dark suit. A gentle rain, barely tickling her face and resting on her eyelashes was falling. Looking to her left her heart stopped as she saw Mr. Roosevelt in a wheel chair being taken to his limousine, plated with heavy black steel. She breathed out. He had polio like her father. Rather than think of the president as a weak and crippled man, she was filled with admiration knowing how much of a fight it was to deal with the disease. Mary felt a pulling in her heart for her father; she missed him and his chewing tobacco smile so much.

Michael had rushed back to the *Washington Post* to file his report. It would be about the speech, not about the fact the president, except when his leg braces were in place and he had someone to lean on, was unable to walk. The press knew, the public didn't. It was not the place of the press to make him seem weak in a time of war.

Bill and Mary stood before the door to her room when Betty popped out of her door.

"It's finally starting to turn from a drizzle into rain! You two look wet as a catfish. Where y'all been?" Betty asked.

Mary spoke up while Bill took off his hat and shook off some rain. "We went to Arlington Cemetery, the old amphitheater, where we heard Mr. Roosevelt was speaking!"

"Oh, I love that man. Why didn't you tell me?"

Bill was about to say they left a note for her and Brigette when he noticed it in her room on the dresser. Betty's eyes followed his, and then she turned to him.

"I can't read."

Bill left for work while Mary and Betty went in and sat on the bed. On the dresser Mary saw more notes and envelopes. She picked up one and read it to Betty.

"Here is the one I left for you two weeks ago when Jonesy called, 'Just found out that they are shipping us out. It's all happening so fast. Is it all right that I write you'?"

"He didn't just leave without trying to get in touch with you."

"I saw that note but I can't read and the most I could figure out was that it probably said something about the rent I owed."

Mary picked up a pile of unopened letters on the thin paper used for international mail.

"You must have had a lot of boyfriends!"

"Jonesy is the only one I thought I might have had a future with. That's why I went all the way. We planned on getting married and starting a family."

Mary abruptly left that room and came back with a book in hand, "We'll start with some simple things from the Bible. You're going to learn to read. I'm sure he'll write you and didn't abandon you, so you are ready to read his letter when it arrives."

The night was dark and deep with the fragrances of early summer, and the sweet scent of late spring. Standing in a pool of yellow light from a street light stood Brigette, her dark blue dress absorbing the light. She was a shadow who stood with her back pressed against the pole. She had to make some progress with her life, to move it forward and away from being holed up in the attic, scraping out rent and the other things she needed from the sale of her landscapes; that now the war had come it seemed no one wanted. Some of it was because a crazy, frantic energy had taken over the city and there was no time for a sedate gallery opening, too somber for embassy parties where she had hung her paintings for sale. She wished she could paint what she felt and not worry about sales, but that was life. The only thing she painted with her soul was how she felt about the men she had dated.

It was time to move on from her fantasies and confront Smith to start the divorce he wanted and marry her; and all that the war had done would be changed into a new life for her. A slick black limo pulled up to the Georgetown townhouse whose house number could have been its price tag, 100980 13th Street. The chauffeur got out and opened the back door as Mr. Smith got out. Brigette headed across the street when Mrs. Smith, looking oh so fashionable, got out of the car. Brigette stopped and stepped back into night's shadows.

The sound of someone running up the back stairs; Mary was sitting on Betty's bed with her, teaching her to read the twenty-first psalm when they stopped and were silent listening. The footfalls reached the top floor and there was a loud knocking. Mary and Betty ran into the hall to see Peter knocking on Brigette's door. Mr. Braille, dressed in robe and night shirt walked into the hall. He was about to grumbled at having his sleep disturbed, but was silent when he saw the look of panic on Peter's face.

"What's happening?" Mary asked. She could feel the charge in the air, the tension, in her skin. Of course, her mind went wild with awful possibilities.

While knocking, Peter said, "The baby is coming!"

"Calm down, honey, babies come all the time. It's kind of normal." Betty took his hand off the door. "She went out some time ago. Besides what is she going to do, paint its face?"

"We just started medical school we don't know what to do about this," Peter said.

The kitchen was crowded not only with dishes and pots, but Mr. and Mrs. G who stood in the doorway to the servant's room where Pock and Cynthia slept. Mrs. G was tying her hands in knots saying, "I never delivered a baby before, not like this."

"I don't know nothing either but I know this is not right." Mr. G instinctively grabbed Mary as she rushed down the stairs and led her into the room where Cynthia lay on the sheets in a pool of blood, as she screamed and pushed. Pock was between her legs either sweating profusely or crying or both.

"He is coming out feet first and head up!" Pock yelled above the moaning.

Mary pushed everyone else aside. Sweat broke out on her upper lip. She knew she could do it, having helped deliver her brother and sister. "It's the chin, I have to insert my fingers…Get me a turkey baster quick!"

After the baby was out and the whole room was crying, after the placenta was delivered and Cynthia had eaten some of it to stop the bleeding, after everyone but Cynthia seemed exhausted, Betty turned around and found Mr. Braille had fainted beside a box of cabbages.

Though both Peter and Pock wished they could take Cynthia and little Louise (an Americanization of his grandfather's name) to the hospital, they both knew that they couldn't.

"We can't," said Peter. "They will report you and put the three of us in one of the internment camps."

"Yes, but we can't raise a baby here. I've been thinking about it. We need to leave."

The next day came so quickly; Mary was still running on adrenaline as they all were, except Mr. Barille, who everyone believed would not talk about what he had seen. He was a timid man with timid eyes but not the type to report a newborn baby and his parents to the authorities.

As she sat at her desk classifying the fingerprints of soldiers, she realized that she had forgotten to take a shower. She hadn't realized she was that drained during the whole birth. She subtly tried to take a quick sniff of her armpits. Good, the extra Taboo she had sprinkled on had worked. Across from her sat Roz. She had slept on the big file drawers in the basement to stay late and be early to make a dent in the piles of prints on her desk, the desk that had once been Marge's. The rustling of papers stopped and Mary looked up to see why Roz had stopped her work. Roz was frozen, with a light tremble to the paper she held she began to cry. Mary rushed around to the other side of the desk.

"What is it, dear?" Mary looked at the paper Roz was holding, tears were running the ink. "Your brother's prints." She stooped down and put her arm around her. "It doesn't mean anything. These were taken a year ago. It just means we are behind, as if we could work any harder."

Mary ached from head to foot. Sitting so much made her legs feel like they were made of iron, her back like a pile of rusty gears. Her feet were sweating in her shoes. But every time she tried to take them off under her desk, the monitor caught her and she had to put them back on. She began to wonder if he had a foot fetish the way he got excited when he found shoeless feet. But now she felt relief from the hot room, her back against the cool white tile wall of the bathroom. It was almost like jumping in the Mississippi River back home on a steamy afternoon. The door to the restroom swung open and slammed against the wall as Roz rushed in. She ran over with words about to bound off her lips when she paused and asked for a ciggy. After she had taken a long slow puff of the Camel she had bummed off Mary, she exhaled a blue fog.

"So, what's up?" Mary asked.

"Don't you live on the corner of 20th and R?"

"Yes, in that big red stone monster."

"Well, I was just talking to a friend during break who works upstairs and he thought I had a friend who lived there. Seems they are running surveillance on the house. I don't know who they think is living there, a spy?"

"We did have a spy there but we caught him. So, I can't imagine..." But she could imagine.

It was after the boarder's dinner of chicken stew and flour biscuits the other boarders had left and only Mr. and Mrs. G, Brigette, Michael, Peter, and Pock remained sitting around the table in the basement. Cynthia was off feeding the baby.

Mr. G nodded to his wife whose expression could turn a sunny day to dark clouds. "Maybe they are watching the place because of the high level people who come in."

"Maybe they just wanted to see Lucille Ball when she came in," Mrs. G said, even though she doubted it.

His chair squealed back and Peter stood up feeling that what he was about to say was his duty, to his family of friends. "They are after me. My father, was the ambassador and though he left the country Pock and I stayed here to go to medical school at GW. Now, they must have tracked me down."

"But they must not know you are here otherwise they would just come in and apprehend you."

Mr. G put his hands around his wife's shoulder. "Mary is right, why not just barge in?"

"And," Mrs. G added, "I have a very important client who comes here from time to time and they might just want to make sure the place is safe."

"Cynthia and I have been talking. We read in the papers that they are releasing some from the internment camps…"

"As long as," Peter injected with concern, "they stay out of government areas of which this city is one."

"I've talked to my parents who have a small fishing fleet up in Maine, through the goodness of their hearts; they will take you all to Nova Scotia. You will be safe in Canada." Michael said.

"It will take us two days to make it up there…"

Mary interrupted Pock, "But it's so risky and with the baby…"

"There are many people on the trains who will notice a man and woman wearing hats and sunglasses, and a baby. Spies don't walk around carrying a baby?" Pock pulled out the train schedule. "The train leaves in two days. We're going to be on it for everyone's safety."

Brigette had been silent till now. "And you Peter, are you going with them?"

There was a long silence. Mr. G finally spoke up, "I don't think they are after anyone. I think the Feds are watching the place because a certain 'woman' visits Mrs. G rather frequently lately. They might be trying to make sure there is no way my wife would betray the confidence of this person. Probably trying to get something to blackmail my wife with, as if she was that interesting." His wife nudged him in the side.

"Peter?" Brigette said with a vicious undertone, almost daring Peter to say he would leave.

"Mr. G, would you like to weigh in on this? More than anything, I don't want to put you in jeopardy."

"They keep saying on the radio that the war will be over soon and everything will return to normal, then you could go back to medical school. I'm not worried about us, my wife has powerful friends. Besides, I need a cook."

Brigette loved her nest as she preferred to think of her rooms. She had moved into the top floor of the Golden Parrot years before the war. She had fled the ugly art scene, full of back stabbing, and the visits to the city from her father, who she wished would stay in New Jersey. It was two rooms that had been convert into an 'apartment' at some point, probably for a butler and his wife. A bedroom and a parlor, that was now used as her studio, where she spent the days working on paintings of monuments to sell and paintings of men and their dark sides, which she kept to herself.

At one point, when the war had started and women were flooding into the city to work for the government, she had almost lost her solitude. She had heard from a friend that a government man had come to her door wanting to know if she had an extra bedroom or anyplace she could have a roommate to help alleviate the housing crunch in the city. Her friend ended up with a small woman who was completely pleasant when she wasn't complaining about something. Brigette had discussed that this might happen with Mrs. G and made a plan while agreeing to pay more rent. Mrs. G was savvy enough to warn Brigette when she was coming up the stairs with one of the room inspectors by calling ahead to her.

"Come in," Brigette called out slipping on her painting smock.

A very average woman in a very average dress came in with Mrs. G and was about to introduce herself when she wrinkled her nose and coughed. She went through the door open to the bedroom and Brigette could hear her coughing in there too. Not needing to explain, she quickly left with Mrs. G who departed with a wink. The place reeked of turpentine since Brigette had spread it like a toxic perfume about the two rooms.

Brigette laughed to herself, a very high and silly laugh she never let leave the room, when she remembered the episode with the turpentine. She didn't mind the smell. She was an artist! It was time to take a nice long hot bath. At the time, everyone to be at work, she could relax in the tub for as long as she wanted.

It was laundry day and Mrs. G had started early in the morning. Each of the boarders had dropped off their sheets, all she was willing to do, at the bottom of the stairs, as they left for the day. She had begun work with help from Cynthia, soaking and washing and wringing out the sheets and pillow cases. To her surprise, Mr. G held the baby. He hadn't held one since their son was born. He had joined the army before he could even have a girlfriend to move his life along and create a family. Mr. G would make a good grandfather.

When the sheets were washed and had hung out back in the warm summer sun drying, Mrs. G saw one of her secretive clients. Her reputation for advice, prophecy, and discretion had spread in Washington social circles and had left her quite busy. After the sheets were dry, she folded them and headed upstairs with her keys to drop them off in the rooms. After she had hit the top floor, humming some song she could not really remember to herself, she suddenly felt cold. She could see her breath hovering in front of her and a feeling of great despair loomed below the surface, about to erupt.

Then she saw it. A figure so pale it was just a smear of white on the air. A trembling in her soul as the specter slowly drifted through the closed door of the storage closet and floated on a breath toward the stairs, pulling along the utter hopelessness behind it.

Then it was gone. Mrs. G felt something behind her and spun around dropping the sheets. There behind her stood Brigette with a look of horror on her face.

The sun had dissolved into a gray smoke and taken the city with it. Dusk was scratching at the window of Brigette's bedroom. Beside her on the bed were envelopes tied in a bundle, unopened. The paisley blue pattern of the bedspread ate up the blue tinted paper of the letters. Beside them were opened letters on expensive stationery. Brigette sat crossed legged in her favorite black flowing dress with dragons embroidered on it. In her lap was a sketchbook opened to a sheet of paper, here pen slid across the paper.

Dear Smitty

You've made your decision, stay with your wife that if I remember right you called an old cow. That is the choice that you have to live with when you could have had me in your bed every night, instead of the cud chewer.

I have one problem you may be able to help me with. I have some letters of yours, but need to keep them in a safe place so your political opponents don't find them. But such a hiding place costs money. And oh can you put in a word with Mr. Goldwyn for me about my screenplay? I'm sure you can be persuasive.

Brigette was just about to sign the letter when she heard a floor board squeaking behind her. She turned the letter over, got up and turned around. There stood Peter with a worried look in his eyes and a nervous smile to his mouth.

"I was waiting for you to say something at the table downstairs, to say that you wanted me to stay."

"You already know that I do. It is just that it's difficult to express myself sometimes."

As Peter stepped closer to her, she knocked the pack of letters and the one she was writing to the floor.

"What were you writing?" Peter asked, confused by the mess she had made on the floor.

"I was doing some work on the story to my screenplay."

"I thought that was finished."

"Is it finished? She loves him but knows the time is wrong. War had changed everything. It is all wrong for her but she feels it is so right, more right than anything in her life."

It seemed a strong wind filled with an abundance of passion swept them up and into her bed and suddenly he was inside her.

Warm and sudsy, scented with lavender the bath water was the warm of her body. But Brigette shivered with a thrill as she remembered their love making, not just sex, but love drew them together like magnets, sealed them with sweat and passion. But the part that lingered was the quiet fingertips wandering over her skin, the words delivered in a whisper. Brigette sank down in the water as she realized this was it. Something she had always wanted deeply but had pressed down low in her consciousness where she could not be disappointed because she knew it could never be fulfilled. But it was now right there before her, severing her heart. She began to cry because she had never felt anything like this before. And now it had crashed through her heart and settled by the fire.

When she walked down the hall back to her room, Mary saw a smile on her face like she had never seen before and would never see again.

Brigette walked into her bedroom and everything collapsed, then before it could settle, exploded around her when she saw Peter sitting on her bed, holding the piece of paper she had knocked to the floor before they made love.

"What are you doing with my things, my personal things?" She almost screamed.

Peter felt slapped on the face. "What are you doing?" He sounded hurt, mad. "This is a bunch of unopened letters from soldiers overseas that you have never written back to. Did you lead them on?"

"It's not like that. What could I do for them? I sent them off with some hope…"

"Some hope. You were going to write to them, but instead you tie up their letters and save them in a pile. For what reason? Sit and go through them some day and smile feeling I was loved? I love you but…"

"But what? You only love me if I haven't been with other men! The war has changed all that. You don't think that these boys should go over there to do nothing but die without ever knowing some passion. I donate my body to…"

"You led me to believe I meant something special to you. Or are you having pity on me? Alone in a basement without a woman to comfort me, I can survive without your pity." He was scrunching the letters in his hand. Blood from a paper cut ran down his hand and on to the paper.

"You know that I love you." She said trembling. Disaster was there looming before her and she could see the outline of it through the haze of her vision. Her ears were ringing.

"Do I? Isn't that what you told all these men?"

Brigette sank to the floor letting her towel drop into the pool of despair around her, revealing her naked body still red from the hot bath. She now saw that it was approaching fast. And then there it was.

"And this letter, you've told this man you loved him and wanted to marry him, and when he chooses to stay with his wife you threaten him. This is the letter you were writing…"

"No, that was a long time ago…"

"The ink is barely dry. You were writing this when I came in."

"You don't understand." Brigette felt the humiliation of begging. There had been a promise of love, of a future her heart had longed for, not wanted but needed. And she had realized for the first time when her heart had been broken open and feelings she could never have expected flooded in. She had seen others 'fall in love', but thought it was some delusion felt by the desperate. But now...

"I don't understand you, or myself." He got off the bed and walked past her wilted body and through the door.

She knew it would be a sign that she was desperate to call after him, but she could not help herself and did.

It was later that evening after her despair had settled into a pool in her soul, that Brigette went down the back stairs to the kitchen with the finished script in her hand. It was a craziness flailing around in her head, confusion, dread, and hope. Hope when she saw Peter that they would pretend a great pretense: that nothing had come between them and their garden could be walked in again, at night, with a kiss, in the shadows of their love. Love, how she hated the way it was making her crazy.

Peter was at the sink chopping carrots and she held out the script to him as if offering roses. Her hand trembled and her eyes burned from the salty vestige of tears. But he wilted her with a look and went back to his work. She turned and went up the stairs.

She had run down to the Mayflower Hotel and saluted the desk clerk with her words. "Is room 1420 in?"

Startled by this brash woman with the tangled long dark hair, the clerk hesitantly said, "1420, but let me call up and tell him your name and if he wants to see you…"

"Oh, he'll want to see me."

Chapter 35

Someone had cleaned the tall windows in the office and the setting sun filled the room with pink roses. And the dust from the petals landed on the group of women in the typing class. Dotty was holding the late class outside Mr. Hobson'ss office, and he had stayed late, waiting for the class to end. Afterwards, Dotty would stay and clean up.

Susan sat uneasily at the typewriter. Once again she wanted to impress Dotty with her skill and speed at typing and jammed the keys. Dotty came over and reached down suppressing a laugh and pulled the keys apart.

"It must be your people that give you the ability to type," Susan whispered.

"Sure, all my relatives were great on the typewriter, only the slave traders forgot to bring over the machines when they put us on the boat."

Mr. Hobson's door creaked open and he looked out, his face was awry and his eyes rimmed red. All the women knew he had been hitting the bottle of Jack Daniels he kept in his file cabinet.

He stood a moment swaying slightly.

"Try not to look down at the keys," Dotty was saying to Susan when Mr. Hobson motion for 'Miss Franklin' to come into his office.

Hobson had taken off his tie and jacket and thrown them across his chair. He stood looking out the window where the incoming light had turned a sour purple.

"Close the door please."

"Another letter?" Dotty sat down, opened her steno book, and pulled a pencil out of her hair.

"You know why I'm staying late. I know it was the night for your class with the others."

"To the point please. This is my free time."

He turned around. "Then let's make the most of it." He moved quickly to grab Dotty by the wrist, twisting it.

Dotty let out a scream, pulled free, and slapped him.

The door opened and Susan and the other women filled the room around Mr. Hobson.

The women, the office, the world seemed to grind to a halt, with the women surrounding him, still as mannequins. Without moving, he waited for the slightest movement from them. Hobson was scared of women, terrified actually, so he had never married. He never dated but had hired escorts for events that he was expected to attend or whores from Thomas Circle for sex, until he discovered he had power. Of course, he had power before, but had paid for it. One day one of the office girls came in his office and shut the door. She was crying. She apparently realized she was not doing the job as well as the other girls in the pool and had heard the rumor she was going to be fired. She couldn't afford to lose her job, she pleaded. She had mouths to feed back home, people who depended on her. And she depended on him. He felt it, knew it, and rejoiced in it. Power, he had power; he couldn't remember what he had said but it must have worked because there she was on her knees, with her luscious red lips smearing lipstick on his Johnson.

It was only a matter of time before he realized how vulnerable women were. He became more confident around women. They were the inferior sex after all. The war was a blessing, no longer an office filled with men but objects for him to watch, watch until he could see the one that was vulnerable, needed a job and money, needed his approval.

But now they were all in his office staring at him, judging him, HIM. He felt his balls draw up into his crotch, a lump in his throat. He could tell by the sour look on their faces, the rigidness with which they stood, that they all knew what had been happening.

Words came out sounding garbled in his ears and he wasn't sure what he was saying. "I think that your appointment here…"

"Unacceptable, Mr. Hobson, I think your boss might have a thing or two to say if I…"

"We're all men and we have our ways…"

Susan stepped forward like a soldier ready for battle. "I realize what's been going on, right, girls." Her words hit the walls.

A voice from behind said, "How would it look on your record if we all resigned?"

Lelia, Barb, Susan and others who were standing in the doorway, by the window and against the file cabinets said, "You'll have to fire me, and me, and me," till everyone was hissing it around him.

"Let's get back to class, girls, I think we know how to control this man, no this pervert," Dotty said waving the girls back to their typewriters.

Whispers of 'the nerve', 'Men think they can get away with anything', 'We have to show we have dignity!'

Billy Joe appeared at the door out of breath. "Dotty, we got to hurry if we be catching that train."

"I'll be right there. Susan, you can take over the class. Use my typewriter rather than this jumble of used ones. You can teach till I'm back on Tuesday, that is if you white girls can learn to type."

Chapter 36

The troubled, scared and sometimes exuberant city of Washington was left behind and Billy Joe realized what is was like to see Dotty's shoulders relax. This was an adventure for him and Dotty knew it. He had been this far north and Harlem only once with Dotty. This was going to be a new world for him again. New York was ever writhing and giving birth to a new city with each dawn. How different would Harlem be when she got home again? How her heart hurt to see her family, her crazy and loving family, scraping and scrapping through the days.

By the time they came up to the sidewalk form the subway station, Billy Joe's eyes were as wide as a full moon. They were running, or rather Dotty was and Billy Joe was being pulled along, up the stairs of a brownstone and up another set of stairs to a door that opened before they knocked. There stood her sister Sarah dressed in her best pink dress with a big hug waiting. And there stood her two nieces, seven and ten, in new stiff starched dresses and their hair braided.

"Sister, it's been too long!" Dotty exclaimed with her head pressed again her younger sister's shoulder, then turning to the girls and ladies, "Have you been good?"

Sarah patted them each on their heads. "Trouble here has been trouble of course, and my oldest here, 'More Trouble', has been more trouble."

A large woman in a bright green dress and ebony skin stood in the hallway. Tears were in her eyes, too choked up to speak or even move.

Billy Joe had met them once before and felt very self conscious about what they might think of this southern boy. But this time he felt like this was family.

In a red, blue and gold room in the federal style, Brigette felt her eyes seep open slowly. There near the corner stood a woman with long dark hair, wearing only some type of dirty white shift. She was bent over pulling hard on a rope that trailed behind her. With nothing on it though, the woman seemed to think it was a great weight that she was dragging. It is almost like she was trying to escape but had to pull it behind her, Brigette thought as her eyes drifted softly closed. Have I seen a ghost in this old but immaculate hotel? But why am I not scared nor struggling woefully, like it might have been Jacob Marley's sister?

Turning over, Brigette observed him naked in the bed beside her. They hadn't bothered to close the curtains the night before and his body hair swayed white and slightly curled in her breath. It was disgusting. She threw back the sheets and reached down on the floor for her clothes finding her stockings. She hadn't worn underwear. Why bother? She knew what he expected from her and she would soon make him pay for it. Continuing to dress, she avoided looking in the mirror that hung across from the bed.

As she opened the door to leave, Mr. "Hollywood" as she called him, opened his crusty eyes and sat up on one arm. "When will I see you again?"

Brigette ran across the room and gave him a quick kiss on his balding head. "Silly, we are meeting tonight for dinner, and you told me to remember to bring the treatment of my screenplay, which I have already started by the way. You promised to show it to a producer and I'm so grateful. I'm looking forward to tonight."

"Me too!"

And she left.

"But you might get your butt shot at!" Dotty said a bit too loud so others on the Coney Island boardwalk could hear her. They understood for many of the women had already had this conversation with their husbands and boyfriends going off to war.

"That's what I signed up for," Billy Joe said softly, suddenly embarrassed. He knew he would leave Dotty behind even though he did not even know her when he had signed up. "I signed up to fight for my country…"

"A country that treats you like shit, won't even let you sit at a lunch counter or use the bathroom."

"When all us colored men come back from the war, things will be different. That is if they actually let me fight…"

"That would be good, but what do you mean, not fight? You are a soldier after all. They don't let colored fight?"

"They do but not this one. They want me to be some kind of assistant 'boy' to some general. They must think that's all I'm good for!" Billy Joe looked over at where the girls were eating bright pink cotton candy. It was making his stomach, all the sweet, queasy.

"Well, they should let you fight! You're just as good as any white man!"

Dotty stopped realizing what she had just said. "Wait a minute, I'm arguing you deserve to get shot at, and in some way, I think that is only fair when other men are willing to give up their life for their country. But I should be glad you will be safe."

Dotty opened her handbag and gave the girls a dollar and they rushed away to spend it as quickly as possible. She realized they were now yelling but couldn't stop herself. The thought of him bleeding was upsetting her to no end but the thought of him being discriminated because he was colored drove her crazy.

"I don't want to be safe."

"Don't you want to come back to me?"

Now this drove him crazy. How could she say that? Didn't she know that he loved her? It was better, he figured, to just walk away. Dotty stood there with eyes flashing at him.

Later, Billy Joe found the girls and was tossing a ball even though he was terrible at it. Mamma had joined them after doing a little gambling on the one armed bandits, and she and Dotty decided to take the Ferris wheel. It was a little attempt to get away. Mamma had lost all her mad money and Dotty was still fuming at herself for being…well she didn't know what she was fuming about.

The world swept by them as they edged to top of the amusement on the boardwalk. The tall buildings of the city glistened in the distance. The Ferris wheel stopped and left them swinging back and forth. Both now focused on their predicament high above the people below that were reconsidering if they wanted a ride with the way the seats swung back and forth, ready to drop Dotty and mamma out. They had been forced to calm down as they clutched the bar that held them in place precariously.

Dotty looked down at the seat dangling below them where the girls had not thrown up yet but Billy Joe sat so still it occurred to her he might be thinking about it.

"Hold very still. I'm holding still, very still. I don't want to rock the boat. Mamma, I'm scared." Dotty felt her hands going numb. Squeezing her eyes so tight together was giving her a headache.

"Are you in love with the man?"

A shock went through Dotty and she felt she was falling through space. Not because the chair they were in was swinging but because the words her mother had asked caused her to hold her breath until finally she could hold it no more. "Yes." She answered quickly; it spilled out of her, as if she could see it falling out all over New York City. Of course, mamma could get it out of her; she had always had that talent. No one could lie to her. Her voice was like Wonder Woman's magic lasso that made one tell the truth.

"That's what I thought, him, a soldier, then a baby all during a horrible war. That's what I'm afraid of. Nothing is sane once a war starts. Look at your cousin, two kids and a husband off to war in Africa. War."

"And I am afraid too. I remember what happened to papa: The sleepless nights, him up sitting in the chair coughing. I tell people he died in the war, not slowly of gas, from the war."

"Sometimes I wish he had too, but those moments I was able to hold him, well…I might not have had you girl. Seven years it took for the war to end in his poor body."

Tears formed in her eyes and slid down Dotty's brown checks, the wet glistening in reds and yellows form the carnival lights. Her mother hugged her. She knew Dotty had boyfriends, perhaps too many, but she was always afraid to fall in love. Some of the boys weren't worth spit, but others were so sweet. But word by word she told her mother she built a wall to separate her from the boy. But now her mother knew something different had happened. Dotty had let the wall be knocked down by this young man. Now, it was over with and her daughter was finally really in love.

With a jolt the Ferris wheel started up again.

Brigette stood naked in front of the window of the hotel room looking out at the imaginary chalkboard on which she had written her dreams. But the rain began and washed them away and the moisture in the air seeped into the room, moist with humidity and the odor of sex. She turned around and saw that, finally, Mr. Goldwyn, or as she now had been asked to call him Mr.

Hollywood, was laying down the last page of her treatment on the sheets where he sat on the bed. His expression was boredom or was it dissatisfaction.

"Well," said Brigette walking over and placing her hand on his back, "How do you like the story?"

"Well, women like that forbidden love stuff," he said as Brigette's heart sank. Women had forbidden love. "But the ending, dear, I only need to change the ending. Instead of our heroine sneaking him over the border to Canada in the truck of her car, let her be a real heroine. She knows he is really a Jap spy and turns him over to the FBI. Her love of her country is greater than her love of this man. People would love it. So, I could make the changes. This is your work, isn't it? Not a copy of some guys story?"

It wasn't disappointment, or anger. It was something greater. He didn't believe that she could have even written it herself, that she had stolen the idea! It was rage, a rage about everything in her life that was building up inside of her. Pure rage filled her body and she grabbed up the treatment and tore it in two, threw the paper to the floor and picked up her clothes to dress.

Chapter 37

Sounds, pings, roars, hellos and goodbyes, ricocheted off the ceiling of Union Station and landed on the crowd of civilians and soldiers below. Pock pushed his suitcase across the floor as Cynthia kicked it on with her foot. The baby in her arms stirred but did not wake. Pock approached the ticket window, his face frozen like porcelain and his head tipped down so his hat shielded his eyes.

"Where to?" the man behind the counter asked. He tried to smile but it had been a long day of hurried and bitchy customers.

"Two tickets on the Eastern to Bangor Maine, please and how much?"

"That's ahh…" The man looked up and being as short as Pock, could see his eyes. He stopped and thought a moment. "Let me check and see…" he muttered walking away.

Pock's heart began to beat too fast. He could feel his pulse beating in the side of his neck. He rubbed his sweaty hands together. The baby seemed to sense the tightening and terror of her mother and began to cry. Suddenly, everyone was looking their way annoyed with the echo from the tile floor. Cynthia tried to comfort it but she just cried louder with a frightened sound, not a dirty diaper cry.

The man was now behind the counter whispering to another man and nodding in Pock's direction. Cynthia noticed the hard stare of a nearby policeman.

The two men walked up to the window saying, "Can I see some kind of identification?" only to find that the Asians were gone, and were lost in the crowd.

Brigette was now out in the rain, which soaked her hair and ran down her face, smearing mascara that had already been smeared with tears. She stopped below the yellow trembling glare of a street light beside a telephone booth and stood there for she didn't know how long. Cars splashed by as their headlights slashed the night. Her hand trembled as she opened the door to the phone booth and stepped inside.

The pavement seemed harder than usual. The morning spun around her with people rushing by chattering to each other a bit too fast to catch any conversation. Her legs felt leaden as she had been walking the streets of Washington half the night and all morning, around corners and across streets. Bumping into the squishy bodies of others every now and then. Night had lifted and the sky was revealed to be as gray as cinder blocks. The sun was just a rumor.

She had tried to sleep but it had eluded her and she ended up tossing and turning round and round like a chicken on a rotisserie. The thought made her laugh and laugh some more. She couldn't hold her laughter and Brigette was aware that passersby were giving her peculiar looks. She didn't care. Incapable of stopping, she continued laughing and it seemed to be getting louder. The air was filled with the smell of cigarettes, car exhaust, after shave and cheap cologne, and with her laughter. She took out a handkerchief from her satin red purse and tried to cover her laugh but it was no use for it stopped suddenly.

By afternoon she had come up to the Golden Parrot as the heavy wooden and glass doors banged open and Mr. G came out with a large grim-faced man in a dark suit on either side of him. The sun slid through the sky and birds began to chirp. But all else was solemn as a hot breeze stirred up trash in the gutter.

As they led Mr. G to one of the police cars that sat in the street, the front doors of the Golden Parrot opened again and three more dark clothed men drifted out with Peter, Pock, and Cynthia. One of the men gingerly held the crying baby. Something inside Brigette screamed as Mrs. G followed them with tears in her eyes. And Peter's eyes assaulted Brigette's. "It was you," they said.

Coming up to her and ringing her hands Mrs. G said, "I know a man, a very important man. He may not be able to help them but he may be able to help my husband." She turned to Brigette and her voice was almost pleading as she said, "What have you done, you silly woman?"

They were all on the steps staring at her, the Schweitzer's, Peg and Betty. Michael. Others looked startled as they turned their gaze to Brigette as the cars drove away.

On Saturday evening, Brigette worked into the night hours arranging her drawings.

On that same evening, Brigette dragged a rope from the utility closet down the hall behind her.

The same evening Dotty with Billy Joe, Mary and Bill, and Betty walked through the grand oak doors with golden handles into the clatter and clank, smoke and music, chatter and laughter, of Harvey's, one of Washington's top restaurants. It was the home of the rich, the famous, and the want to be famous. Mr. Smith and his wife were there celebrating their twenty-first anniversary though none of the customers from the boarding house knew them.

Dotty saw the maître d' coming toward them wearing a shiny tuxedo and a frown on his face, "You can't afford this place," he said curtly, his pencil mustache twitching in a way that almost made Betty laugh.

Dotty stepped closer to the man and he took a step back. "I saved for this. I made a reservation for five."

The maître d' stepped forward so close to Dotty she could smell body odor that his sweet cologne could not cover. "I didn't know when you made the reservation by phone that…We don't serve…"

"…white folk? Well I see some here," Betty chimed in.

"All our tables are taken for tonight." There went that mustache and Betty laughed to cover the fact that she was starting to get mad.

"I see a table over there," Dotty said to a table for five in the center of the room.

The group began to walk to the table as a hush fell over the room.

Betty whispered to Dotty, "I don't think this was such a good idea."

"I chose this place to make a special announcement." The band began to play 'Humpty-Dumpty Heart' as the singer eyed what was going on and continued to sing. She was a Negro and had never seen another Negro customer in the restaurant.

Don't mean to criticize, or say I'm wise,
But if you will just recall, you sat on a garden wall,
And you know what happened
You'll still have a chance won't you?
You sure want romance don't you?
Hope you're lucky, Humpty-Dumpty Heart

As they sat down at the table, the maître d' was not giving up but not sure how to enforce the rules of the restaurant. "You'll have to leave at least these two." He said pointing to Billy Joe and Dotty.

"He is military just like I am," said Bill.

Betty couldn't help but say, "How are you serving your country in white gloves and a tuxedo?"

Billy Joe said loud enough for the table to hear, "I think maybe we should go."

"You sit your black ass down in that chair that has only been touched by white asses," Dotty insisted. Billy Joe did as she said as the maître d' walked away making a huffing noise.

Betty turned to Dotty as a Negro waiter rushed up with five glasses of champagne and as quickly as he could lay them down in front of each of them. Mary picked up her glass and held it up. "Better make your announcement quickly and then I have something to say."

"Before they call in the storm troops," Billy Joe added.

"Don't worry," said Bill, "this is too classy a place to make a big scene."

Billy Joe stood up into the silence and said, "Dotty and I are getting married."

Before he could sit, Bill stood up and said, "We were going to wait to say this but Mary and I are getting married. We were going to wait but I'm being sent down to North Carolina then overseas." They lifted their glasses and downed the champagne. And the band played Chopin's wedding march. Clapping erupted from a few tables as an elderly couple came up to the table holding an open bottle of champagne which they put on the table, "Congratulations and thank you for defending our country."

Chapter 38

As Brigette stepped out of the service closet in the hallway, the rope slithered silently behind her. And this is what she wanted most, clean and pure silence rising up around her, snaking around her neck loosely. As she tightened it around the banister on the third floor, the stairwell echoed with silence and it filled her ears and then her eyes as she saw the ghost which was her soul that had already begun to haunt the halls even before this moment of silence. The apparition nodded and Brigette felt a smile crack across her lips. Soon there would only be silence; she mounted the railing and leaned over, falling into the silence her heart had craved.

Chapter 39

Pale pink slipped by on the invisible clouds and suddenly, as the sun dipped toward the west, spilled out oranges and deep magentas onto the clouds which surrounded them like a barrier, the battle front of the war. Here it was. Filled with the swish of a sudden breeze and retreated into silence as they reached the cool marble of the Jefferson Memorial. They lay their shopping bags filled with spring clothes in front of the still stature of Thomas Jefferson. Betty, Roz, and Mary, whose feet were sore and tired, sat on the steps. But Dotty stood, her deep brown skin shining in the light.

"Let's make a pact," she said almost in a whisper.

"A what?" a confused Roz asked.

Mary got up. "A pact, my brothers were always making them with each other or their friends." She smiled to herself as memories of a more innocent time surrounded her.

Betty stood, nervous. "But no blood, I thought of becoming a nurse until I realized the sight of blood…" she shuddered as the light began to shiver.

"Just friends," said Dotty, "friends always."

"Because I can't make it through without my friends," said Mary as she helped Betty and Roz up.

"Friends, always," said Dotty.

Betty said thoughtfully, "Things will never be the same."

"But we will always be friends," Mary said as a smile drifted across her face.

"And everything else will be different. This war having brought all these women together here, doing the jobs that only men had done," Dotty added.

"Women will never be the same," said Betty.

Roz laughed and said, "And neither will men. Thank God!"

"Colored people, we will never be the same," Dotty said with tears in her eyes.

"And our daughters," Mary stared out into the distance. "They will be more…"

"Independent," Dotty replied.

"And brave," said Roz.

Betty had to add, "And all because of this horrible war."

"War changes everything," Mary said realizing how true it was. "So, let's go and see if we got clothes for a wedding."